TROUBLE IN THE TEXAS HILLS

"Ma!" Mandy whispered. "Look!" And she pointed.

The latch was moving. Slowly, quietly, as someone outside tried to open the door.

Blue let out a *whuff* and a loud growl. He pawed at the bottom of the door, his claws digging into the wood.

The latch became still. Then the door itself moved slightly as pressure was applied to the outside.

"They're pushing on it!" Mandy whispered.

"If they get in, shoot at their heads," Philomena instructed. A head shot to man or beast, her grandfather always told her, was the surest way to put something down. "We'll retreat down the hall, and if we have to, barricade ourselves in an upstairs bedroom."

"Listen," Estelle whispered.

Now there was a scratching sound, as if a fingernail were being run over the outside of the door.

"What are they up to?" Mandy whispered.

"If they want in, they'll have to batter it down," Philomena said grimly.

The next moment, the door shook violently.

Ralph Compton

TEXAS HILLS

A Ralph Compton Novel
by David Robbins

A SIGNET BOOK

𝄞

SIGNET
Published by New American Library,
an imprint of Penguin Random House LLC
375 Hudson Street, New York, New York 10014

This book is an original publication of New American Library.

First Printing, November 2015

For more information about Penguin Random House, visit penguinrandomhouse.com.

ISBN 978-0-451-47320-2

Printed in the United States of America
10 9 8 7 6 5 4 3 2 1

Penguin
Random
House

THE IMMORTAL COWBOY

This is respectfully dedicated to the "American Cowboy." His was the saga sparked by the turmoil that followed the Civil War, and the passing of more than a century has by no means diminished the flame.

True, the old days and the old ways are but treasured memories, and the old trails have grown dim with the ravages of time, but the spirit of the cowboy lives on.

In my travels—to Texas, Oklahoma, Kansas, Nebraska, Colorado, Wyoming, New Mexico, and Arizona—I always find something that reminds me of the Old West. While I am walking these plains and mountains for the first time, there is this feeling that a part of me is eternal, that I have known these old trails before. I believe it is the undying spirit of the frontier calling me, through the mind's eye, to step back into time. What is the appeal of the Old West of the American frontier?

It has been epitomized by some as the dark and bloody period in American history. Its heroes—Crockett, Bowie, Hickok, Earp—have been reviled and criticized. Yet the Old West lives on, larger than life.

It has become a symbol of freedom, when there was always another mountain to climb and another river to cross; when a dispute between two men was settled not with expensive lawyers, but with fists, knives, or guns. Barbaric? Maybe. But some things never change. When the cowboy rode into the pages of American history, he left behind a legacy that lives within the hearts of us all.

—*Ralph Compton*

Chapter 1

A beanpole with hair the color of ripe corn ambled into the Crooked Wheel Saloon in Kerrville early on Saturday night. His high-crowned hat, his clothes, and his jangling spurs told everyone what he did for a living. Cowhands were as common as horses in some parts of Texas.

Smiling, the stranger jangled to the bar, paid for a drink, and brought it over to the table where Owen Burnett, Gareth Kurst, and Jasper Weaver were playing poker. Once every month or so, the three settlers came down out of the hill country to indulge in a few drinks and a sociable game of cards.

Owen Burnett came up with the idea. He'd thought it would be nice to get better acquainted. They were neighbors, after all. So what if they lived ten miles apart, or more? In the West, "neighbors" didn't mean the same thing it did back east.

Owen was from Kentucky. He wasn't all that big, but he was solid. He had short, sandy hair, a rugged complexion, and pale blue eyes. When the cowboy came to their table and asked if he could sit in, Owen smiled and gestured at an empty chair. "Help yourself, mister."

Jasper Weaver grinned like a cat about to pounce on a sparrow. "If you won't mind us taking your money," he remarked. Which was a funny thing for Jasper to say given that he was the poorest card player west of the Mississippi River. Everyone thereabouts knew it. So did he, but Jasper never let it discourage him from playing. He was lean and gangly, with a face like a ferret's and a neck like a buzzard's. His brown hair stuck out from under his hat like so many porcupine quills.

Gareth Kurst grunted and eyed the cowboy with suspicion. He and most of his sons had the same features: black hair, blunt jaws, and eyes like shiny pieces of coal. "Why'd you pick our table, boy?"

About to set his drink down, the cowboy scowled. "First off, I'm not no infant. I'm eighteen, I'll have you know. And second, you three looked friendly, although I might have been wrong about that."

"We're friendly," Owen said.

"Speak for yourself," Gareth said. "I never trust anybody until they prove they deserve it."

"It's not as if I'm out to rob you," the cowboy said.

"You couldn't if you tried," Gareth said. "I give a holler, and three of my brood will be on you like hawks on a prairie dog." He nodded at three of his sons over at the bar.

"What's all this talk of robbing?" Jasper said. "We're here to play cards."

"Me, too," the cowboy said. He took a sip and sighed with contentment. "They call me Shoe, by the way."

"Peculiar handle," Jasper said.

"Not really," Shoe said. "I got hit by a horseshoe back when I was a sprout, and everyone took to calling me Horseshoe. Later that became just Shoe."

"I should reckon you'd want to use your real name," Jasper said.

"My folks named me Abimelech Ezekiel Moses. All three are from the Bible."

"Maybe not, then," Jasper said.

"Are we here to jabber or play?" Gareth Kurst said.

"You're awful cantankerous tonight," Owen said. He was in the process of shuffling the deck. "We'll deal you in, Shoe. Jacks or better to open. The limit is ten cents."

"That much, huh?" Shoe said.

"Ain't none of us rich," Jasper said.

Taking another swallow, Shoe offhandedly said, "You

could be if you wanted to bad enough. Most anyone can these days."

Jasper chuckled. "How does that work, exactly? We wish for money and it falls into our laps?"

Gareth uttered a rare laugh.

Pushing his hat back on his head, Shoe said, "Any of you gents know where to find longhorns?"

Owen nodded. "The hill country is crawling with them." It was a rare day when he didn't spot some off in the brush as he went about turning his homestead into what he hoped would become a prosperous farm.

"There you go," Shoe said.

"You're talking nonsense," Gareth said.

Shoe looked at each of them. "You haven't heard, then? How valuable they've become?"

"Longhorns?" Jasper said, and cackled.

Owen couldn't help joining in. The notion was plumb ridiculous. Longhorns had been around since the days when Texas belonged to Spain. Left on their own in the wild, they'd bred like rabbits. To a lot of people, they were a nuisance more than anything. They were good to eat but not much else.

"We don't like being ribbed," Gareth said.

"Ribbed, hell," Shoe said indignantly. "You're behind the times. Cattle drives will be the next big thing. Everybody thinks so."

Owen thought he knew what Shoe meant. "You mean those gents who took some longhorns up to Missouri to sell?"

"And now can't anymore because the folks in Missouri are worried about diseases the longhorns might carry," Jasper said.

"That's a lot of trouble to go to for nothing," Gareth said.

Jasper bobbed his chin. "Rounding up a bunch of contrary longhorns can't be easy. And for what? Four dollars a head, if that?"

Shoe sat back. "Shows how much you know. How about if you sold them for ten times that much?"

"Forty dollars a head?" Jasper said in astonishment.

"That's right," Shoe said. "And not in Missouri, either. You'd take them to Kansas. The people back east are so beef-hungry, they'll pay anything to have steak on their table."

"You're making this up," Gareth said.

"As God is my witness," Shoe said. "I left the ranch where I've been working to sign up with an outfit planning a drive." He chuckled. "I can't believe you haven't heard about it. Last year a fella named Wheeler took the first herd up to Abilene. They say he made over ninety thousand dollars."

Jasper's jaw fell, Gareth's coal eyes glittered, and Owen set down the deck he was about to deal. "You're not joshing us?"

"As God is my witness," Shoe said again.

"If that's true," Gareth said, "why aren't you out rounding up a herd of your own?"

"By my lonesome?" Shoe said. "Might be I could collect a couple of dozen head, sure, but where would I keep them until I start the drive? I don't own any land. The smart thing for me is to join a drive going north and learn how it's done." He grinned. "Besides, the pay is better."

"Ninety thousand dollars," Jasper said, and whistled. "Think of what a man could do with a fortune like that."

"I'm thinking," Gareth said.

"Sounds like too much risk for my taste," Owen said. "Longhorns aren't kittens."

"It's not too much risk for me," Gareth said.

"I bet my missus would like me to," Jasper said.

"You can't be serious." Owen couldn't begin to imagine the work involved. And then there was all the time they'd be away from their families. The cowboy drained his glass and grinned. "Looks as if I've started something here."

"You sure as blazes have," Gareth said.

Chapter 2

Harland Kurst took after his ma more than his pa. Tell him that, and he'd wallop you. Harland's pa was tall and muscular, his ma as broad as a barn door. Harland was tall and bulky. Truth was, he liked being big. He liked throwing his weight around and squashing anyone who made him mad.

Harland was the oldest of the five Kurst boys. On this particular night, he and the second oldest, Thaxter, had gone into town with their pa and their brothers but parted company to go to a different saloon. Harland told his pa he hankered to see a dove, but he really just wanted the freedom to do as he pleased.

His pa had a habit of reining Harland in when Harland didn't want to be reined in.

Once Harland had enough whiskey in him, he liked to pick fights. Because he was so big, he nearly always got the upper hand. And he made sure to have Thaxter close by to back his play in case the person Harland picked on resorted to a six-gun. Thaxter was quick on the shoot. So much so, folks fought shy of him.

The Kurst Terrors, people called them behind their backs. Which tickled Harland to no end.

So now, while their pa was off playing cards at the Crooked Wheel, Harland leaned on the bar at the Brass Spittoon. The Spittoon wasn't much as saloons went: a bar, tables, and a roulette wheel. The doves were dumpy and not all that friendly. Not to Harland, anyway. He liked it there anyhow.

"I see how you're looking around, big brother," Thaxter said after taking a swallow of bug juice. "You're in one of your moods."

"I'm always in a mood," Harland said.

"Who will it be tonight? That gambler yonder? Him with that frilly shirt and those big buttons on his vest?"

For reasons Harland had never understood, Thaxter was always critical of others' clothes. Harland didn't give a damn what people wore. Thaxter, though, took it as an affront if he saw clothes he didn't like. "Gamblers usually have hideouts up their sleeves."

"So?" Thaxter patted the Colt he wore high on his hip.

"We don't want you shooting anybody. The marshal won't take kindly to that."

"So?" Thaxter said again.

Harland chuckled. He wouldn't put it past his brother to gun the lawdog, should it come to that. But then they'd be on the run. "I don't aim to spend the rest of my days dodging tin stars."

"Wouldn't bother me any."

Just then the owner of the saloon, Rufus Calloway, came down the bar, wearing his apron. "You boys need a refill?"

"When we do, you'll know it," Harland said.

Rufus was well into his middle years and had a balding pate and bulging belly. "I don't like the sound of that. No trouble tonight, Harland, you hear me?"

"Or what? You'll hit me with your towel?"

Thaxter laughed.

"I mean it, boys," Rufus said. "I can't have you causing trouble all the time. It scares the customers off."

"Oh, hell," Harland said. "It's not as if I ever really hurt anybody."

"My brother does as he pleases," Thaxter said.

"Your pa won't like it if you do," Rufus told them.

Bending toward him, Harland growled, "Anyone tells him, they better light out for the hills."

Rufus swallowed and made a show of running his towel over the counter. "Just behave, is all I ask."

"Behaving ain't fun," Harland said.

"Go bother somebody else," Thaxter said.

Rufus went.

"I swear," Thaxter said in derision. "He's got as much backbone as a bowl of butter."

Harland thought that was funny. He tilted his glass to his lips, then narrowed his dark eyes as someone new came strolling in. "Well, lookee there. What is it the parson is always saying? Ask and you'll get what you want."

The newcomer was about their age and wore city clothes: a bowler, a suit, polished boots, but no spurs. He had a ruddy complexion and red hair, and smiled at everybody.

"It's Mr. Perfect," Thaxter said.

"He sure thinks he is," Harland said. Nudging Thaxter, he drained his glass, set it down, and moved toward where the man in the bowler was joshing with several men at a card table. Coming up behind him, Harland said, "As I live and breathe. If it isn't Timothy Pattimore."

Pattimore turned, his smile becoming a frown. "Hell in a basket. Leave me alone, you two."

"Is that any way to talk to a good friend?" Harland said, and wrapped his arm around the smaller man's shoulders.

"We are anything but," Pattimore said. "Get it over with. Knock my hat off. Call me a dandy. Have your brother make me dance with his six-shooter. I won't raise a hand against you. I learned my lesson the last two times."

"Well, listen to you," Harland said. "You're no fun."

An older man at the table said, "Leave him be, you Kursts. You're always stirring up trouble."

"Who asked you, you old goat?" Thaxter said.

Another player chimed in with, "You hill folk. Always riding in here like you own the place. This town has grown up. Your sort of antics aren't welcome anymore."

"I should pistol-whip you," Thaxter said.

Harland saw that others were giving them looks of disapproval. He was used to that. The weak always resented the strong.

"There's something you should know, though," Timothy Pattimore said. "The marshal is right across the street, having a smoke. You start a ruckus and he'll be in here before you can blink."

"Have a look," Harland said to his brother.

Thaxter stepped to the batwings and peered out. "There's someone over by the general store smoking, all right. I can see the glow. Can't tell who it is because of the dark."

"It's the marshal," Pattimore insisted.

"I believe you," Harland said. "You're too much of a chicken to lie to us." His mood suddenly evaporated. Removing his arm, he said, "To hell with all of you. This place has gone to the dogs."

"We're civilized now," Pattimore said. "We have law and order. You Kursts should get used to it."

"Your law only goes as far as the town limits," Harland reminded him. Beyond lay hundreds of square miles of mostly uninhabited hill country, of wilderness as wild as anywhere. He strode toward the batwings. "Come on," he said to Thaxter. "The air in here has gotten too righteous for my liking." He pushed on out into the cool of the night and heard someone make a remark that simmered his blood.

"Those Kurst boys. Mark my words. They're going to come to a bad end. Every last one of them."

Chapter 3

Owen Burnett didn't give much more thought to the cowboy and his news about the cattle drives. Sure, the notion held some appeal. So did prospecting for gold. But as anyone with any common sense was aware, few gold hounds ever struck it rich.

Owen didn't deem it worth mentioning to his wife when he got home. He had land to clear, ground to till, daily chores to do. A farm didn't run itself.

Owen liked being a farmer. He'd liked it in Kentucky, where they were from. He'd helped to work his pa's farm in Caldwell County growing up, and when he struck out on his own, he continued doing what he liked best. He'd still be there if it hadn't been for his wife.

Philomena shocked him one day by sitting him down in the parlor and informing him that she'd like to move. It came out of the blue. They'd been happy where they were, or so he thought. Granted, their farm was small, and with their two sons and two daughters, more land and a larger house would be nice.

Recovering from his surprise, Owen had suggested looking for a bigger farm right there in Kentucky. Philomena, though, had been studying up on the homestead law, and she'd taken it into her head that having the government give them one hundred and sixty acres would be just about the greatest thing in the world.

"It's an opportunity we can't pass up," she'd said in that tone she used when she wouldn't brook an argument.

Then she'd stunned Owen even more by saying that she had thought about it and thought about it, and she'd like for them to move to Texas.

In the past, Owen had been willing to go along with her notions. But *Texas*? It might as well be the moon. At least the moon didn't have Comanches and other hostiles. And outlaws. Texas had a reputation for being wild and woolly that put other states to shame. He brought all that up, but Philomena refused to be swayed. Texas was a land of opportunity—there was that word again—where a hardworking family could prosper like nowhere else.

"If it was good enough for Davy Crockett and Jim Bowie, it's good enough for us," Philomena had concluded her pitch.

Owen hadn't seen what that had to do with anything. Neither Crockett nor Bowie were farmers. And Philomena seemed to have forgotten that those men went off to Texas and had gotten themselves killed. Still, in her mind only Texas would do.

Now here they were nearly three years later at their new homestead, the work harder than it had ever been in Kentucky. They had a bigger, if plainer, house, built with their own hands, and had cleared about fifty of their one hundred and sixty acres.

Philomena picked the spot. She liked the hill country. It reminded her of Kentucky, what with the rolling hills, woods, and grass. And the soil was good for growing crops.

When they first settled there, they'd had their part of Creation all to themselves. Jasper Weaver and his family showed up about six months later. Jasper, his wife, Wilda, and their son, Reuben, lived farther back in the hills, practically hidden from the world.

Gareth Kurst and his large clan had only been there a year or so. Gareth chose a site on Wolf Creek, about ten miles from Owen. With his five grown sons to help, Gareth could easily have cleared his land and had a fine farm by now. But the Kursts weren't farmers. They were hunters. They'd built a cabin barely big enough to contain them, and that was it.

Which was why what came next surprised Owen so much.

On a sunny spring morning, Owen was downing trees. He'd stripped to the waist and was wielding his axe with relish. He liked the exercise, liked the feel of working his muscles, liked the sweat it brought to his brow. With each stroke, the axe bit deep into the oak he was cutting down and sent chips flying. He was so engrossed in his work that he didn't realize riders had come up until a horse nickered.

Stopping, Owen turned. He thought it might be one of his sons come to help, but it was Gareth Kurst and two of his own boys, Harland and Thaxter.

"Neighbor," Owen said, nodding. "Don't see you over this way much." He mopped his forehead with his forearm.

"We need to talk," Gareth announced. "I've been to Jasper's and he agrees, so now I'm paying you a visit."

"You make it sound serious," Owen said.

"It's life or death," Gareth said.

Alarmed, Owen said, "Are the Comanches on the warpath?"

"No," Gareth said. "I'm here to talk about that cow business."

"Oh." Owen smothered a snort of amusement. "That's hardly life or death."

"In a manner of speaking, it is."

"How so?" Owen asked. He'd never cottoned to Gareth all that much. The man could be surly, and ruled his roost with an iron fist. When he told his brood to do something they jumped, or else. Philomena once confided in him that Gareth's wife, Ariel, had confided in her that Gareth slapped her on occasion. Owen never could abide men who abused their womenfolk.

"Moneywise," Gareth said.

Owen rested the handle of his axe across his shoulder. "The ninety thousand dollars got to you, did it?"

"Hell, twenty thousand is a fortune as far as I'm concerned," Gareth said. "However much, it's more than any of us would make in our entire lives."

"What are you saying?"

"It should be as plain as the nose on your face," Gareth said. "I'm proposing that you and me and Jasper go into the cattle business together and fill our pokes with more money than we ever imagined having."

"God in heaven," Owen blurted. He couldn't believe what he was hearing.

"God," Gareth Kurst said, "has nothing to do with this."

Chapter 4

Philomena Burnett didn't like some of the Kurst clan. Not from the moment she met them. Gareth Kurst was one of those men who looked down their noses at everyone female. Gareth's boys—most of them, anyway—were ill-mannered. Gareth's daughter was a flirt. And Gareth's poor wife worked herself to death to please her man and keep her brood happy. Ariel, her name was, and she wasn't much more than their servant.

Philomena could never live like that. She had too much pride. Too much gumption. And she wasn't shy about giving someone sass if they imposed on her in ways they shouldn't. Fortunately, her Owen was as considerate a man as was ever born. She loved him dearly, and the feeling was mutual.

When Owen showed up with Gareth and the two oldest Kurst boys, she picked up right away that this was more than a social visit. The men had something serious to talk about. They roosted at the table while she put coffee on the stove. They didn't ask her to sit in but she could hear every word. And she didn't like what she heard.

"Something like this doesn't come along very often, if at all," Gareth was saying. "It's a godsend, dropped right into our laps."

"I thought you said God doesn't have anything to do with it," Owen remarked.

"We're in the right place at the right time," Gareth said. "There are more longhorns in these hills than you can shake a stick at. Hell, in a month, I bet we could round up a couple of thousand."

"I'll thank you to watch your language around my wife," Owen said.

Philomena grew warm inside, and not from the stove. She liked how he always insisted she be treated like a lady. It showed Owen respected her. Which was more than could be said about Gareth's feelings for Ariel.

"And that seems a mite high," Owen had gone on.

"Maybe, if only one family went about it. But not if all three of our families work together," Gareth said. "We do it right, each of us stands to make twenty to thirty thousand dollars."

Philomena couldn't understand why they were talking about such large sums of money. Make thirty thousand dollars? Why, they should walk on air while they were at it. She wanted to take the coffee over and stand next to Owen, but when she touched the pot, it wasn't hot enough.

"A third for each of us," Gareth said.

"And all we have to do is round up two thousand long-horns and drive them, what, almost a thousand miles?"

"Only about seven hundred," Gareth said. "I did some asking around in town and that's how far a gent who has been there told me it was."

"Still a long way," Owen said, "and we're not cattle-men."

"How hard can it be? There'll be more than enough of us. There's me and my five boys and you and your two and Jasper and his son. That makes eleven. Plus Lorette wants to help, too, and she can ride as good as anyone."

"It sounds too much like wishful thinking," Owen said.

Gareth placed his elbows on the table. "Look. Let's say we only round up a thousand head. That still comes to forty thousand dollars. Which is pretty near fourteen thousand for you, me, and Jasper. I don't know about you, but to me, even fourteen thousand is a lot of money."

Philomena was unable to contain her curiosity any longer. She left the stove and went over and stood beside

Owen. Forcing a light laugh, she said, "The sums you're throwing around. What's this business about, anyhow?"

"If you've been listening, you should know," Gareth said archly. "I'd like your man to join me and Jasper Weaver in a cattle drive to Kansas."

"Word is," Owen said when Philomena looked at him, "up there they'll pay forty dollars a head."

"For a longhorn?" Philomena found the notion amusing. Longhorns were big but they were spindly critters. All horns and legs, was how she thought of them. And they didn't fetch more than four dollars a head in Texas.

"Cattle is cattle," Gareth said. "And the brush is crawling with the critters, just waiting to be rounded up."

"I can't farm and go after longhorns, both," Owen said. "I couldn't grow the crops I need. My family would suffer."

"Not much," Gareth said. "Your root cellar is well stocked, you once told me. And it'll be worth it once you have more money than you'll know what to do with."

"I don't know," Owen said.

Philomena was startled. She knew that tone. Her husband was considering the idea. "Owen?"

"It's tempting, is all," Owen said.

"It's what anyone with half a brain would do," Gareth said, and then gestured. "Not that I'm saying you don't have one, Burnett. But a chance like this doesn't come along but once in a man's life, if then."

"You've made your point," Owen said.

"And?"

"I told you. I don't know."

"Jasper didn't hesitate. He jumped right on it. Or, rather, his wife did and he jumped on right behind her."

"I'm not Jasper. I have to talk it over with Philomena and ponder on it some."

Gareth gave Philomena a glance that hinted he would be happy if she made herself scarce. She wasn't about to. "Maybe I should sit in," she suggested, "and we'll hash this over right here and now." She tactfully added, "So Mr. Kurst won't have to wait days for our answer."

"A good idea, woman," Gareth said. "Beats me why he has to consult you, anyhow. A female needs to know her place. My Ariel, I tell her how things will be and she goes along."

"Isn't she lucky to have you for her husband?" Philomena said.

Chapter 5

Luke Burnett had snuck off to practice. His ma would have a fit if she knew. She was always on him about it. "Stop playing with that thing," she'd say, and warn him, yet again, that no good would come of it.

The "thing" was a revolver. A Remington Navy given to him by an uncle before the family headed West so he could deal with "snakes and Injuns and such." The gift had almost brought Luke to tears. No one had ever given him anything so grand.

On their long trek to the Mississippi River, Luke kept it bundled in an old blanket and only took it out at night to admire it and practice drawing and twirling it. Once they crossed into the frontier, where law was rare and the lawless ran rampant, Luke strapped the Remington on and never took it off except to sleep and when doing work that would get it dirty.

His ma didn't like that. She said he didn't need to "traipse around with that thing strapped on all the time."

His pa, though, sided with him. His pa told his ma that in the West, a man had to be able to protect himself and his loved ones. His pa also secretly confided in Luke that he was glad one of them was going around armed. When Luke asked why his pa didn't wear a pistol, too, his pa had shrugged and said he'd never worn one back east and just couldn't get used to the idea. Luke suspected there was more to it. Luke suspected his ma was against it. His pa nearly always did whatever his ma wanted.

Luke loved his ma dearly, but he wasn't about to let her dissuade him. Which was why, every chance he got, he snuck off to practice drawing and twirling and flipping.

Unfortunately, Luke rarely got to practice shooting. Percussion caps, lead, and black powder cost money. And he seldom had any to spare.

In all the months Luke had owned the revolver, he reckoned he'd fired it less than twenty times. He could draw and cock it "like lightning," as his brother, Samuel, was always saying. But he wished he got to shoot it more.

Now, in a grove of trees not far from the barn, Luke spun the Remington forward and backward, flipped it and caught it by the handle, and twirled it into its holster.

Behind him, someone clapped and chuckled. "That was slick as can be," his brother said.

Luke and Samuel were born three years apart. At eighteen, Luke had taken on the aspect of the man he'd become, but Samuel was still boyish. Luke more resembled their pa; Samuel had their ma's hair and cheeks. Both wore homespun and boots, and Samuel was fond of a floppy-brimmed hat that Luke thought looked silly but Samuel liked because it kept the sun and the rain out of his eyes.

"Shouldn't you be hoeing Ma's garden, little brother?" Luke playfully scolded.

Sam had leaned the hoe against his side to clap. Gripping it, he grinned. "I've done for the weeds."

"So you snuck over to watch me." Luke didn't mind. He sort of liked how his brother looked up to him.

"And to let you know we have company," Sam said. "I take it you didn't hear them ride up."

About to practice his draw again, Luke said, "Who?"

"Some of those Kursts," Sam said. "The pa and the oldest two."

Luke frowned. He didn't like the Kurst family much. Especially that Harland, and Thaxter.

"Their pa is inside talking to our pa," Sam mentioned. "The other two are over at the pump with Amanda and Estelle."

A flush of resentment deepened Luke's frown. His sister Amanda was seventeen, Estelle sixteen. He adored them both, and disliked the way the Kurst boys sometimes looked at them. "Let's go see."

"You're not too fond of them Kursts, are you?"

"I surely am not," Luke admitted.

"How come?"

"They're ill-bred," Luke said. It was a word he'd picked up from his grandmother, bless her soul. She had been big on manners, and on showing respect for others.

"They sure think they're God's gift to the world," Sam said.

"Even you've noticed."

"What's that supposed to mean? I notice things."

They came around the barn and Luke felt a flush of anger. Harland Kurst had his hand on Amanda's shoulder and was bent close to her ear, saying something that made her cheeks grow pink. "What's this?" he demanded loudly to get their attention.

Harland and Thaxter both turned, Thaxter with his hand near his Colt.

"Well, look who it is," the latter said, and glanced at Luke's Remington. "The gunhand."

"Be nice," Harland said. "You remember what Pa told us."

Amanda and Estelle stood side by side, their backs to the pump, a bucket at their feet. Their dresses were plain, their shoes the kind a fancy city girl would scoff at. Amanda, or "Mandy" as they called her, was taller, almost as tall as Luke, with the bluest eyes in the family. Folks were always saying how pretty she was. Estelle had their ma's broad shoulders, and a nose much too long and wide for her face. She hated it.

"They behaving themselves, sis?" Luke asked.

Her cheeks still pink, Mandy nonetheless nodded. "Harland, here, was saying how he'd like to come courting sometime."

"What?"

"I said it polite," Harland said. "No disrespect intended."

Luke stepped up to him so they were practically nose to nose. "You *better* treat her with respect."

"Don't threaten me."

"Be nice, brother," Thaxter said, mimicking Harland, and laughed. "You remember what Pa told us."

For a moment Luke thought Harland would take a swing at him. Instead, Harland's mouth curled in an odd sort of smile.

"That's right. We need you Burnetts, if it's to work out."

"If what is?" Mandy asked. She was staring at Luke, and gave a slight motion of her head. Reluctantly, Luke took a step back.

"We're going into the cattle business together, girl," Harland said. "Your family and mine."

"We're farmers, not ranchers," Luke said.

"You thought you were," Thaxter said.

"Everyone knows we farm," Luke said, and couldn't resist adding, "It's more than you do for a living."

Thaxter glowered and went to take a step, but Harland held out a hand, stopping him. "Those longhorns won't herd themselves."

"Longhorns?" Mandy said.

"Money on the hoof, little lady," Harland said. "Even as we speak, our pa and your pa are striking a deal to make all of us rich."

"That's ridiculous," Mandy said.

"Is it?" Harland pointed at the house.

Their fathers had just come outside and were shaking hands.

"Yes, sir," Harland declared. "We're going to be right close from here on out." He chuckled and winked at Mandy.

Chapter 6

Jasper Weaver was getting drunk. Again. Jasper liked to get drunk. He liked the euphoric feeling that came over him, liked the fact that all his cares melted away and he could drift along, as it were, on inner tides of peace and happiness.

Lord knew, his life was anything but peaceful. For starters, there was Wilda. Or, as Jasper liked to think of her, "the Shrew," with a capital S. Wilda never stopped carping, never ceased criticizing. She'd complain and she'd complain, and then she'd complain some more. To hear her tell it, he'd never done a thing right in his entire life.

The funny thing was—if by "funny" you meant "sad"— she hadn't been such a shrew before they got hitched. No, Jasper distinctly recollected that she'd been as quiet as the proverbial mouse, hardly ever saying a word unless he asked for her opinion, and even then, her replies never once gave a hint of her true nature. No, that came later.

Jasper got his first whiff of the foul odor his marriage would become on their wedding night. He'd looked forward to finally being able to do what he'd hankered after ever since their first kiss. Not that the kiss had been all that memorable. It was more of a peck. But it was his first time kissing a girl, and amazingly, she hadn't slapped him and hit him with a rock.

Jasper knew he wasn't much of a prize. Not when it

came to his looks. His own ma used to call his face ratty, and his neck was long enough for two men. Add that to his hook nose and buckteeth, and he was about the least handsome man alive.

Girls had taken to him about the same as they would to smallpox. When he was little, they were always poking fun. One even went so far as to say he should put a burlap sack over his head to spare them misery.

No, when it came to females, Jasper had about resigned himself to living his life alone. Then along came Wilda. They had a lot in common. She was an only child, like him. She was shy, like him. Awkward, like him. And, the truth be known, about as attractive as a bedbug. She was all bone, with a face as ratlike as his own. When he first saw her, he had the impression he was looking into a strange sort of mirror. She was a female version of him. So, naturally, they were drawn to each other.

Jasper courted Wilda for a year before she agreed to say "I do." With her mother as chaperone, he'd sit in their parlor and make small talk the best he knew how. Now and then they'd go for a stroll, and after eight months or so, she let him hold her hand.

Jasper remembered that day fondly. It had been in the fall. The leaves were rustling. It was a windy day with a chill in the air. They'd bundled up and gone for a stroll to a pond near her house, and halfway around, without really thinking about it, he'd covered her hand with his. He did it because his fingers were cold and he thought hers would warm him. But her fingers were ice. She didn't pull away, though, which encouraged him to squeeze her hand. When she squeezed back, he thought he'd died and gone to heaven.

The day of their wedding, Jasper was so nervous he could hardly get his brain to work. It was a small ceremony: her folks and his, and a few kin and friends.

The pastor was old Reverend Willis, whose perpetually red nose was a testament to his fondness for whiskey. When Reverend Willis said that Jasper could kiss the bride, Jasper had eagerly pressed his mouth to hers. All Wilda did was stand there as stiff as a board. She didn't kiss back. That should have told him something right there.

That night, the true Wilda, as Jasper liked to think of her, showed her real self for the first time.

They had prepared for bed. Jasper put on a nightshirt and couldn't wait to strip it off again. He'd entertained naughty notions about Wilda for so long, he was anxious to consummate their marriage, as folks put it. Unknown to him, his idea of consummation and hers were two different things.

"Now before you start in," Wilda had said, sitting with her back to the headboard and pressing her hand to his chest to stop him from reaching for her, "we have to set the rules."

"The what?"

"The rules. Like my ma taught me. She says that without rules, all sorts of unpleasant things can happen."

His body so hot he felt like he was on fire, Jasper had said in confusion, "All I want to do is to make love to you."

"And that's your right as my husband," Wilda said. "So long as you do it proper."

Jasper had wondered if maybe his pa had neglected to pass on an important fact of life with regards to matrimony. "We can't just do it?"

"I should say not. The proprieties must be observed."

"I didn't know there were any."

"Exactly my point. So here's how it will be." Wilda had paused. "We do it clothed—"

"What?"

"Don't interrupt. We do it with our clothes on. Or our nightshirts, rather, since we're only to do it at night, after we retire, and then only on nights when I feel up to it and don't have a headache or a womanly complaint. I'll allow kissing but only with your mouth shut. None of that tongue stuff. Tongues are too wet for my taste. And don't touch me more than you absolutely have to. I don't like being touched. Now, I don't know how many times a month you expect me to give in to your needs but my ma says once a month was good enough for my pa and it should be good enough for you."

Jasper had been so stunned, he hadn't known what to say. So he'd blurted the first thing that popped into his head. "What the hell?"

"None of that," Wilda had said sternly. "My ma didn't put up with any of that kind of language from my pa, and I won't abide it, neither. There's not to be any swearing around me."

Jasper had sat back in bewilderment. No cussing, and hardly any lovemaking? What had he gotten himself into? "Is there anything else?" he'd asked, half in jest.

"There are lots of things that will help us get along better," Wilda said. "You're not to track dirt in. You're not to use the chamber pot when I'm in the room. You're not to try and boss me around like some men do because I simply won't stand for it. You're to always open doors for me and treat me like a perfect lady. And once we have a child, we'll sit down and have another of these talks since I'm not sure I want more than one and it seems pointless to keep on doing, well, you know, if nothing is ever going to come of it."

Jasper had actually pinched himself, pinched his own leg, half-thinking he was imagining this, but no, there she sat, as rigid as at the altar and as cold as winter snow, smiling happily now that she had laid down the matrimonial law.

That was the start. The next morning, at breakfast, she'd mentioned how she didn't like that he chewed with his mouth open, and did he have to slurp his milk instead of swallow it, and he should do something about his cowlick.

Now, alone in their kitchen, Jasper glumly raised the whiskey bottle to his mouth and took a long swallow. The sound of footsteps on the stairs galvanized him into quickly rising and shoving the bottle into the cupboard and sitting back down again, his hands folded in front of him, before she came down the hall.

"What are you doing?" Wilda asked suspiciously.

Jasper shrugged. "Thinking about things."

"Don't think too much. It's not good for you." Wilda went to the counter and filled a glass with water from the pitcher. "I'd like a few more words with you about this longhorn business."

"You already made it clear you want me to do it," Jasper said.

"Why wouldn't I? You expect me to live like this forever?"

"You knew I was a farmer when you married me. And living out in these hills was your idea, not mine."

"Don't nitpick," Wilda said. "As for the longhorns, Gareth Kurst is right. This is a once-in-a-lifetime proposition. Think of what we could do with ten or twenty or thirty thousand dollars."

"I never gave much thought to being rich."

"Another of your faults. But that's all right. I've been doing the thinking for both of us for a long time. You're to help the Kursts and the Burnetts, and when you get our share of the money, you're to come right back here and give it to me." As an afterthought, Wilda added, "And don't forget to take Reuben. It will do him a world of good."

"I never knew making money mattered that much to you," Jasper said, not without a touch of bitterness.

"Why wouldn't it? I'm normal, like everybody else. We can start a whole new life. Be happy, for once."

"I wouldn't mind more happiness in my life," Jasper bleakly conceded.

"Just so you don't get carried away with it," Wilda said.

Chapter 7

Gareth Kurst heard himself whistling and stopped. He hardly ever whistled—or hummed, for that matter. People who did were usually in a good mood. He was hardly ever in a good mood. But at the moment Gareth was as pleased as he'd ever been about anything. The prospect of being rich did that to a man.

His two oldest were riding single file behind him, on their way home after their visit to the Burnetts. They came to where the trail widened, and his sons gigged their mounts up on either side of his.

"That was slick, Pa," Harland said, "you talking them into it."

"Burnett did most of it," Gareth said. "He was the one who convinced his missus. That contrary female had her nerve. Why he lets her get away with it, I'll never know. But then, a lot of men do. They go around with whip marks on their backs."

Harland laughed. "At least she agreed we can try the roundup for a week or so, and see how things go. If they go well, we can keep on until we have our herd, and off to Abilene we go."

"I can't believe how he lets his woman butt in like she does," Thaxter said. "None of his women know their place."

"It's not like the old days, boys," Gareth said. "A lot of women think they should have the same say as men." He remembered something he'd heard a while back. "There's even talk of giving them the vote."

"The hell you say, Pa," Harland said. "Female brains don't work like ours. They can't savvy stuff like that. Giving women the vote will send this country straight to the dogs."

Thaxter grinned. "That Burnett gal must have a good brain, seeing as how you're so sweet on her."

"Just because I might court her doesn' t mean I think she's smart," Harland said.

Gareth's interest perked. "What's this about courting?"

"Harland is smitten by that Mandy," Thaxter said. "He probably dreams about her at night."

"Keep it up," Harland said.

"Is this true?" Gareth asked, and could tell by his oldest's expression that it was.

"She's the prettiest gal in these parts, Pa," Harland said. "Who wouldn't want to court her? I let her know I'm of a mind to, is all."

"No and no," Gareth said.

"Now hold on, Pa," Harland began.

"No. You listen, and listen good," Gareth said. "I won't have anything spoil this longhorn business. We need the Burnetts and we need the Weavers. Doing it all ourselves would take forever. You picked a bad time to be randy. Save your courting for after we've sold the herd and have our money."

"Damn," Harland said.

"Think about it, boy," Gareth said. "Think of the courting you could do with a thousand dollars in your poke. That's how much I aim to give each of you if this comes to pass."

"A thousand dollars?" Thaxter said, and did some whistling of his own. "Why, I could get a new Colt, one with ivory handles."

"You can get anything your heart desires," Gareth said, and turned back to Harland. "So long as you keep your pecker in your pants."

"She's not like that, Pa," Harland said sulkily. "She doesn't work at a saloon. I'd have to court her proper."

"No courting, and that's final." To soften the sting, Gareth said, "I'd take it as a personal favor, son. I don't often ask much. But this here is one of those golden opportunities folks talk about. We can have more money than we'll know what to do with if we play our cards right."

"I suppose," Harland said.

"How hard do you reckon it will be?" Thaxter asked. "Corralling all those critters?"

As fate would have it, just then there was a loud snort from up ahead, and a longhorn strode out of the brush into the middle of the trail and stood staring.

Gareth and his sons drew rein, Thaxter exclaiming, "Lordy, look at the horns on that thing."

A brindle bull, it packed close to a thousand pounds on its big-boned frame. The horns had to be pretty near seven feet from tip to tip.

Gareth suddenly had an inspiration and reached for a rope. "Let's give it a try and see how it goes."

"Pa?" Harland said.

"Help me catch it." Gareth wasn't much of a hand at roping but he had roped cattle before and could toss a fair loop. He got ready, watching the bull. All it did was stand there and stare.

"You ask me, I'd rather shoot it," Thaxter said uncertainly. "It'd be safer."

"The meat buyers in Abilene don't pay for dead longhorns," Gareth said, holding the loop close to his leg. "You two set?"

"If he lets us rope him, I'll be plumb amazed," Harland said.

The moment Gareth started forward, the bull snorted and plunged into the brush. Gareth used his spurs. He was determined not to let this bull get away. Reining right and left, he glimpsed its hindquarters and tail.

Thaxter let out a holler. "Keep after him, Pa!"

It wasn't easy. The bull picked the thickest brush to plow through, no doubt to throw them off, and some of that brush was thorny. Gareth winced as what felt like a handful of nails tore at his left leg. Jabbing his spurs harder, he sought to end the chase quickly but the bull pulled ahead, and before Gareth knew it, was out of sight and making good on its escape.

Gareth drew rein in disgust and came to a stop.

"Well, that didn't go well," Harland said.

"I've torn my pant leg," Thaxter said.

"So did I." Gareth looked down. He was bleeding from cuts caused by the thorns. "We'll need chaps for each of us."

"You still aim to try and corral a herd?" Harland said.

"This doesn't prove anything," Gareth said. "We have a chance to be rich, and I'm not letting anything or anyone stand in our way."

Chapter 8

The Burnett family had just sat down to supper when there was a knock on their front door. Owen stood and said he'd see who it was.

Philomena promptly rose, too. "I'll go with you."

"There's no need, dearest," Owen said. "Sit there and relax."

"I don't feel like relaxing." Philomena was peeved that he'd told Gareth Kurst he'd give the longhorn business a try even though she'd made it plain she didn't think it was a good idea.

As they walked down the hall, Owen placed his hand on her arm. "You're still upset, aren't you?"

"You ignored my wishes and forced me to give in."

"All I did was agree to try it for a while," Owen said. "I haven't committed to anything."

"You only think you haven't," Philomena said.

Whoever was outside knocked again.

Philomena stepped in front of Owen and opened the door to show she didn't need a man to do it for her. She was so annoyed, she hadn't given any thought to who their visitor might be, and was momentarily startled by the apparition that greeted her. "Mr. Troutman!"

Ebidiah Troutman was as old as the hills, or so folks said. He certainly looked it. Troutman had more wrinkles than Methuselah, and a large scar on his left cheek that split his face so deeply it made Philomena's skin crawl. A tomahawk had done that to him back in the early days, or so rumor had it. The old man had been in the hills for decades. He made his living trapping. Another rumor claimed he'd once been a mountain man, up north during the beaver days, and had come south after the beaver trade died out. A scrawny bundle of sinew dressed in buckskins that were almost as old as he was, Troutman held his coonskin cap in his hands. Knee-high moccasins protected his feet. "I didn't mean to scare you, ma'am."

"You didn't," Philomena replied, embarrassed.

"I apologize for disturbing you folks," Troutman said, shifting his weight from one leg to the other. In the crook of his left elbow was a Sharps rifle, and an ammo pouch and possible bag crisscrossed his thin chest. On his left hip hung a bowie knife.

"Not at all, Mr. Troutman," Owen said, offering his hand. "It's always a treat to see you."

"That's awful kind," the old man said, shaking. "The reason I'm here is I got me some new furs. Your missus liked that fox skin so much last time, I reckoned she might want first look at my new batch." He motioned at his mule, Sarabell, and the bundles she bore.

"Tell you what," Owen said. "We're about to eat. Why don't you join us, and we'll look at your furs after we're done?"

Philomena liked the old trapper and didn't mind feeding him, but it would take some doing to get used to the smell he gave off. If she were to guess, he hadn't taken a bath since he was ten. "Yes, by all means, please join us," she said to be polite.

Troutman shifted his weight again. "That's awful kind. But I wouldn't want to impose on you and your family."

"Don't be silly, Ebidiah," Owen said, and beckoned. "Come on and make yourself at home."

"If you say so." Nervously coughing, Troutman entered. He stared at the door as Owen closed it as if he were thinking about bolting. Then he gazed at the ceiling and the walls and gave a little chortle. "I ain't used to being closed in. It's like being in a box."

"You've been in houses and cabins before, surely," Philomena said.

"Yes, ma'am," Troutman said, "and never much liked it. I'm the same about caves. I get a feeling like I can't breathe." He hesitated, then leaned his Sharps against the wall. "Will this do?"

Owen nodded. "Follow me."

Philomena went last, scarcely breathing. She supposed she should be grateful. Having the old trapper there would take her mind off the longhorn predicament for a while.

"I trust you remember everyone else?" Owen said. Pointing at each in turn, he said, "Luke, Sam, Mandy, and Estelle."

Philomena was pleased that her children dutifully nodded. She'd raised them to be well-mannered.

"How do you do, young'uns?" Troutman said.

"Sam, fetch the extra chair from the parlor," Owen directed, "so Mr. Troutman has a place to sit."

"Sure thing, Pa."

Philomena moved to her own chair. To make small talk she asked, "What kind of furs did you bring this time, Mr. Troutman?"

"Oh." Troutman coughed. "I have a bearskin that would make a fine rug. Black bear, a big male. I also have bobcat and a coyote pelt and a few rabbit furs." He scratched his rather poor beard. "And a longhorn hide."

"Isn't that interesting," Owen said.

"I don't care to hear any more about longhorns, thank you very much," Philomena said.

"How's that again, missus?" Troutman asked.

Owen caused Philomena's blood to simmer by saying, "Pay her no mind. I'd like to talk to you about that hide after we're done eating."

"Whatever you'd like, Mr. Burnett."

For their supper, Philomena—with Mandy's and Estelle's help—had made stew and biscuits. Stew was a favorite of hers because it was so easy to make. All she had to do was take some meat—rabbit or venison or beef or what-have-you—carve it up, chop some carrots and potatoes and maybe green beans, throw it all together in their big pot, add water and salt and pepper, and she had enough for everybody without going to that much effort.

Ebidiah Troutman stared at the china bowl and wooden spoon Estelle placed in front of him as if he didn't know what to do with them.

"Here. Let me fill that for you," Mandy offered. She ladled stew into his bowl, careful not to spill any on the tablecloth.

"I'm obliged, young miss," Troutman said, sitting back until she was done. "Your family is nice as can be."

"My folks taught us to always show respect for our elders," Mandy said.

"Your ma and pa are good people," Troutman said. "There's some hereabouts who aren't."

"Who do you mean?" Mandy asked, but the trapper didn't answer.

The family ate mostly in silence. Normally, the children would chat up a storm. Philomena always encouraged them to talk about anything they wanted during meals.

Owen kept glancing at Troutman. Clearly, he was eager to have their talk.

Unfortunately, Philomena couldn't think of a way to discourage him without coming across as a harpy. Which was something she'd never do. She wasn't Wilda Weaver.

Finally Troutman spooned the last morsel into his mouth and sat back and patted his belly in contentment.

Owen cleared his throat. "Now, then, I'd like to ask you a few questions, if you don't mind."

"About furs and skinning and such?" Troutman said.

"About longhorns."

Chapter 9

It had occurred to Owen that if anyone knew anything about longhorns, it was Ebidiah Troutman. The old trapper had lived in the hill country longer than any white man, and was familiar with all the wildlife, with their habits and their dispositions.

"What do you want to know, Mr. Burnett?"

"Everything," Owen said, and went on to explain about the rising price for meat in the markets back east, and about the new cattle trails for taking them to market.

Troutman cocked his head quizzically. "And you aim to do that with longhorns?"

"We're considering it," Owen said. "But I'll be honest with you. I know next to nothing about them. Oh, I see them from time to time, but they nearly always run off."

"Be thankful they do. There's no more fierce critter in God's whole Creation than a longhorn when it's riled."

"You see?" Philomena said.

"My wife is somewhat against the idea," Owen said. "So I'd like to hear your take. Is it feasible, Ebidiah? Will longhorns be hard to corral?"

The old trapper chuckled. "It won't be any harder than corralling a passel of grizzlies."

"I'm serious."

"So am I." Troutman pursed his thin lips. "Let me tell you what you're up against, Mr. Burnett. Longhorns are . . . what's the word I want? I heard it a few times when I was younger." He gnawed his bottom lip, then brightened.

"Now I remember. *Formidable*. That's longhorns, right there. They're as strong as buffalo and can knock a horse over if they get up enough steam."

"You hear that?" Philomena said.

"Longhorns aren't cows," Troutman went on. "They have minds of their own."

"Worse and worse," Philomena said.

"But they can be tamed with a heap of doing."

"What?" Philomena said.

"I don't want to tame them," Owen said, "just get them to market."

Troutman crossed his legs and folded his arms. "It can be done, I reckon. The Spanish used to round up wild ones for their herds. The Mexicans, too. Those vaqueros are right fine cowboys."

"What tricks did the Spanish use?" Owen was curious to learn.

"Sweat and brains, mostly," Troutman said. "I never saw it, myself, but an old Mex friend of mine claimed he'd heard all about it from his grandpa."

"I'd like to hear the particulars."

"Well, as best I can recall, the Spanish would cut down a lot of trees for rails and build a big corral, then drive the longhorns in."

"That was all it took?"

"Of course not. Rails won't keep a longhorn somewhere it doesn't want to be. But fire will. The Spanish would get a lot of small fires going, all around the herd. And after a few days or a week—I can't remember exactly how long—the longhorns would get used to the vaqueros, and quiet down."

"Fires, huh?" Owen said.

"What you need for the trail is a leader," Troutman said. "A big old bull to go out in front for the rest to follow. But the big bulls are the hardest to catch and as likely to gore you as to let you tame them."

"Do you hear that?" Philomena said.

"Always keep a gun handy," Troutman said. "You never know when one will turn on you."

"Oh, Owen," Philomena said.

Apparently to mollify her, Troutman said, "Your husband just has to be careful."

"No amount of money is worth losing him over," Philomena said. "I am more than ever dead set against it."

"I'm still interested," Owen said. If vaqueros could do it, so could they.

He was going to ask if there was anything more the old trapper could remember, when Mandy spoke up.

"Mr. Troutman, what did you mean when you said there are some folks hereabouts who aren't good people?"

"I'd rather not say, young miss," Troutman said.

"Besides us, there's only the Weavers and the Kursts," Mandy said.

"I know."

"And the Weavers aren't bad people."

"I know that, too. Jasper is a little too fond of coffin varnish, but that's not a sin. His missus has a tart tongue, but that's not a sin, neither."

"That leaves one family."

"I'd still rather not say."

Mandy looked at Owen. "Did my pa happen to mention that he'd be partners with the Kursts in the longhorn venture?"

"Thank you, daughter," Philomena said.

"I don't believe he did, no," Troutman said.

"I couldn't do it with just my sons," Owen said, "and Jasper only has Reuben. We need more hands."

Ebidiah Troutman frowned. "Something tells me you've already made up your mind, Mr. Burnett. And far be it from me to say you're making a mistake. If I had a family, I'd want to provide for them the best I could, the same as you. But you be mighty careful, you hear? The longhorns are worrisome enough. Those Kursts, they're not to be trusted."

"What can possibly make you say that?" Owen said. "Granted, they're rough around the edges, but it's not as if they're snake-mean."

"I learned a long time ago to trust my instincts, Mr. Burnett. And I'd no more trust a Kurst than I would a rabid wolf."

Chapter 10

The next morning Owen went for a ride. He often did that when he needed to think. He would go off into the cedar scrub to clear his head and sort things out.

Not that Owen expected to change his mind about the longhorns. The more he thought about it, the more he liked the idea. Even if that meant partnering up with Gareth Kurst. He appreciated the old trapper's advice, but he believed Gareth was sincere about wanting to work together. As for Gareth's hotheaded and sometimes ill-mannered sons, Owen was sure Gareth wouldn't let things get out of hand. Not with so much money at stake.

The money. Owen never thought of himself as a greedy man, but Lordy, it was tempting. To have more than he ever dreamed. Enough to last him and his family the rest of their lives.

Philomena was still dead set against the notion. Her "womanly instincts," as she called her intuition, warned her to have nothing to do with it.

Owen could recall other instances of Philomena's instincts. Like the time she'd persuaded him to buy a pony for Mandy when Mandy was eight because her instincts told her the pony had the sweetest disposition this side of heaven. Owen gave in because it would be good for Mandy to learn to ride and to have the experience of taking care of the pony. But not a week later it threw her and tried to kick her head in. Turned out, the pony had a mean streak, which was why the buyer sold it.

Then there was the time Philomena's instincts told her an approaching thunderstorm would spawn a tornado. She'd insisted they all go down into the root cellar and stay there until the tornado passed. So they'd huddled with the potatoes and carrots for almost two hours, only to have the thunderstorm fade harmlessly away.

Philomena's instincts weren't always reliable. And as much as Owen cared for her, this time he decided to stand firm and do what his own instincts told him to do.

His kids were the real issue. A good father liked to provide for his children. It was as natural as breathing. He'd always done the best he could raising Luke, Sam, Mandy, and Estelle, and he was as close to them as a father could be. They respected him. Looked up to him. Counted on him to be there for them should they need him.

Here was a chance to give them something his own folks could never give him. Not that they wouldn't have if they could—but for his parents, the opportunity never arose.

Owen could give each of his children "financial security," as the bankers called it. How could he *not* say yes to the idea? The answer was obvious. He had to go through with it, and Philomena would have to live with his decision. Eventually, she'd come around to his way of thinking, just as he'd always come around to hers when the situation was reversed.

Now, rounding yet another thicket, he drew sharp rein.

Not twenty feet away stood a longhorn. A cow of average size, red with white spots. She didn't snort or tear at the ground with her hoof or show any alarm whatsoever. She just stood and stared at him and chewed whatever she was chewing on.

To amuse himself, Owen said, "How do you do, ma'am?"

The longhorn swished her tail.

"I wonder," Owen said and gigged his chestnut forward. Slowly, to test what the cow would do. She looked at the horse and then at him and went on chewing.

Owen was careful of her horns; cows could be just as dangerous as bulls when they were riled. He came up next to her, halted, and waited for her to react. "Well?"

The cow gave a slight toss of her head. Not because she was angry, but to shoo a fly.

"That's all?" Owen said. "You're not going to try and gore me?"

Owen had seen a lot of longhorns around his place, but he'd never once tried to get close to them. He always went his own way and left them free to do as they pleased.

On an impulse, Owen cautiously reached over and touched a finger to the longhorn's back. She didn't do anything. Elated, he straightened and chuckled and shook his head. "Don't this beat all."

Without warning, the longhorn took a step.

Thinking she might be about to attack, Owen stiffened. But no, she went walking off as calmly as you please.

"I'll be," Owen said, and laughed.

He knew an omen when he saw one. This cow was as much as telling him that their brainstorm could work. That some longhorns were docile enough that they could gather up a herd and make the long drive to Abilene and come home with more money in their pokes than he'd ever dreamed.

Gazing skyward, Owen said, "Thank you."

Making no more noise than if she were a ghost, the cow melted into the brush. A feat Owen had observed before. How they could be so stealthy, given their size, was a mystery.

Turning around, he flicked his reins.

Owen would inform Philomena that he was sorry to disappoint her, that he was going to go into the cattle business with Gareth Kurst and Jasper Weaver. She'd no doubt put up an argument, and he'd remind her that no one could predict the future. Maybe it would work out.

Maybe it wouldn't. The important thing was that he had to try. For their children's sake, if nothing else.

"For our children's sake," Owen repeated out loud.

He'd do as he'd so often done and leave everything in God's hands.

Come what may.

Chapter 11

Gareth Kurst called a meeting of his clan. In the hills of Tennessee where they were from, "clan" was what most folks called their families. Gareth's wasn't as large as he'd have liked; he'd wanted four or five more young'uns. It hadn't worked out.

Gareth blamed his wife. Something had gone askew inside of her. That was the only explanation. His body worked fine. Proof of that was in their five sons and one daughter. So it had to be her body that was at fault. Something had gone wrong in her womanly parts.

Gareth had told Ariel so, more than once. She always cried and said she was sorry, and how he shouldn't ought to blame her because she didn't have any control over whether she got pregnant.

Gareth thought that was a poor excuse.

Harland, Thaxter, Wylie, Silsby and Iden were their boys. Lorette, the lone girl, could ride as well as any of them, and hold her own and then some in a scrap.

Because he'd always been fond of hound dogs, Gareth tended to think of his offspring as a litter. And as with any litter where no two pups were ever the same, his own brood had distinct traits.

Harland was the pup that lorded it over the rest. That he was the oldest had something to do with it. So did the fact he was the biggest. He just naturally liked to tell his siblings what to do.

Thaxter was the fast pup. The one that always got to

the mother's teats first. He was fast on his feet and fast with his six-shooter, and eager to show off how fast he could be.

Wylie was the thinker of the litter. There was always a pup that didn't play much but sat off by itself and seemed to study on things all the time. That was Wylie.

Gareth had never seen it fail that in most litters there was a dumb one, a pup that would run into things, that had as much coordination as a drunk, and that was always yipping and yapping even when there was nothing to yip or yap about. Silsby, sad to say, was the brainless pup of their bunch.

That left Iden. His youngest son, as with many litters, had turned out to be the runt. Five-feet-two in his stocking feet, Iden had been mercilessly picked on when he was little. Now he was sixteen, and still the runt. Only he wore an Arkansas toothpick on his right hip, and no one picked on him as much anymore.

Growing up around nothing but boys, Lorette was practically a boy herself. She could shoot like a boy, ride like a boy, rope like a boy. She even dressed like a boy in britches and a shirt instead of a dress. She was so boyish, Gareth had half-taken to thinking of her more as a son than as a daughter.

Lorette didn't mind. She swaggered around saying how she could lick anything on two legs. These days, any man who made the mistake of poking fun at her over how she acted or dressed regretted it. She didn't take any guff, that gal.

Truth to tell, Gareth was proud of her. He felt that pride yet again as he gazed out over his entire clan.

With the blue of day giving way to the gray of twilight as the sun dipped below the far horizon, Gareth stood with his arms folded. They were gathered outside their cabin rather than inside where the heat of the day hadn't dissipated yet.

Harland, Thaxter, and Silsby had their heads huddled and were talking in low tones.

Gareth cleared his throat to get their attention, and when they didn't look up, he barked, "Whatever you three are jawing about can wait. We have something important to discuss."

Gareth glanced at Ariel, seated on a stump he'd never gotten around to clearing. There were a lot of stumps. Removing them was hard work, and if there was one thing Gareth hated more than work, he'd yet to make its acquaintance.

"We know why you called us together, Pa," Harland said. "The longhorn business."

"I don't see what there is to talk about," Thaxter said. "We can round up cattle as good as anybody."

"Let Pa speak," Wylie said. "He knows what he's doing."

Iden nodded. "Go ahead, Pa."

"As if I need your permission," Gareth said. He'd already worked out part of what he was going to say, and he began with, "All of you know about the cowpoke I ran into in town. How he told Owen Burnett and Jasper Weaver and me about the money to be made if we take a herd of longhorns north to market. The meat packers are paying forty dollars a head, if you can believe it."

Silsby chuckled. "How dumb is that when a longhorn can be had for four or five dollars hereabouts?"

"It's not dumb at all." Gareth set him straight. He had to do that a lot with Silsby. "They cut the cattle up and sell the meat by the pound and make twice what they pay, if not more."

"We should cut the cows up and make that much, too," Silsby said.

Gareth reminded himself that Silsby was the slow one, and he must be patient. "What do you know about butchering?"

"I can carve up a deer," Silsby said.

"Not the same," Gareth said. "And how would we get the meat to market even if we did? It would rot long before we got to the meat buyers. That's just not practical, boy."

"You use that word with me a lot, Pa," Silsby said.

Lorette, who was chewing on a stick, spat it out. "That's because you don't use your thinker, brother-mine. You ain't got no common sense."

"Do, too," Silsby said.

"Who was it threw rocks at that hornet's nest the other day, and had to run when they swarmed him?" Lorette laughed. "And who nearly shot his toe off a while back when he stuck his six-gun in his holster with the six-gun cocked, and it went off? Who rigged a rope to swing out over the creek but didn't tie the knot tight and got tangled in the rope when it fell in with him?"

"What's your point?" Silsby said.

"Enough," Gareth said. If he didn't intervene, they'd bicker endlessly.

"We're listening, husband." Ariel broke her silence.

"You better be, all of you," Gareth said. "We have a chance here to make a lot of money, and I won't let any of you spoil it. Which is why I'm laying down the law. I'm going to tell you how it will be, and you damned well better do as I say."

"You want us to be nice to the Burnetts and Weavers," Lorette said. "We get that."

"You only think you do," Gareth said. "Listen. Jasper Weaver is a weak sister, and his son's not much better. I have nothing but contempt for both, but do you know what? I never let on. You never let anyone outside our clan know how you feel about them."

"Why not?" Silsby asked.

"So they'll never suspect if you have to stab them in the back," Harland said.

Gareth nodded. "In this case, we've got another reason. We can use their help gathering a herd and getting it to market. The same with the Burnetts, although they're not the no-accounts the Weavers are. The Burnetts are hard workers, so we need them even more."

"So you want us to be nice?" Iden said. "Is that your point?"

"Nice as can be. Some of you have tempers, and you're quick to rile." Gareth gave Harland and Thaxter pointed looks. "There's to be none of that with the Burnetts or the Weavers. You hear me?"

"I don't like Luke Burnett," Thaxter said. "He acts like he's a gunhand when he ain't ever shot anybody."

"I don't like any of them," Harland said.

Lowering his arms, Gareth balled his fists. "No matter how you feel, you're to treat them decent. If one of them makes you mad, go off somewhere until you simmer down."

"All this trouble you want us to go to," Harland said resentfully. "What's in it for us?"

"You'll all get a share of the money."

"But you'll get most of it, I bet," Harland said.

"I'm the pa. I should," Gareth declared. "Until then, remember. I want each of you on your best behavior. Or else." He raised a fist to accent his point.

"Well, hell," Lorette said.

Chapter 12

You'd think Jasper was going to be gone for a year, the way his wife carried on. "I don't know how long it will take to round up enough cattle," Jasper said as he adjusted the cinch on his sorrel. "It depends on how hard it is."

"You be careful, you hear?" Wilda said. "Watch out that nothing happens to our son."

About to climb on his own horse, Reuben rolled his eyes. "I'm not a little boy anymore, Ma." At seventeen, he was as thin as a rake and took a lot after Jasper. Which was to say his face was all bone and sharp angles, and he had no chin to speak of.

"Anything happens to you, it would break my heart," Wilda said.

Jasper almost snorted in amusement. The notion of his wife having a heart had never occurred to him. A mouth, yes, the way she carped and carped.

"I won't let any harm come to him."

"Those longhorns aren't puny," Wilda reminded him. "And there's hostiles and rattlesnakes and polecats to watch out for."

"When you say polecats, Ma," Reuben said, "do you mean the smelly kind or the kind who stick you up?"

"Both."

Jasper wished he could take a nip from his flask. He hadn't had a swallow in over an hour and was in dire need. Being around his wife had that effect. "There haven't been any outlaws in these parts in a coon's age." None that he'd heard of, anyway.

"Even so," Wilda said.

"Even so what?" Jasper said.

"You know."

No, Jasper didn't, but he would be darned if he'd ask her to explain. She had a habit of putting on airs, of acting as if she was smarter than him, when the truth was, he let her think she was smarter because they had fewer spats that way.

"Where are you going, anyhow?" Wilda asked.

"I told you already," Jasper said. "Up near—what's that creek called? Comanche Creek."

"Why so far out?" Wilda clasped her hands together as if she were about to pray. "You do know they named it that because Comanches used to be seen up that way?"

"Long before we came here," Jasper said.

"Even so," Wilda said a second time. She was fond of using the same expression again and again.

"You take care of your own self while we're away," Jasper felt compelled to say. He went to kiss her but she averted her face like always. He settled for pecking her on the cheek.

"Don't worry none about me. I have the shotgun."

Jasper's saddle creaked as he stepped into the stirrup and swung up. He was wearing a well-used brown hat, and touched the brim. "Be seeing you."

Wilda stepped over and put a hand on Reuben's leg. "You listen to your pa, son. Do as he says unless it's something that might get you hurt, then do what you think I would say."

"Honestly," Jasper said.

"What?" Wilda said.

Jasper got out of there before he said something that might earn him a tongue-lashing. When her dander was up, Wilda used her tongue like a bullwhip. He glanced back and gave a little wave but only because she expected him to and would complain about it the next time he saw her if he didn't.

Reuben waved, too. "I reckon I'm the luckiest boy alive to have a ma like her. She's always looking out for us."

"That's because if we died," Jasper said, "she wouldn't have anybody to gripe to."

"Oh, Pa," Reuben said, and laughed. "You sure are a hoot."

Jasper sighed.

The Texas hill country was in the green lush of early spring. Wildlife was everywhere, deer and rabbits and squirrels and the like. Longhorns, too.

Jasper and Reuben were about halfway to Comanche Creek when they spied several longhorns off in the brush, watching them. It prompted Jasper to bring up something that had been weighing on his mind.

"We need to talk, son."

"About what, Pa?" Reuben was grinning at the world as he usually did. He seemed to find living a delight.

Wait until he's married, Jasper thought. That will cure him. "This cattle affair can mean a lot to us if things go right. To hear Gareth Kurst talk, we'll have more money than that old king what's-his-name."

"Who?"

"Some king in Greece or Persia or somewhere who was rich. My point is that we can be rich, too, or as close to it as we'll ever get. All we have to do is play our cards right."

"How do I do that, exactly? I've hardly ever played cards. Ma won't let me. She says gambling is the devil's work."

"Don't I know it," Jasper said. There was a whole list of things Wilda didn't approve of. Drinking was at the top but he did it anyway, sometimes right in front of her to show her he hadn't been entirely strangled by her apron strings. "I'd take it as a favor if you'd go out of your way not to make the Kursts mad at you. You know how some of Gareth's boys get."

"That girl of his, too," Reuben said. "Lorette is always laughing at me. Half the time, I don't even know what she's laughing at."

"The Burnetts are nice," Jasper mentioned.

"They treat me real good," Reuben agreed. "Estelle even talks to me when I see them in town. She's the sweetest gal there is."

Jasper had thought the same, once, about Wilda. Back then he couldn't look at her without getting excited. Then came their wedding night, and she made it plain that she didn't share his desire. Being intimate, to her, was a duty she was required to perform as wife, nothing more. She allowed it, but only under her terms. She was ice, that woman.

Jasper never said anything, but Wilda crushed him that night. She took all his passion and threw it over a cliff, and it crashed to bits on the hard rocks of bitter knowledge that he'd married an icy shrew. Any love he'd felt evaporated like morning dew under a hot sun in the glare of her stern disapproval of nearly everything about him.

There were days when Jasper wondered why she'd wed him. To listen to her, he had so many faults, he was next to useless. It occurred to him that all he was to Wilda was a pair of ears to listen to her endless gripes.

Now, hoping to nip his son's interest in Estelle Burnett in the bud, Jasper said, "Love ain't always what we figure it to be. You fight shy of her, you hear? Her brothers won't like you fawning over her."

"Who will fawn?" Reuben said. "I can barely get up the courage to say howdy."

"Maybe so. But you treat her as a friend and nothing more. We don't want Owen and Philomena mad at us. We need to stick by them against the Kursts."

"Against?"

"Gareth Kurst has always treated me the same way Lorette treats you. Oh, he doesn't come out and laugh in my face, but I can see it in his eyes. He has little regard for me. His son Harland has even less. Harland proved that at the saloon one time when he told me flat-out he reckons I'm next to worthless."

"He didn't!"

"I'm suspicious of the Kursts, son. I don't trust them. Owen Burnett does, but they don't treat Owen the same as they treat me."

"If you don't trust them, I won't, neither."

Jasper wasn't done. "The whole Kurst clan is like a nest of rattlers. You can't predict when one of them might strike."

"This complicates things, doesn't it?" Reuben said.

"So long as we keep our wits about us, we'll be fine," Jasper assured him. "I'm not keen on the notion of being away for so long when we drive the cattle to market, but all that money will make it worthwhile."

"So long as we live to get our share."

"There's that," Jasper said.

Chapter 13

Comanche Creek was as far into the hills as most settlers ever went. Ebidiah Troutman had gone farther, but then, the old trapper had been everywhere.

Ebidiah loved the Texas hill country. The first time he set eyes on it years ago, he'd made up his mind then and there that it was where he'd spend the rest of his days. For decades he'd trapped in the High Rockies, but trapping was hard, sometimes brutal work, and when a man got on in years, it became more difficult to do what needed doing. His mind was willing but his body had aches and pains where it never had aches and pains before. Each day was a reminder he wasn't as spry as he used to be.

Ebidiah never bothered to build a cabin. He despised having a roof over his head. His more-or-less permanent camp was a gully, a place where he stashed his packs when he didn't need them. Rimmed by thick forest, it was well-hid from the rest of the world.

On this particular morning, seated cross-legged close to his fire to warm himself against the chill morning air, Ebidiah sipped coffee and pondered on the revelation that the Burnett family was going to go into the cattle business with the Kursts.

Ebidiah liked Owen Burnett and his family. They were nice folks. They always treated him cordially.

Ebidiah didn't like Gareth Kurst, nor any of that brood. They were filled with spite and venom. He'd seen it with his own eyes, many a time. How they yelled at each other, and were always squabbling. He'd seen how Gareth lorded it over them. Twice he'd witnessed Gareth cuffing one or another of the boys, and once he saw Gareth cuff his missus.

Ebidiah had seen a lot, thanks to his most prized possession. Thinking of it, he opened a pack next to him and took out his brass spyglass. Back in his trapping days, a lot of trappers owned one. A spyglass kept a man alive; he could spot enemies far off.

Not many people used one, these days. Which was a shame, in Ebidiah's opinion, because for sheer entertainment, nothing beat spying on folks with a telescope.

Ebidiah did it all the time. He'd roost half a mile from a homestead and watch the settlers go about their daily doings. Since the Kursts and the Burnetts and the Weavers were the closest, he spied on them the most. He'd learned a lot of their habits, seen them do things. Which was how he knew the Kurst clan was snake-mean, and why he was worried for the Burnetts.

Ebidiah shouldn't let it bother him. He told himself Owen was a grown man and could do as he pleased. But Mrs. Burnett was always especially nice to him, and that sweet oldest gal of theirs, Mandy, treated him like he was her grandpa instead of a stranger.

It was plain to Ebidiah that Owen didn't know what he was getting himself into. As sure as the sun rose and set every day, something bad would come of their cattle venture.

But what could Ebidiah do? He wasn't their kin. He wasn't anything except an old man past his prime with nothing to do anymore except spy on people.

"Listen to me," Ebidiah said to Sarabell, who was dozing. Her ears pricked but she didn't muster the effort to raise her head. Like him, she was getting on in years.

On Ebidiah's last visit to the Burnetts, Owen had mentioned that he and Gareth and Jasper Weaver were going to Comanche Creek to scout around for longhorns.

Ebidiah figured he'd mosey up that way, too, and keep an
eye on things, as it were.

With his spyglass, he could lie low in the hills and
watch what was going on.

He wasn't worried about being caught. When it came
to being stealthy, he could be as sneaky as a Comanche.

And who knew? It might be a spectacle in itself, those
settlers trying to catch longhorns and the longhorns not
wanting to be caught. Some might put up a fight, and
blood might flow.

Five hundred to a thousand pounds or more of muscles and horn was nothing to sneeze at.

Ebidiah only hoped that if someone were gored or
trampled, it would be one of those mean Kursts.

Chapter 14

The Texas hill country boasted an abundance of vegetation. Several kinds of oaks, and junipers, were the most common trees. Occasional pecan groves added variety. Interspersed with grassland of predominantly grama, and watered by creeks and streams, the hills were a haven for wildlife.

Longhorns thrived. A hardy breed able to live off the land where other cattle couldn't, longhorns enjoyed a feast of plenty in the hills. Intimidated by their size, predators left them alone. They wandered where they wanted, with no one to stop them.

In recent years their population soared. No one had done a count, simply because no one could. There were too many, spread over an area larger than some Eastern states.

For the most part, they avoided contact with humans. They'd rather make themselves scarce than charge. There were exceptions, though. Tales of the unwary being gored were common.

Owen Burnett was reflecting on those tales as he and his two sons neared the vicinity of Comanche Creek. All three had rifles in their scabbards, and Luke and Samuel had revolvers, besides. Luke never went anywhere without his Remington. Samuel had an old Walker Colt that he needed two hands to shoot and was too big to strap around his waist. It nestled in a saddle holster that hung from his saddle horn.

Owen had never owned a six-gun, himself. He had a Spencer repeating rifle that held seven rounds. To feed them into the chamber, he had to work the lever. His particular model used .56-56 ammunition. Some shooters didn't think that was powerful enough to drop big game, but he'd never had any problems with it. Then again, the only large animal he ever shot was a wild boar, and it had run off.

"We'll be there shortly, Pa," Samuel announced.

Owen smiled. His youngest was so excited, he couldn't stop fidgeting. "Relax, son. We're not heading out after longhorns right away. It will be tomorrow morning at the earliest."

"A whole night with those Kursts," Luke said, bringing his horse up on Owen's right.

"Don't start," Owen said. "There will be a lot of nights. You have to learn how to get along with them, or you might as well not take part."

"It's not me you have to worry about," Luke said.

Owen didn't dispute the fact. Luke could control himself. The Kurst brood were the ones to watch, particularly that Harland, and Thaxter. Owen would as soon they didn't take part—but without the Kursts, the roundup was doomed before it started.

"Did you hear me, Pa?" Luke said.

"My ears work fine."

"You didn't answer me."

Owen shifted in the saddle and beckoned for Samuel to bring his mount up on the other side. "I want both you boys to listen to me. I know this won't be easy. Those Kursts are always on the prod. But you need to tuck your spurs and not take offense."

"What if they prod too hard?" Luke asked.

"Like if they lay a hand on you?" Owen said. "Or come out with an insult you can't abide and still look at yourself in the mirror?"

"Something like that," Luke said.

"Do the best you can. Neither of you have ever had tempers. Keep them in check and you'll be all right."

"Do you reckon Lorette will be there?" Samuel asked.

"Where did that come from?" Owen asked.

"Pa?"

"I'm talking about not getting shot by any of the Kurst boys and you bring the girl up. Were you paying attention?"

"She's pretty, is all," Sam said, and did more fidgeting. "It would fluster me some, having to work with her around."

"Wonderful," Owen teased. "Don't tell me you're in love. That's the last thing we need."

"Shucks," Sam said. "I don't even know what love is."

"Keep it that way," Luke said.

"Who are you to tell me what to do?" Sam rejoined.

"Boys, boys," Owen said. They weren't even to Comanche Creek and his sons, who rarely argued, were about to have one over a Kurst.

"You heard him, Pa," Sam said. "Just because Luke hates them doesn't mean I have to."

"Lorette is no different from the rest of her kin," Luke said. "She's trouble, through and through."

"I don't believe that," Sam said.

"You haven't seen how she sashays around town? She practically throws herself at every boy she meets."

"Take that back."

Owen seldom raised his voice but he raised it now. "Enough! We'll treat her like we do the rest of the Kursts. Be civil, but nothing more."

"Fine by me," Luke said.

"Sam?" Owen said.

"I'm not looking to get hitched, if that's what you're worried about."

"I should hope not," Owen said. "Keep your mind on the longhorns. Daydream about her, and you're liable to get a horn through the chest."

"That would never happen in a million years," Sam declared with great conviction.

"Glad to hear it," Owen said.

Chapter 15

Comanche Creek meandered through the hills like a lazy snake. It flowed year-round, unlike a considerable number of Texas waterways that dried up in the summer.

The spot Gareth Kurst had chosen was where the creek bisected almost a mile of grassland flanked on both sides by hills thick with cedar scrub, oaks, and brush.

"This is near perfect," Owen Burnett complimented Gareth when he drew rein at the camp the Kursts had made at the west end of the grass. "Those hills must be crawling with longhorns. They can hide up there and come down to drink and graze whenever they want. How did you find it?"

"We came across it when we were hunting once," Gareth said. "I remembered it because I thought at the time it would be a good place for a ranch."

A fire had been kindled, and Gareth's sons—and Lorette—were sitting around drinking coffee, and talking.

"Luke, Samuel," Gareth greeted Owen's own boys with a bob of his chin.

"Mr. Kurst," Sam said. "Isn't this exciting?"

"Making money excites me," Gareth said. "Not all the work we have to do to earn it," he added. "Not that we'll shirk our part, mind you. We're all in this together."

Owen saw Luke and Thaxter swap hard looks. "I just hope everyone can get along."

"My brood will, or else," Gareth said. "Any of them

acts up, you tell me and I'll deal with it." He turned and scanned the approaches to the south. "Still no sign of Weaver and his boy. They live closer than you, and you'd think they'd have gotten here sooner."

"Jasper will show," Owen said. "He gave us his word."

"So did Wilda, and hers counts for more," Gareth said. "Jasper doesn't breathe without her say-so."

Sam chuckled.

"That's not funny, son," Owen chided. He felt sorry for Jasper, and was eternally thankful that Philomena was nothing like Wilda Weaver.

"Let it be a lesson, boy," Gareth said to Samuel. "When you tie the knot, tie with a gal who won't ride roughshod over you. A man who lets a woman do that doesn't have any backbone."

Owen felt compelled to say, "A marriage should be a fifty-fifty proposition. The man and the woman should work together, make decisions together, that sort of thing."

"You have strange notions sometimes," Gareth said. "Men should be the masters in their house. Look at my Ariel. She's too dumb to make decisions. I make them for her, and she lives with that whether she likes it or not."

"I don't know if I could do that, Mr. Kurst," Sam said.

"You'd better learn, or you'll have another Wilda on your hands. When a man doesn't keep a female in her place, she becomes uppity."

Owen hardly considered Gareth an authority on matrimony, and didn't want him giving Sam and Luke bad ideas. He noticed that Lorette was listening, too, and changed the subject with, "Have you seen any longhorns since you got here?"

"A few have come to the edge of the trees, seen us, and gone back in. But there's a heap more up there. And I can prove it." Gareth motioned. "Come with me and I'll show you something."

Dismounting, Owen went with Gareth to the creek. Gareth pointed. The ground on either side of the water was pockmarked with hoofprints, many hundreds of them.

"See what I mean?" Gareth said.

The prints were so mingled that telling one set from another was next to impossible, although a few exceptionally large ones stood out.

"Must be some monsters up there," Owen remarked.

"More meat for the butcher," Gareth said.

The sun was on its westward slant. A few hours of daylight were left. Then the Texas night would descend in all its starry glory.

"I suggest we have a leisurely supper and get a good night's rest and start early in the morning," Owen proposed. "It shouldn't take more than a day or two to get the lay of the land. Then we can go to town, buy the supplies we need, and begin in earnest."

"I reckon we can't take more than a month or two to round up the cattle," Gareth said, "not if we want to get them to market before winter sets in. Kansas is a far piece."

That sounded right to Owen. He recollected the cowboy in the saloon told them that a drive took two to three months, and they'd want to reach Abilene well ahead of the cold weather or the ride home would be hellacious. "Sounds good to me."

Gareth glanced over his broad shoulder toward the fire, and lowered his voice. "My youngest came up to me earlier and claimed he saw a redskin watching us from off in the woods. I went for a look and there was nothing. Not even tracks. I gave Iden a smack for jumping at shadows. Comanches haven't been seen in these parts for a couple of years or more."

"I know," Owen said. "The longhorns worry me more."

"We can handle them."

Owen admired his outlook. Say what people would about Gareth Kurst, one thing the man didn't lack was confidence.

"Well, look who it is," Gareth said.

Owen looked up.

A pair of riders were coming around a hill. One rose in the stirrups and waved.

"Jasper and his boy," Gareth stated the obvious. "I bet if they hadn't seen our smoke, they'd have missed us and gone on by."

That set Owen to wondering who else might see it. "You're sure your son didn't see a Comanche?"

"Even if he did, they won't bother us, as many guns as we have."

Thinking that there was a fine line between confidence and foolhardiness, Owen said, "They raid when and where they please. They're not yellow."

"They're Injuns," Gareth said, as if that had meaning in itself. "Let's go greet our partner."

Jasper Weaver and his son held their mounts to a walk. Jasper smiled and waved a second time.

"Will you look at that simpleton?" Gareth said.

"Jasper is a good man," Owen came to his friend's defense.

"He's a lush. We'll have to keep an eye on him. He needs to do his part, the same as the rest of us."

Owen didn't argue. Everyone knew about Jasper's fondness for liquor. Indeed, when Jasper climbed down and offered his hand, exclaiming how pleased he was to see Owen again, Owen smelled whiskey on Jasper's breath. He shook without saying anything.

Not Gareth. "Been hitting that flask of yours again, have you?"

"Only a little," Jasper said, sounding hurt that Gareth had brought it up. He gave a mild start when Gareth draped a big hand on his shoulder.

"Listen, Weaver. If you want to drink yourself into an early grave, go right ahead. But you're to hold off on this roundup. You can take a chug now and then, but if I catch you reeling in the saddle, or too unsteady to stand on your own two feet, I'll thump you to within an inch of your life."

"Now see here," Jasper said. He went to say more, but Gareth held up a finger.

"That's all that needs be said, Weaver. Do your part

and we'll get along fine." Wheeling, Gareth strode toward the fire.

"The nerve of the man," Jasper said to Owen, but not loud enough that Gareth would hear.

"We're off to a grand start," Owen said.

Chapter 16

They were up at the break of dawn, roused by Lorette, who took delight in hollering, "Up and at 'em, you lazy menfolk. We've got work to do." She kicked a few of her brothers who were slow in rousing.

Breakfast consisted of biscuits that Gareth had ordered his wife to make. He'd brought an entire sack, and didn't seem to mind that Ariel's biscuits were too hard and too brittle. When it came to food, the Kursts could eat anything. He passed some out to the Burnetts and the Weavers, and young Sam grimaced with each bite.

The sun was a blazing orb on the eastern rim of the world when they forked leather.

Gareth reined his mount in front of the rest and turned to face them. Leaning on his saddle horn, he announced, "We'll go in pairs and spread out to cover more of the countryside."

"Is that wise, what with the Comanches and all?" Jasper asked.

"There hasn't been a Comanche in these parts in a long while," Gareth said. "Your scalp is safe." It amused him that Weaver was so paperbacked. "Jasper, you and Reuben might as well pair up. Harland, you ride with Thaxter. Wylie, you're with Silsby. I'll take Iden with me. That leaves Owen and Luke."

"What about me, Mr. Kurst?" Sam Burnett wanted to know.

"I guess you'll have to ride with Lorette," Gareth said.

"There's no one else left. And behave yourself, boy. Don't run off and marry her behind my back." He chuckled when Sam flushed scarlet with embarrassment.

"I'd never do that, Mr. Kurst."

"Shucks," Lorette said. "I had my hopes up there for a second."

"None of your shenanigans, daughter," Gareth warned. "Treat him like he's one of your brothers."

"Ah, Pa."

"Any questions?" Gareth said to the others. "If not, we'll meet back here about an hour before sunset."

"You sound like a general commanding his army," Jasper said.

"Someone has to take charge," Gareth said. "Unless you're up to directing the hunt yourself."

"No, that's all right," Jasper said quickly. "You're better at it."

Gareth looked at Owen. "Any objections?"

"Working in pairs is best," Owen agreed.

Gareth regarded the others. "Today we're just counting. Keep a tally of how many longhorns you come across. Don't spook them or shoot them if they come at you. Run away."

"I don't like turning tail," Harland said.

"Me, neither," Thaxter threw in.

"These are cattle, not men," Gareth said. "You'll tuck tail if I tell you to. What have I told you matters the most?"

"The money comes before all else," Harland quoted him.

"Damn right it does. And every longhorn is money on the hoof."

Owen spoke up with, "Our lives are more important than any amount of money."

"To you, maybe," Gareth said. He laughed so Owen and Jasper would think he was joshing when he wasn't. "Now let's scatter."

Without further to-do, Gareth reined to the north. His youngest was quick to join him, swelling with pride.

"Thanks for picking me, Pa," Iden said.

"Someone has to tell you what to do, and it might as well be me."

"Still," Iden said. He'd been born with the misfortune of taking after his mother, at least as far as his looks went. "I won't let you down."

"You'd better not." One trait that Gareth didn't like about his youngest was that Iden was a chatterbox. The boy could talk rings around a tree. "And none of your usual gabbing."

"I can't help it if I'm friendly."

"You don't need to be friendly with me. I'm your pa." Gareth had always been annoyed by Iden's air of innocence. Try as Gareth might, he couldn't disabuse the boy of the silly notion that the world was basically a decent place. That was the problem with young boys. The only one more naïve than Iden was Samuel Burnett. Reuben Weaver wasn't so much naïve as dumb.

No sooner did they enter the brush than they encountered a pair of longhorns, cows that turned tail and melted away without so much as a snort or a flick of an ear.

"Golly, they can be quiet when they want to," Iden exclaimed.

"What did I tell you about flapping your gums?"

"Sorry, Pa."

If there was one rule of parenting that Gareth had learned over the years, it was to rule his roost with an iron hand. Not that he'd believed any different before he married. His pa had not been one to spare the rod and neither was he, although Gareth preferred an open hand or a fist to a birch stick. When his kids were little, he'd often rattled their teeth with a hard cuff.

Not sixty yards higher they came on a clear space, and four longhorns that stood their ground, and stared.

"We'll go around," Gareth said. He purposely rode close to see what the longhorns would do; the animals didn't do anything.

"Why are they looking at us like that?" Iden asked.

"They're wondering if they should gore you."

Gareth had heard stories about men who had been

run through. The tale he recollected best was told to him in a saloon by a Mexican freighter who drank tequila like it was water. According to the Mex, he'd been with a freight outfit that stopped at a spring to water their oxen. It was late in the day, and the seven drivers were more than a little spooked when a longhorn bull stepped out of the shadows. They'd stood still, thinking that it wouldn't attack if they stayed quiet. Instead, the bull bellowed and barreled at them like a grizzly gone amok. Before they could collect their wits, the man closest to the bull was impaled through the chest and flung aside. A second man screamed and turned to run, and a horn sheared completely through his body to burst out the other side. He died thrashing and gurgling blood. In a panic, the rest fled. The bull came after them. A third driver was knocked down and had his head stove in by an iron-hard hoof. A fourth man was butted low in the back. The Mex who told Gareth the story shivered as he related how he'd heard the man's spine snap with a loud *crack*. Only three drivers made it into the brush. The Mex said he flung himself flat and hugged the ground, sure the bull would find him and do him in as it had done in the others. After a long while another man called out to him that the bull was gone. So scared he had to pee, the Mex ventured to the spring, and never forgot the sight that greeted him.

"It was horrible, *señor*. The most terrible thing I have ever seen, and I have seen the work of Apaches."

Gareth had heard another account, about a rancher who kept a longhorn as a pet. This was back in the days before anyone had any use for them. The rancher liked to show his pet off to his friends, and treated it no different than he did his dog. One morning he went out to the corral to feed it, and the moment he stepped inside, the longhorn was on him like a bear on honey. The longhorn gored him not once but half a dozen times, then tossed the lifeless body on its horns as if the rancher were a plaything. The rancher's wife saw it all, and was never quite right in her head afterward. Every time she saw a longhorn, she'd scream.

Gareth put all of that from his mind and concentrated on the count. By the middle of the day he was upwards of a hundred. And he'd only had to go about four miles.

Even Iden saw the possibilities. "There's an awful lot of those critters out here," he commented when they drew rein on a hill to survey the tract ahead.

"Is there ever," Gareth said excitedly. "We'll be rolling in money."

Iden hesitated, then said, "Are we fixing to play fair with them, Pa?"

"Who?"

"Mr. Burnett and Mr. Weaver."

"What makes you think I wouldn't?"

"The night before last, Harland told me that we might wind up with more than our share."

"Your brother said that? Flat-out?"

"He sort of hinted it. His exact words were, 'Wouldn't it be nice if we ended up with their shares, too?'"

"I'll have a talk with him," Gareth said.

"It's not true, then?"

"I gave them my word, didn't I? All that need concern you, boy, is doing the work I give you and not getting gored. Leave the rest to me. And don't pay any attention to your big brother. He says things he shouldn't all the time."

"It wouldn't bother me any if it was true," Iden informed him. "I'm your son and I'll do whatever you say."

Gareth smiled in relief. "Good to know," he said.

Chapter 17

For Samuel Burnett, the day didn't seem real. It was more like a dream come true. He even pinched himself to be sure he was awake, and since the pinch hurt, he must be.

Sam had never told anyone, but he thought Lorette Kurst was about the most beautiful female he'd ever laid eyes on. Not that Sam had laid eyes on a lot. Except for the family's infrequent visits to town, his ma and his sisters were the only females he was around.

Sam would be the first to admit he didn't have much experience with women. Until the last year or so, he'd hardly paid them any mind. Girls were girls, and women were just bigger girls. But something changed. Something inside of him. He began to notice the ladies in town more than he ever had. And then there was Lorette.

Lordy, she was gorgeous, Sam couldn't help thinking as he rode behind her in their search for longhorns. He couldn't believe his incredible luck in being paired up with her. When Gareth Kurst said it, he'd half-feared his pa would say he shouldn't. But his pa didn't say a thing, and now here Sam was, alone with the girl of his daydreams and nighttime imaginings.

"What the blazes is the matter with you?"

Sam glanced up and drew rein, startled to find Lorette had stopped and was staring at him in puzzlement. "Ma'am?" he said.

"Let's get some things clear, handsome," Lorette said.

"Don't call me 'ma'am.' Call my ma 'ma'am' if you want. That's what you call older ladies. But I'm the same age as you, or pretty near. So no 'ma'am's for me."

Sam's ears began to burn. He'd distinctly heard her call him "handsome." She must be joshing, because as far as he knew, he was as plain as anything. "I'm sorry. I didn't know."

"Are you a man or a mouse?"

"What?" Sam said in confusion.

"Never mind. Now answer my question. Why did you have that peculiar look on your face?"

"What was peculiar about it?"

"You looked like my little brother Iden used to when he ate pie or cake or candy. A sort of dreamy, stupid look."

"I don't want to look stupid," Sam assured her in all earnestness.

Lorette had a fine laugh. "Just so you're paying attention. I've counted twenty-three longhorns so far. How many have you counted?"

Sam wanted to die, he was so ashamed. He'd barely paid attention to the cows and bulls. All he was interested in was Lorette. "The same," he fibbed.

"Good." Lorette gestured. "Why don't you ride up here next to me so we can talk?"

"You sure?"

"Why not? Don't tell me you're like my brother Wylie and hardly ever say a word unless you're spoken to."

"Oh, I can talk plenty when I have a reason to."

"Then what are you waiting for? Or don't you like female company?"

Sam clucked to his roan and brought it beside her. "I like female company just fine. Who wouldn't?"

"Some of my brothers, for starters," Lorette said, "and men in general."

"I'm not sure how that works," Sam said. "My pa likes women. And Luke has never said he doesn't."

"My family is different. My pa and my brothers think females are a nuisance more than anything. They've said so to my face."

Before Sam could stop himself, he blurted, "I'd never say such a terrible thing to a face as pretty as yours."

A slow smile spread across Lorette's. "Well, listen to you. Are you fond of me, Samuel Burnett?"

Now it felt like Sam's whole body was on fire. "'Fond' is a strong word," he replied, his voice sounding strange.

"Oh, my," Lorette said, and laughed again. "This hunt might be more fun than I thought it would be."

"Ma'am?" Sam said, then coughed and said, "Sorry. It's a habit. My ma says I'm to always call ladies that."

"I'm not no lady. I'm sitting here in men's clothes, in case you ain't noticed."

"Oh, I've noticed," Sam said.

"Have you, now?" Lorette grinned and continued with, "So what would you like to talk about?"

"You're the one who wanted to talk. You tell me."

Around them, the hills were lush with the colors of spring, with greens and browns, and here and there splashes of yellow and blue wildflowers. Songbirds warbled, butterflies flitted about, a red hawk screeched. Occasionally, deer bounded off. Once, there was a rabbit. Then there were all the longhorns.

"Tell me about yourself, Sam Burnett."

Sam shrugged. "There's not much to tell. I came west with my family and we've lived here ever since. I haven't seen much or done much. The states we passed through, I hardly remember them."

"Sounds kind of dull," Lorette said.

"How about you?"

"I try to make my life as exciting as I can. I hate to be bored. I hate it more than anything."

"How do you excite yourself?"

Lorette snorted, then stared at him for so long, he grew uncomfortable.

"What?"

"You were serious."

"I wouldn't have asked if I wasn't. I've never had much excitement. Mainly, I just go about doing my chores and whatnot."

An impish gleam lit Lorette's green eyes. "You're down-right adorable. Has anyone ever told you that?"

Sam was sure he blushed from his head to his toes. "You shouldn't call a man that. It's not fitting."

"So you're a man, are you?"

"Well, I'm not no boy anymore."

"I'm beginning to see that," Lorette said. She flicked her eyes over him, and grinned. "Yes, sir. The possibilities are commencing to occur to me."

"The which?"

Instead of answering, Lorette asked, "Where'd you get that hand cannon, anyhow?"

Sam placed his hand on his saddle holster. "My Walker Colt? It was my grandpa's. My pa gave it to me for my twelfth birthday."

"Can you hit anything with it?"

"If I hold it real steady."

"I heard Harland say once that you can judge a man by his gun. Can I judge you by your gun?"

"I don't see how," Sam said. "My Colt is old and I'm not."

"That wasn't what I meant," Lorette said, and laughed anew.

Sam grew flustered. Some of the things she was saying confused him. To get back on firm footing, he brought up something he had been wondering about. "Is there a fella in your life, if you don't mind my asking?"

"Why do you want to know?"

"Curious, is all."

"No, there's not. I haven't hitched myself to a man yet. My ma says I shouldn't rush it, like she did. She says I should enjoy myself while I can, that once I say 'I do,' I'm stuck. And I don't want that. I don't want my life to be a repeat of hers." Lorette had grown unusually somber but now she gave her head a toss, and chortled. "Listen to me."

Her voice was so musical to Sam's ears, he could listen to her all day. Without thinking, he blurted, "I like hearing you say things."

"You better be careful," Lorette teased. "The next thing you know, you'll be falling in love with me."

"I'd never . . ." Sam began, and stopped.

"Why not? Aren't I good enough for you?"

Sam felt as if his tongue were tied in knots. Clearing his throat, he got out, "You're plenty good."

Suddenly serious again, Lorette reached out and touched his arm. "That's all right. For your sake, we'll take it slow."

"Take what slow?"

"Yes, sir," Lorette said, nodding. "There's a lot I can teach you."

"About what?"

"About everything," Lorette said.

Chapter 18

"We can do it, son. We can by God do it."

Luke Burnett had seldom seen his pa so excited. An excitement he didn't share. Not when they had to work with the Kurst clan. "If you say so, Pa," he replied without much enthusiasm.

"We've seen over three hundred longhorns alone," Owen said. "If the others have counted as many or more, it won't take us half the time I thought it would to round up enough for our herd."

"Counting them and rounding them up are two different things," Luke pointed out. In his estimation, his pa was putting the cart before the horse.

"Think of it! We could end up with twenty to thirty thousand dollars."

"You're starting to sound like Mr. Kurst," Luke said. Which was the last thing his pa should do.

"I'm not as money hungry as he is," Owen said. "But money is nothing to be sneezed at, neither. It lets a family do things they've only ever dreamed about doing."

"We're getting along right fine, Pa. You've never heard any of us complain, have you?" Luke glanced to the west. The sun had slipped low, painting the sky with streaks of pink and yellow. "We should be heading back soon."

"A few more minutes."

Luke had half-hoped his pa would change his mind

about taking part in the drive, but now, with the long-horns so plentiful, there was no turning back. It put him in a funk. To be around the Kursts for that long would grate on his nerves. Frowning, he stretched to relieve a cramp in his back, and happened to gaze at a tangle of brush about forty feet off to their left. For a few moments what he was seeing didn't sink in; a swarthy face, with crow-black hair parted in the middle, and dark eyes that seemed to glitter. "Pa!" he cried.

The instant he did, the face disappeared. It was there, and it was gone.

"What is it?" Owen asked, drawing rein and turning.

Luke had his six-shooter out but didn't remember drawing. "A Comanche!"

His pa shucked his Spencer and raised it to his shoulder. "Where?" he anxiously asked, looking all about.

Luke pointed. "Yonder. He was watching us but he's gone now."

Owen swung the Spencer from side to side. "Where there's one there are always more. We're getting out of here. You go first and I'll cover you."

"We go together." Luke wasn't about to leave his pa to be slain and mutilated. Tales of Comanche atrocities were legion. Whether they were true, Luke couldn't say.

Lowering his rifle, Owen brought his horse around and they started down the hill side by side. Thick vegetation hemmed them uncomfortably close.

"If they jump us," Owen said, "shoot and light a shuck. We're no match for a war party."

"I won't die easy," Luke vowed. He concentrated on the brush, looking for movement, for anything that might give the Comanches away. He'd never fought Indians but had heard they could be like ghosts and slit a man's throat before he realized they were there.

At the bottom the growth thinned, and they moved into the open. Behind them a twig crunched, and Luke whipped around, his Colt up and cocked.

"I heard that, too," his pa said.

Luke glimpsed buckskins but when he focused on the spot, nothing was there.

"If they're on foot we have a chance," Owen said. "I'll count to three and we use our spurs."

Luke nodded.

"One."

Luke thought some scrub moved, but there was nothing to shoot at.

"Two."

Gripping his reins tighter, Luke tensed. At "Three!" he jabbed his spurs and his mount exploded into a gallop. His skin prickling at the expectation of taking an arrow, he bent over the saddle horn. Without meaning to, he pulled ahead of his father, then realized his pa had let him pull ahead so his pa could protect his back. He went slower so his pa could catch up.

For half a mile or more they raced pell-mell over and around hill after hill. Finally his pa called out to halt and they brought their mounts to a stop, both of them turning in their saddles with their guns ready.

"I don't see any sign of them," Luke said.

"Maybe they were on foot."

Luke doubted that. From what he'd heard, Comanches practically lived on horseback. Centaurs, Texans called them, not as an insult, but as a compliment to their riding ability. Comanches were taught to ride almost as soon as they were old enough to sit a horse, and by the time a warrior was full grown, could ride like the wind.

"We're safe, thank heaven," Owen said, and let his rifle drop to his side.

Luke kept his Colt in his hand. Comanches were notoriously tricky. The war party, if such it was, might be holding back, waiting for them to make a mistake so the Comanches could take them by surprise.

"Didn't you hear me?" Owen asked, shoving the Spencer into its scabbard. "We can stop worrying."

"You, maybe," Luke said.

They rode on. The birds and the insects had gone quiet, and they didn't see a single longhorn. It was as if the wild creatures were holding their collective breath, waiting for something to happen.

In a low voice, Luke remarked, "It's too still. I don't like it."

"Nerves, is all," Owen said.

Luke cared for his father dearly and considered him to be as fine a farmer as ever used a plow, but when it came to Indians, his pa was as green as grass. So was he, but at least he knew enough not to let down his guard. "It's a good thing you're not a scout. You wouldn't have lasted long."

"What a thing to say."

"You didn't see that Comanche. He'd have killed us if he could have."

"We don't know that. Comanches don't kill every white man they come across."

"Enough," Luke said.

The silence became oppressive. Luke almost let out a bark of joy when a robin burst into song and a longhorn appeared and watched them go by with no more concern than if they were wild turkeys.

"Things are back to normal," Owen said in relief.

Not for Luke. Things wouldn't be normal again until after the drive. Until then, he'd have a host of dangers to deal with.

"We'll tell Gareth what you saw," Owen said. "But I doubt he'll call off the roundup."

"We should go home."

"Because of one Comanche?" Owen shook his head. "No. I agree with Gareth. The Comanches will leave us alone, as many guns as we have. I want to see this through to the end, son."

"Just so it's not the end of us," Luke said.

Chapter 19

Philomena Burnett wasn't happy. It was bad enough her husband and sons were going to go off on a drive and leave her and her girls alone for months. Now he was fixing to spend a lot of the money they'd socked away for emergencies and whatnot on things the family didn't need.

Owen had to buy supplies to purchase for the roundup and the drive. Victuals, and the like. Rope, and a lot of it. Lucifers, for starting campfires. The list was as long as Philomena's arm.

"You've been mighty quiet," Owen mentioned as he examined a pile of blankets in the general store.

"I'll miss you."

"I'll be back once the roundup is over and stay a few days before we head for Abilene."

"Provided nothing happens."

"First Luke and now you," Owen made light of her concern. "I never realized what worriers you two are."

"You don't worry enough," Philomena said. "Or doesn't it bother you that the girls and me will be all alone out there? Miles from anywhere, with Comanches about. And who knows what else."

Owen glanced around as if to be sure no one could hear him. "Don't tell Luke, but I'm still not convinced he saw one. I didn't. And we never found any tracks when I went back with Gareth."

"You're accusing your own son of lying?"

"No. But our eyes can play tricks on us. Maybe he only thinks he saw a Comanche." Owen set down a blanket and took one of her hands in both of his. "I've been thinking about you and the girls not having a man about the place while me and the boys arc away. And I have the solution."

"You'll take us with you?"

"I'll ask Ebidiah Troutman to keep an eye on you. On Ariel Kurst and Wilda Weaver, too. He's reliable. Plus, you like him, don't you?"

"I do," Philomena admitted, "but . . ."

"I knew there'd be one."

"He's not you," Philomena said. "It won't be the same. And he's getting on in years. How much use would he be if the Comanches attack?"

"They haven't bothered us once the whole time we've been here," Owen said. "Why should they pick now?"

"I don't know. I just have a bad feeling."

"One of your instincts?"

"Don't you dare poke fun. Female intuition isn't to be scoffed at. My ma and my grandma both had powerful premonitions that came true. And I have one that this drive will end badly."

Owen did something he rarely did in public. Looking her in the eyes, he said tenderly, "You know I love you more than anything on this earth?"

Philomena coughed and glanced around to see if anyone was watching. They had the aisle to themselves, thank goodness.

"Do you think I want to lose you, or put our family at risk? I've thought about it and thought about it, and I've come to the conclusion it has to be. Gareth Kurst is right about this."

Philomena opened her mouth to remark that she wouldn't trust Gareth Kurst as far as she could throw him.

"Hear me out," Owen cut her off. "I know you don't like him. To be honest, I'm not all that fond of the man, myself. He thinks too highly of himself, and his views on a lot of things don't match mine. But he's exactly right that this is an opportunity we can't afford to pass up. You're going to say that the money doesn't matter, that our lives are more important. And I agree. But the money isn't unimportant, either. Not as much as we might make from selling the cattle."

"But—" Philomena got out.

"I'm not done." Owen gently squeezed her hands. "I could have told Gareth I wasn't interested. I could have gone on as we are and not given the money another thought. Only I couldn't live with myself if I did."

"Owen, please . . ."

"Let me finish. I'm a husband and a father. Those roles come with obligations. A good husband does the best he can to provide for his wife. A good father tries his best to prepare his young'uns for leaving the nest and going off into the world. If I were to let this opportunity go by, I'd fail on both counts. I couldn't live with myself, sweetheart. Not with failing those who mean the most to me. I'd be miserable the rest of my days. Oh, I'd hide it from you and the kids. But in my quiet moments, when I was alone, I'd feel a misery I could never shake."

Philomena was deeply touched. He seldom talked about his deeper feelings. And it wasn't just him. Men, by their nature, tended to keep their emotions to themselves. "I'm grateful you're opening up to me."

"I'd like your blessing."

"Owen, I just don't know," Philomena said uncertainly.

"Please."

"Owen, don't do this."

"I need it. So I'll be right with myself, come what may."

"Do you know what you're asking?" Philomena asked. Because if something terrible happened, it would be on her head as well as his.

"I'm asking the woman I gave my heart to, to give me her support."

"Oh, Owen."

"I'll only ask this once."

Philomena gazed into his eyes, saw the love and adoration there, and was lost. Her throat constricted and her eyes moistened. She barely got out, "You have my blessing."

"Thank you," Owen said, and did another thing he rarely did in public. He kissed her.

God help me, Philomena thought, *what have I done?*

Chapter 20

The grassland bordering Comanche Creek became riotous with sounds. The loud *thunk* of axe heads biting deep into trees echoed off the hills. Horses whinnied and stamped. The nearly dozen men and the young woman with them were constantly yelling back and forth.

From his vantage point atop one of the nearby hills, Ebidiah Troutman watched the goings-on with amazement and amusement. The Burnetts and Kursts and Weavers scurried around like so many ants, laboring mightily to prepare their cattle camp. They erected lean-tos to store their packs. They built a corral for their horses out of poles of trimmed saplings. They strung rope to serve as a corral for the longhorns they'd soon go after. They also prepared a lot of small campfires around the perimeter, evidently to use once the cattle were caught.

Ebidiah didn't see the sense in that, but then he didn't see much sense in a lot of the antics of his fellow man. It was part of the reason he had so little to do with other human beings.

From an early age, Ebidiah never could understand why so many people busied themselves to death. From the moment they woke up until the moment they turned in, they buzzed around like bees, doing this and doing that, and for what?

All those folks never really did anything of any consequence except keep busy.

Ebidiah first got a sense of the preposterousness of it

all when he was a boy and his folks made him do chores. Every day was a repeat of the day before. Get up at dawn, milk the cows and feed the chickens, eat breakfast, shovel the cow manure, spread straw. There were always a thousand and one things that needed doing.

Ebidiah hated it. When he was in his late teens, he struck off on his own and headed west, where he'd heard a man could live as free as he pleased, with no one to tell him to do this or that. When he learned of a man organizing a trapping brigade, he signed on.

The trapping life suited him. He checked his traps, collected any beaver that were caught and skinned them for their hides, and generally had the rest of his time to himself.

Not that the work was easy. Sometimes the water was so cold, his fingers and toes half-froze. And setting the traps took some doing. So did toting those dead beaver. But all in all, the work fit him down to his marrow. Which was why he left the brigade and became a free trapper, and had been trapping ever since.

When beaver hats went out of fashion and the beaver trade fell off, Ebidiah turned to other critters. For long decades he'd roamed the Rocky Mountains, trapping anything with a pelt that would put money in his poke. He wasn't a fanatic about it, though. He trapped enough to get by, and that was all. Not like some trappers who went on sprees and trapped entire regions out.

In his wanderings, he'd traveled the length and breadth of the Rockies. From up near Canada, clear down to the Davis Mountains in west Texas. He'd ended up in Texas late in life, having drifted further and further south each year. Part of it had to do with his endless quest for furs. More of it had to do with his aching joints and muscles.

Ebidiah was pushing ninety. He was spry for his age, and got around fine, and his mind hadn't given out on him like it did with some. But he felt his years with every breath he took. Cold weather made it even worse, which was why he'd left the mountains for the hill country where it was warmer. He still trapped, and sold the hides to settlers like Mrs. Burnett and Mrs. Weaver.

He'd never sold anything to the Kursts.

Ebidiah had gone to their homestead once to introduce himself. He'd brought Sarabell and his pelts, thinking he might sell a few.

Gareth Kurst rudely informed him that the family skinned its own hides and wouldn't be buying any from an "old goat" like him. The oldest boy, Harland, had opened one of Ebidiah's packs, "to see what this old buzzard has," as Harland put it, and then played catch with a couple of his brothers, tossing a marten fur back and forth and not letting Ebidiah have it until their pa told them to give it back. And the daughter, Lorette, had sashayed up to him, pulled at his beard, and teased him about his wrinkles.

It was all Ebidiah could do not to shoot one of them. When he left, he'd vowed that he'd never set foot on their place again. He did see various Kursts now and then, when they were out hunting and such, always from a distance. He went the other way. They were trouble, that bunch.

And now Owen Burnett and Jasper Weaver were partners with those troublemakers in the cattle enterprise.

Ebidiah liked Owen. The man was as honest as the year was long, and never spoke ill of another soul. Ebidiah respected that.

He didn't have much respect for Jasper Weaver. Jasper was a drunkard. Not the loud, brawling kind, but the sort who drank in secret, or at least in the privacy of his own home, and never imposed on anyone else.

What drove Jasper to drink, Ebidiah couldn't say. Usually it was a tragedy of some kind. But as far as he knew, Jasper had been spared any deep sorrows. Maybe the wife had something to do with it. Or maybe Jasper drank because he liked it.

A shout from below put an end to Ebidiah's musing. Extending his spyglass, he pressed it to his right eye and the scene below came into sharp focus. It was as if he was right there; he could see the sweat on their brows, the dust on their clothes.

The one who had shouted was Reuben, Jasper's boy. Reuben was pointing to the north and saying something, and his pa and Gareth and Owen were hurrying over.

Ebidiah raised his telescope to the hill the boy was pointing at and swept the slopes. He spotted a few longhorns and a couple of deer but nothing to account for the boy's shout.

The sound of hooves drew Ebidiah's attention. Harland and Thaxter Kurst and Luke Burnett had climbed on their horses and were riding to the north. They had their rifles out.

Ebidiah wondered if Reuben had seen a bear or a mountain lion. Settlers were always spooked by meateaters even though bears and the like hardly ever attacked people.

He did more scanning with his spyglass and was about convinced that they were making a fuss over nothing when movement caught his eye. Something fast, that went from cover to cover. Centering the spyglass, he cussed in surprise. He shouldn't have been surprised, but he was.

It had been a spell since any of their kind were seen in those parts, and it didn't bode well for the would-be cattle wranglers.

For high up on the other hill was a Comanche warrior. He had stopped moving and hunkered to watch the settlers.

And his face was painted for war.

Chapter 21

Luke Burnett, his hand on his Remington, rode with Harland and Thaxter Kurst toward where Reuben Weaver claimed he'd seen an Indian.

The Kurst boys weren't happy about having to go up the hill to check.

"An Injun, my ass," Thaxter complained. "Most likely it was a deer and we're wasting our time."

"Pa said to have a look, so we'll have a look," Harland replied.

"You know and I know that Reuben Weaver is scared of his own shadow," Thaxter said. "He thought he saw a mountain lion two days ago, but it was only a danged squirrel."

"He'll be of help when we round up the cattle," Harland said.

"Not much."

Luke had never met a family that bickered as much as the Kursts. They argued about everything, every hour of the day. He'd come to suspect, as strange as it seemed, that they liked to spat. "I saw an Indian about ten days ago, remember?" he reminded them.

"You say you did," Thaxter said over his shoulder. "But your pa was right there with you, and he didn't."

"Are you calling me a liar?" Luke demanded.

Before Thaxter could respond, Harland called back to him, "Don't forget what pa told us about getting along."

Frowning, Thaxter glared at Luke. "No, I wasn't calling you no liar. But our eyes can play tricks on us. Maybe you saw a Comanche and maybe you didn't."

"I did, damn you," Luke said, controlling his anger with an effort.

"Hush, the both of you," Harland said.

Luke rose in the stirrups to see ahead. They were making so much noise, any Comanche would be long gone. Unless it was a war party, out to count coup. From what he understood, warriors proved their courage by striking or killing an enemy. He wasn't sure if it applied to all tribes, but the word on the Texas frontier was that the Comanches did.

Suddenly stones rattled from under the hooves of Thaxter's mount, and his horse slipped. Smacking it, Thaxter cussed.

That was another thing Luke didn't like about the Kursts. They were forever cussing. His folks had raised him to keep a civil tongue, especially around others. He couldn't recall ever hearing his ma swear, although his pa had a few times.

"There's the spot," Harland called out.

They were nearing a patch of brush below a large boulder, which was where Reuben claimed he'd seen an Indian. Harland slowed, and with one hand, pressed his rifle to his shoulder.

Thaxter drew his Colt.

Luke relied on his Remington rather than his rifle. He was better with a six-gun, especially up close. Drawing rein, he said, "I'll cover you while you investigate."

"Investigate, hell," Harland said. "It would be a fool's proposition to go into that thicket."

"Don't look at me," Thaxter said. "I wasn't born stupid."

That made no kind of sense that Luke could see. "One of us should check," he insisted.

"Be our guest," Harland said.

"Serves you right if you get your throat slit," Thaxter said. He didn't sound upset at the prospect.

"All three of us should go in," Luke proposed. They had to find out if Reuben had in fact seen an Indian.

"It was your idea," Harland said. "*We'll* cover *you*."

Thaxter snickered.

Reluctantly, Luke climbed down. "If this is how you are with one hostile, how will you be with a whole war party?"

"We'll do our part, don't you worry," Harland said gruffly.

Thumbing back the Remington's hammer, Luke crept into the heavy tangle of juniper and other growth. Except for the buzzing of a bee, all was still. He crept higher, wincing when a leaf crunched under his left boot.

Luke had a feeling that unseen eyes were on him. His mouth went dry as he warily advanced. He searched for tracks even though the ground was so hard, a longhorn wouldn't leave any.

"You all right in there?" Harland yelled, and Thaxter laughed.

Luke didn't see what was so funny. The warrior could ambush him at any moment. Skirting a trunk, he bent as low as he could without lying flat, and looked for sign. The quiet mocked him. "I know you're there," he bluffed. "Show yourself."

"As if Comanches speak our tongue," Thaxter said in ridicule.

Luke had heard of some who did. They were exceptions rather than the rule, just as whites fluent in the Comanche tongue were as rare as hen's teeth. He'd never had any interest in learning another language, not even Spanish, which was spoken all along the border country.

The sense that he was being watched grew stronger.

Luke became molasses, alert for the slightest sound, or anything else out of the ordinary.

"You're taking long enough," Harland said. "What's going on in there? We can't see you."

"He's taken up knitting," Thaxter said.

Luke would never tell them, but his ma had, in fact, taught him how. The basics, anyway. She thought it was something a man should know. "For when you're older, and if you should find yourself on your own," was how she justified it. Cooking, ironing, he could do it all. So could Sam.

"Did you see that?" Harland whispered.

"See what?" Luke had let himself become distracted. He glanced about but saw only plants, and up a short way, the boulder. "See what?" he asked again when Harland didn't answer.

"Off to your left," Harland said.

All Luke saw were oaks and high grass. He moved closer. The grass was undisturbed; if a grown man had passed through it, the blades would be bent or flattened. "Nothing."

"Come on back, then," Harland said.

Luke was glad to. Once clear of the thicket, he stood and shook his head. "Not a sign anywhere."

"We wasted our time," Harland said.

"Told you," Thaxter said. "We should take a rock to Reuben Weaver's skull for this wild-goose chase."

"You let him be," Luke said.

"Or what?" Thaxter taunted.

"You'll answer to me."

"I'm real scared."

"You two cut it out," Harland snapped. "Thax, I won't remind you again. Pa told us to leave them be. There's a time and a place to stand up to him, and this isn't it."

Luke wondered what that was about. "Stand up?" he said.

"None of your business," Harland said.

"Aren't you the diplomat, big brother?" Thaxter said sarcastically.

"For thirty thousand dollars," Harland said, "I'll do whatever I have to."

Chapter 22

Ebidiah saw the whole thing through his spyglass. He saw the Comanche melt away before Luke Burnett and the Kurst brothers climbed within rifle range. He saw Luke Burnett dismount and search a bit, saw them give up and head down. And he saw the warrior reappear and hunker where the three couldn't see him. Thanks to the spyglass, Ebidiah saw the warrior's sly smile at having outwitted them.

Ebidiah went on watching the Comanche. There was a saying to the effect that where you saw one, there were always more. But he saw no sign of others. An advance scout, he reckoned, for a war party. Or maybe a lone warrior on a killing spree. That happened from time to time, he'd heard.

Whatever the case, it spelled trouble for Owen and the rest. The warrior would bide his time and pick the most advantageous moment to strike.

Ebidiah had to decide what to do.

He could ride down and warn Owen. But then he'd have to explain how he saw the warrior through his spyglass, which might lead to embarrassing questions about him spying on the Kursts.

He could deal with the Comanche himself. He'd fought a few Indians in his time. But he wasn't about to delude himself. He was well past his prime. Neither as strong nor as spry as he used to be. He'd be putting his life at risk.

The sun climbed, and the Comanche didn't move.

Ebidiah considered using his Sharps. Once, years ago, he'd dropped a buffalo at six hundred yards. But that was on an open plain, on level ground. Where he'd had a clear line of sight. Where he didn't have to take elevation into account or worry about other factors.

Ebidiah lowered the spyglass, rubbed his eyes, and raised it again. He calculated the range to be pretty near eight hundred yards from his hill on the south side of the creek to the hill the Comanche was on, on the north side. Much too far for him to try.

His only recourse was to get closer. That in itself was dangerous. The warrior didn't have a spyglass, but Comanches were known for their fine eyesight. They were like hawks, able to pick things out at a distance that baffled most whites.

Ebidiah turned his attention to the camp below. The men, and that one gal, were busy preparing for the roundup. No one was standing guard. Maybe they thought they'd scared the Comanche off.

"Blamed fools," Ebidiah said to himself. He'd seen it before. Overconfidence killed more pilgrims than disease. Emigrants who loaded down their Conestoga with a piano and cabinets but neglected to bring enough food and water because they were sure they could find plenty on their own, and died of thirst on a dry stretch. A cavalry officer who believed that hostiles would run at the sight of him and his men, and was turned into a pincushion with arrows when the hostiles proved him wrong. Or the hunter who poked his head into a grizzly's den without first tossing a rock in to see if the grizzly was there, and lost his head to a swipe of the bear's paw. Overconfident, one and all.

Ebidiah fixed his spyglass on the girl. Her name was Lorette, if he recollected right. She was trouble, that girl. She sashayed around like a she-cat on the prowl, and seemed to have attached herself to young Sam Burnett. The kind of girl, his ma used to say, who was always up to no good. Even so, she didn't deserve to spend the rest of her days in a Comanche lodge. And there was a very real possibility that she was the one that warrior was after.

Comanches took white women for wives now and then. They weren't like the Apaches, who thought white women were too weak to make good wives.

It could be that warrior wasn't out for blood. It could be he was out for romance.

Ebidiah went back to pondering how to stop him. He could sneak down close to the camp and wait for the warrior to move in, and hope he picked him off before he struck. Or he could go after him. Hunt the warrior down as if he were a buck or a bear.

Ebidiah balked at the notion of killing him, though. His whole life he'd never liked to kill other people. It felt wrong.

Some whites claimed that killing redskins was all right because they weren't human. They were animals. Which was ridiculous, in Ebidiah's estimation. It wasn't the color of the skin that made a person human. It was what was under the skin.

In that regard, Indians weren't any different than whites except in some of their beliefs. Even there, whites had so many different beliefs of their own, they took to waging wars over who was right and who was wrong, with each side thinking it was better than the other.

Ebidiah shook himself. He was straying off the mental trail again. The issue was the Comanche, and how to stop the warrior from hurting anyone.

By the position of the sun, it would be six to seven hours yet before nightfall. Plenty of time for him to make up his mind.

Opening his possible bag, he took out a bundle of pemmican, broke off a piece, replaced the bundle, and set to chewing and thinking.

He remembered his ma and his pa, good people who'd done the best they could by him, and how he'd heard about their passing more than a year after the fact when a letter from his sister caught up to him. His pa went first, of cancer, and his ma died three months later. She'd refused to eat or drink, and wasted away. One of Ebidiah's regrets was that he'd never gone back to see them. They would have liked that.

Ebidiah remembered a Crow gal he'd lived with for several seasons. She wasn't much of a looker, by white standards, but to him she'd been downright beautiful, with as tender a heart as ever beat. He'd lost her to an avalanche one winter's morning when she went to the stream for water. He'd hated snow ever since.

Ebidiah recalled as many good times as came to him, and the few friends he'd had, and the pleasures of smoking a pipe, and the taste of apple pie, and the sheer delight of chocolate pudding.

All things considered, the Good Lord had granted him a fine life. He could go to his grave content.

Careful not to show himself, Ebidiah turned and descended the far side of the hill to Sarabell. She was dozing, as usual, and looked up when he took hold of her lead rope.

"Wake up there, girl," Ebidiah said. "I've made up my mind. We've got us a Comanche to kill."

Chapter 23

Sam Burnett was doing as his pa had told him and making a final check of the rope they'd strung to hold the longhorns. To Sam it seemed pointless. He didn't see how a puny rope would keep a longhorn from going wherever it hankered to go.

His pa also wanted him to check that the ring of small fires were set to be lit. Sam had helped gather the wood for the fires, and extra wood, besides, plus a lot of kindling. Supposedly, the fires, and the smoke, would hold the longhorns in check if the rope failed. It was a trick the Spanish used.

He came to the third and dismounted. Just as he thought, there was nothing more to do. Turning, he was about to climb on his dun when a mare came out of the trees.

Her rider grinned like the cat that ate the canary.

"Here you are," Lorette Kurst declared as if she'd been hunting him for a while and was glad to find him.

Which made no sense to Sam. "You heard my pa tell me what to do," he reminded her. "You saw me ride off."

"Well, true," Lorette said, and laughed that impish laugh of hers. "You caught me, you handsome lunk, you. I'm guilty of following you."

Sam wished she wouldn't talk to him like that. Her antics puzzled him sometimes, in that he was never quite sure if she was serious. "Don't you have work of your own to do?"

"Not at the moment," Lorette said, "so I thought I'd help you."

Forking leather, Sam said, "I don't need any help, but thanks."

"Dumb as a stump, you know that?"

Sam would have been insulted, except she was smiling like it was a joke. "I am no such thing." He wasn't as quick-witted as Luke but he wasn't stupid, either.

"Don't get your dander up, handsome."

"I'm not that, either." When it came to looks, Sam knew that Luke had those over him. He was as plain as rawhide. "I'm not much to look at, and I won't be teased about it."

"Who's teasing?" Leaning on her saddle horn, Lorette raked him with those green eyes of hers. "To me you are, and that's what counts."

"You need spectacles."

Lorette laughed louder and longer than Sam thought was called for. Then, sitting back, she ran a hand over the front of her shirt as if to smooth it. The effect was to have her bosom sort of thrust out at him.

Growing warm all over, Sam said, "You might as well go back. There's other work you can do."

"I'd rather help you."

Sam continued on. Within moments Lorette caught up and gave him another of her strange womanly looks.

"What would you like to talk about?"

"Nothing. I'm working. Go on back and leave me be." Sam figured that would be the end of it but she stayed at his side. "You don't listen very well."

"I have my own mind, thank you very much."

"Your pa might get upset," Sam grasped at a straw.

"Pshaw. As if he cares what I do. So long as I'm not unladylike when he's around, I can do as I please. And it pleases me for the two of us to become better acquainted."

"Why?"

"Dumb as a stump and then some," Lorette said.

"There you go again. I wish you'd stop playing games with me."

"I'm not no child," Lorette said. "And you are no game. I'm sort of surprised at myself, but there you go."

"What are you talking about?"

Lorette chuckled, and shook her head. She idly gazed skyward, and her grin widened. "Look up there. What do you see?"

Sam did, and told her. "A pair of hawks."

Lorette nodded. "A male and a female."

"So?" Sam said. Hawks hunted in pairs all the time. Once the female laid her eggs, that would change, and the male would do most of it. He mentioned as much.

"Listen to the egg expert," Lorette said.

"You say the strangest things."

"I'm not about to lay any eggs."

"See?" Sam said.

"Honestly," Lorette said, sounding annoyed.

Sam was flustered. Again. She had that effect on him. To be fair, so did most any young female except his sisters.

Unexpectedly, Lorette swung toward him and asked, "Do you like me or not? Tell me true."

"You're fine," Sam said in confusion.

"That's not what I said. Do you *like* me?"

"What's not to like?" Sam hedged. Besides her smirking at him all the time, as if she knew something he didn't, and how she kept comparing him to a tree stump.

"I swear," Lorette said. "If men aren't the most aggravating critters God ever made, I don't know what is."

"What did I do?"

"I asked you if you like me and you won't give me a direct answer. You keep beating around the bush."

To shut her up, Sam said, "I like you."

Lorette went from mad to sweet in the bat of her eyelashes. "What about me do you like the most?"

Sam indulged in a rare cuss, glad his ma wasn't there to hear. "Hell and tarnation. I just said I like you and now you want more?"

"You're stalling again, Sam Burnett. What about me do you like?"

Sam said the first thing that popped into his head. "Your hair, I guess."

"You guess?"

"It's sort of pretty."

"Sort of?"

"Just like your eyes. They're sort of pretty, too."

"I could just shoot you."

"What did I do?"

"You're male."

Sam almost cussed a second time. "Why are you making such a fuss over this? Maybe you should be asking Luke or Reuben Weaver questions like this."

"Reuben Weaver?" Lorette said, and cackled. "I'd rather be poked by a Comanche. And your brother doesn't interest me. He's like Thaxter. All they care about are their pistols."

Her mention of pokes had caused Sam to break out in a prickly itch. "A lady shouldn't talk about things like that."

"Pistols?"

"No. Pokes."

Lorette laughed. "Maybe I've taken it into my head that I'd like a poke. You ever think of that? Maybe I'd like it with a certain fella my own age."

Sam could have been knocked from his saddle with a feather. "Are you talking about me?"

"I'm not talking about your horse."

Sam was flabbergasted. This was beyond his experience with women, by a long shot. "Why, you come right out with it, don't you?"

"If I waited for you to come out with it, I'd have gray hair and be using a cane." Lorette grinned and winked. "Mull it over. You might cotton to the notion. I'm told I'm pleasing to the eye."

Sam swallowed hard.

Raising her reins, Lorette said, "I'll leave you to your work, like you want. But some day or night soon, you and me are going to get a lot better acquainted." She blew him a kiss and used her spurs.

"Lord in heaven," Sam said. "What do I do now?"

Chapter 24

As Ebidiah Troutman worked his way around a hill to the west of the cattle camp, he had second thoughts about his notion to kill the Comanche. He was putting his life at risk for folks he hardly knew.

Sure, Ebidiah liked the Burnett family. They were friendly, and always treated him decent when he paid them a visit. They'd even invited him to partake of their meals, something no one else ever did. Yet for all that, he knew very little about them. They were acquaintances, was all.

He didn't care a fig what happened to the Kursts. The Comanches could count coup on the whole clan and he wouldn't lose a wink of sleep. For that matter, he wasn't much fond of the Weavers, either. Jasper was all right, but he was a drunk. Wilda Weaver was a shrew. Their boy was nice but a mite simpleminded.

Why die for any of them?

The Burnetts, yes. That was the crux of it, right there. He'd grown fond enough of Owen and his family that he was willing to hazard his life to save them from harm. Which was peculiar in itself. He'd seldom grown attached to anyone the past few decades.

"It's my age," Ebidiah said to Sarabell. He was growing soft in his twilight years. Back during his beaver days, the only person he'd cared a whit about had been himself. Except for that Crow gal. He'd liked her considerable.

There had been something about her, something special. The day she'd died, he thought his heart died, too.

So he was doing this for the Burnetts. If he was smart, he'd go tell Owen about the Comanche and ask for their help in driving the warrior out of hiding. But here he was, bound and determined to do it by his lonesome.

"I have rocks for brains, old gal," Ebidiah told Sarabell.

She flicked her ears.

Ebidiah grimly clenched his jaw, and continued on. There came a time in everyone's life when they had to do what needed doing, and the consequences be damned. He told himself that in his head, several times, but it didn't make the doing any easier.

Deep down, Ebidiah was afraid to die. He might be close to the grave in years alone, but that didn't make a violent end any easier to contemplate. And no mistake about it, if the warrior turned the tables and took him by surprise, he'd be in for the most violent death imaginable.

It was do or die.

Circling wide to the north, he came up on the hill where he'd seen the warrior from the rear.

His thumb curled around the Sharps's hammer, Ebidiah drew to within fifty yards, and stopped. He looped the lead rope around an oak, gave Sarabell an affectionate pat, and whispered, "I didn't tie you tight. If I don't come back, get loose and go to the Burnett place. They'll take you in if anyone will."

Loosening his bowie in its sheath, Ebidiah crouched and snuck to the bottom of the hill. Butterflies took wing in his belly, a feeling he hadn't had in a coon's age. It brought back memories of the old days: that time the Blackfeet chased him for a day and a half; the time a bull buffalo charged him; the time he was nearly bit by a rattlesnake.

The hill was covered with scrub and trees. Ideal cover for the Comanche. It would make sneaking up on him hard. To make matters worse, the vegetation was so dry, it would crackle and rustle and give him away if he wasn't careful.

Easing down onto his elbows and knees, Ebidiah sank flat. He would stay flat, pretend he was a snake.

As he started up the slope, the butterflies multiplied. His throat became so dry, it hurt to swallow.

Off to one side, sparrows chirped and flitted. He crawled extra slow, so as not to spook them and cause them to take abrupt wing.

A little farther, and he spied a small rabbit, motionless except for its ears, which moved back and forth, and the twitching of its small nose. It was alert for the sounds and smells of any predators.

Ebidiah stopped to avoid scaring it.

The rabbit shuffled a couple of steps, nibbled at a plant, then raised its head and looked around.

Ebidiah figured his scent had given him away, but if so, the rabbit didn't show any alarm. Unconcerned, it hobbled off, its tail bobbing.

He crawled higher. Twenty feet. Thirty. More. The top was still a ways off, crowned by growth.

Ebidiah figured that was where the warrior would be. He skirted a cedar, intent on the crest above, and almost missed spotting a buckskin-clad form with raven-hued hair crouched in shadow not ten feet from him.

The next instant the figure sprang.

Ebidiah heaved upright to meet the attack, but he was only halfway to his feet when steel flashed. He got the Sharps up and blocked the knife, only to take a kick to the thigh that buckled his leg. He went to one knee and tried to jam the Sharps's stock to his shoulder to shoot, but the Comanche was on him in a heartbeat, the knife striking at his throat. Again he barely blocked it.

The warrior was young; it was doubtful he'd seen twenty winters. He kneed Ebidiah in the chest and Ebidiah sprawled onto his back. Instantly, the young warrior pounced, his knee gouging Ebidiah's gut.

Stars exploded before Ebidiah's eyes. For a few harrowing moments he thought he would pass out. Iron fingers clamped onto his throat, and his breath was choked off. Then his vision cleared, and he saw the Comanche, the knife raised high, about to plunge it into him.

The young warrior was grinning; he thought Ebidiah was a goner.

Not if Ebidiah could help it. He drove the Sharps into the Comanche's ribs and had the satisfaction of causing him to grunt in pain. Swinging the barrel, Ebidiah sought to slam it against the warrior's temple, but he jerked back and the barrel only clipped him.

Still, it was enough that the Comanche let go and dived to one side.

They scrambled to their feet at the same moment. Before Ebidiah could level his Sharps, the warrior seized the barrel and shoved it aside, then thrust his knife at Ebidiah's heart.

Ebidiah sidestepped, barely, and did the last thing the warrior would expect. It was a dirty trick from the many wrestling matches Ebidiah took part in at the annual rendezvous back in the beaver days. He butted the young warrior in the face.

Giving voice to a wolfish snarl, the Comanche skipped backward, scarlet spurting from his nose. In the same motion he wrenched on the Sharps and tore it from Ebidiah's grasp. Casting it aside, he swiped at his nose, then poised on the balls of his feet, his knife glittering in the sunlight.

Ebidiah clawed for his bowie. The last thing he wanted, at his age, was to become embroiled in a knife fight.

The Comanche screeched his war cry, and pounced.

Chapter 25

"Did you hear that, Pa?" Luke asked.

Owen Burnett paused in the act of filling their coffeepot with water. He was on his knees by the creek, the sun warm on his face, the water cool on his fingers as he dipped the pot in. "Hear what?" His son had sharper hearing than he did. Sharper eyesight, too.

Luke was quizzically scanning the hills to the north. "A scream of some kind, or a yell."

Owen listened, then shook his head. "I don't hear a thing."

"There was only the one," Luke said, "but I'm sure I heard it."

"I've been told that mountain lions scream on occasions," Owen recalled. And the hills were known to harbor the big cats. "Never heard it myself. They say it sounds just like a woman screaming."

"This didn't sound like a woman."

"Someone in trouble?" Owen said skeptically. They were so far back in the hills, there was no one else around.

"I don't know." Luke shrugged. "Maybe it was my imagination."

"If you hear it again, let me know." Owen bent, lifted the full pot, which took both hands, and stood. He headed back, saying, "Things are going well."

Falling into step, Luke said with less enthusiasm, "Well enough."

"Is there a problem?" Owen asked. They were all set

to commence the roundup in the morning. In a month or two, if all went well, they'd have enough cattle for the drive.

"I don't trust the Kursts."

"Not that again," Owen said. "They've behaved themselves, haven't they? And held up their end of our pact? I haven't seen a single one shirk their work."

"You won't, as much as their pa hankers after the money," Luke said. "It's all that matters to them. And that worries me."

"You're worse than your ma," Owen muttered, and then said, "Why does it worry you?"

"Where do we stand with the Kursts?"

"How do you mean?" Owen saw Gareth with Harland and Thaxter over by their mounts, talking. "We're their partners. Same as the Weavers."

"I doubt they give a damn about any of us."

"That's harsh, and uncalled for, unless they've done something I don't know about."

"It's their attitude," Luke said. "They act as if we're here to help them out, and nothing more. They don't treat us as equals."

"Gareth has treated me with nothing but respect."

"I can't say the same about his brood, especially the older two. They act like I'm the dirt on their boots."

Owen sighed. "You three have been at each other's throats since I can remember."

"Can you blame me? I've told you how they act."

"Does your brother feel the same way?" Owen probed. If so, he'd sit both of them down and have a long talk, sort out the resentments on both sides so the roundup and the drive went more smoothly.

"Sam is too bothered by Lorette to pay much attention to anything else."

This was news to Owen. "Lorette? What does she have to do with anything?"

"You haven't seen how she acts around him? Sam thinks she's set her sights on him. You ask me, she's teasing to set him up for a fall. That's something those Kursts would do."

They were almost within earshot of the others, and Owen stopped so what he said next wouldn't be overheard. "You need to stop this. It can lead to arguments, or worse."

"You make it sound as if it's my fault they treat us so shabby."

"I very much doubt that Harland and Thaxter have complained to Gareth about you. You're the one who keeps griping about things."

"You've always told us to be honest with you," Luke said, looking hurt.

"Sam hasn't mentioned anything about Lorette, and I haven't noticed her misbehaving."

"She wouldn't around you or her pa."

Owen shifted the coffeepot from one hand to the other. "Look. I grant you, the Kursts are rough around the edges. In fact, I'll go so far as to say that their social graces, as your ma would call it, leave a lot to be desired. They don't get along with others very well. That's their nature. It doesn't mean they're up to no good. It's just how they are."

"If you say so," Luke said, but he didn't sound convinced.

Owen sought to mollify his son by adding, "I'll also grant you that they don't give a hoot about anyone but themselves. People like that, they look down their noses at everybody else."

"That's the Kursts, sure enough," Luke allowed.

"Once you take them as they are, as rude and overbearing, they won't bother you as much. You come to expect it."

"Is that why it doesn't bother you any?"

"I never said that," Owen replied. "I wish they would be nicer. But there are a lot of people like them in this world. People who only care about their own wants, and the devil take everyone else. You ask me, they've never grown up. They're like little kids. Everything is me, me, me."

"I never thought of it like that."

"If everybody in this country was like the Kursts, things would be a mess. There'd be squabbling all the time, with everyone wanting to ride roughshod over everyone else."

"So I should try harder to get along with them?"

Mightily pleased, Owen smiled. "Give it a try. For me. Swallow your pride and ignore them and things will work out fine."

"I hope so, Pa. I truly do."

"Good." Owen clapped him on the arm. "Now why don't you go find your brother and send him to me while I get this coffee on?"

Owen went to their campfire and hunkered. He was greatly relieved that he'd finally gotten his oldest to quit being so suspicious. Philomena was bad enough in that regard. He loved her dearly, but she was the most suspicious person on God's green earth.

Humming to himself, Owen prepared the coffee. He didn't pay much attention when Gareth and his two oldest rode off. Wylie was over by the packs, doing something or other. Silsby and Iden were across the way, with Reuben Weaver.

It was a while before Samuel showed. He reported that he had checked the rope corral, and it was secure. He ended with, "Luke says you wanted to see me."

Owen patted the ground. "Have a seat."

Sam plopped down, cross-legged, and placed his elbows on his knees and his chin in his hands. "What is this about?"

"Lorette Kurst."

Sam sat up so fast, it was a wonder his spine didn't snap. "What has Luke told you? Consarn him, anyhow."

"Are you and her getting along?"

"If we got along any better, I'd have to marry her."

"How's that again?"

Sam squirmed and puckered his mouth as if he'd bitten into a lemon. "I wasn't going to say anything. But since you brought it up, she treats me like I'm some of that hard candy at the general store, and she wants to take a lick."

"Samuel Guthrie Burnett," Owen said. "That's no way to talk about a lady."

"Honest to goodness, Pa. She makes eyes at me, and everything. She gets me so flustered, I can't hardly think."

Owen laughed. "Girls her age sometimes do that, son. It doesn't mean she wants to haul your britches down."

"Oh, Pa," Sam said, and blushed.

"Your sisters aren't like that, but I have known of girls who like to flirt with boys to no end. It's how they test the waters, your ma tells me. They tease and they play but they're not serious."

"So it's a game with her?"

"Yes," Owen said with absolute conviction.

"All her talk about me being handsome, she's just teasing me?"

"Do you think you're handsome?"

"I'm ordinary as dishwater," Sam said.

"Well, then."

Sam's face mirrored immense relief. "I've been worried silly, and all for nothing?"

"I believe so, yes."

"Why, that ornery female. I could just spank her."

"That wouldn't help matters," Owen said. "Let her tease and playact. You go on about your business and eventually she'll lose interest."

"You're sure?"

"Women don't keep after a man if he doesn't warm to them."

"So no trouble will come from her antics?"

"None whatsoever," Owen assured him.

"Thanks, Pa. I feel a lot better."

"Trust me, son," Owen said. "You and your brother, both. Things will work out fine."

Chapter 26

Ebidiah Troutman saved his life by a whisker. He swept his bowie high and blocked the young Comanche's blow. Blade rang on blade, the shock jarring Ebidiah's arm down to his marrow. He retreated to gain space but the warrior came after him, swinging his knife like a cleaver.

Ebidiah had no time to think, no time for anything except to rely on pure instinct. He was cut on the arm, but not deep. His left leg was nicked. He stabbed his bowie at the Comanche's neck, but the man skipped back out of reach.

Suddenly crouching, the young warrior said something in his own tongue. His face was aglow with bloodlust, the effect all the more unnerving because of the blood that still trickled from his broken nose.

"I don't want this," Ebidiah got out. "Just leave those settlers be. We don't have to fight."

The young warrior showed no sign of understanding. A vicious sneer curled his lips, and he returned to the attack.

Ebidiah backpedaled. He was no match for his adversary. Not if the fight went on for more than a few minutes. The warrior had the advantage of youth and vigor. Ebidiah would tire, his reflexes would dull. He must end it quickly, but how? he asked himself in desperation.

Moving his knife in small circles, the young warrior feinted, laughed, and feinted again.

The warrior was toying with him, Ebidiah realized.

When the Comanche flicked the knife at him yet again, he retaliated with a short, quick thrust. The tip of his bowie sheared into the other's hand above his knuckles, drawing blood.

Springing away, the warrior looked down at his hand. Fury replaced his sneer. He growled a few words, and with his eyes blazing like the fire pits of hell, he came at Ebidiah in a rush.

Ebidiah blocked, countered. For a little bit he held his own, but he could feel his arm tiring, feel fatigue nipping at his body. He was too old for this, much, much too old.

The Comanche delivered his most powerful blow yet, a swing that would have decapitated Ebidiah had it connected. Ebidiah jerked his bowie up and spared his throat, but the sheer force sent him stumbling. He tried to right himself but his right heel caught on something, and the next thing he knew, he was flat on his back.

Quickly placing his free hand flat on the ground, he tucked his knees to his chest, intending to roll and stand.

With a fierce yip, the Comanche loomed over him. The young warrior's arm arced high.

Without thinking, Ebidiah slammed his feet against the Comanche's knees. He was only trying to knock him back. Instead, there was a loud crack. The warrior cried out in pain and pitched forward, directly toward Ebidiah. In a panic, Ebidiah flung his arms out to push the warrior away. But the weight was too much. The young warrior crashed down on top of him. Ebidiah yelped and heaved and kicked, and only then realized that his bowie was buried to the hilt in the warrior's chest, just below the sternum.

Riveted in shock, Ebidiah lay still as the Comanche tried to rise. The younger man's eyes locked on his. The warrior started to raise his knife, and collapsed.

Ebidiah scrambled to free himself. He didn't know if the Comanche was dead or only wounded. He shoved clear, yanked his bowie free, and sat up.

The young warrior lay on his side, his arms limp, his eyes open and glazing with the emptiness of death.

A reaction set in. Ebidiah quivered from head to toe,

and gulped deep breaths. He had been lucky, oh-so-lucky. He stared at the blood on his bowie, then hugged his arms to his chest, bent over, and shook violently. His teeth chattered so hard, his jaw hurt.

Ebidiah lost track of time. He didn't know how long he sat there. Finally the shakes faded and his breathing returned to normal and he was himself again. Sitting up, he wiped his bowie on the grass, then stood and stared down at the body. "Will wonders never cease?" was all he could think to say. By rights, it should be him lying there.

"Thank you, God," Ebidiah said reverently. He replaced the bowie in its sheath and reclaimed his Sharps.

Belatedly, it occurred to him that there might be more Comanches about. Squatting, he studied the undergrowth and strained his ears, but apparently there had only been the one.

"What to do with you?" Ebidiah said. He considered taking the body down and showing it to Owen Burnett and the others. But the Kursts might wonder what he had been doing so near their camp, and he couldn't very well say he'd been spying on them. No, he reckoned the smart thing was to leave the body there, and go.

Standing, Ebidiah took a couple of steps, and stopped. The body might draw buzzards. The settlers might not notice or care to investigate if they did, but if there were other Comanches in the vicinity, they certainly would.

Ebidiah changed his mind. He should bury the warrior and hide the grave. There were still a couple of hours of daylight left, more than enough time to have it done by dark.

First things first. Ebidiah went down the hill and brought Sarabell back up with him. He wouldn't risk losing her to the Comanches. With her safe, he found a broken tree branch thick enough for his purpose, sharpened it with his bowie, and set to digging a hole long enough and wide enough. Within a short while his shoulders ached something awful. Grimacing, he persisted.

As he dug, he reflected. This business of keeping an eye on the Burnetts had unforeseen dimensions. He hadn't counted on tangling with a Comanche. Who knew what else might be in store? He liked them, but he wasn't willing to die for them.

By the time he'd scooped out a shallow trench, Ebidiah had come to a couple of new decisions. It would take the settlers weeks to collect enough cattle. He wasn't about to hang around that long. He'd go his own way, maybe drift by now and again to see how they were doing.

He wouldn't tell them about the Comanche, either. They might want to see the grave, and what use would that be? Besides, the Bible said something about doing good deeds in secret. Well, Ebidiah would keep this a secret. He'd take it with him to his grave.

Finally the hole was big enough. Mopping his brow, Ebidiah stood. Brief dizziness came over him, and he had to steady himself. "I am definitely too old for nonsense like this. Don't you think, gal?"

Sarabell went on dozing.

Stepping to the body, Ebidiah hooked his hands under the warrior's arms and dragged it over. He laid the warrior on his back and folded the hands on the chest. Covering the body took a while. He had to be sure to spread the dirt over every square inch.

To make doubly certain the body was never found, he added rocks and brush and branches. He tried to arrange things so the grave appeared to be part of the landscape, in case other Comanches happened by. If they found the dead one, there would be hell to pay.

Finished, Ebidiah wiped his hands on his pants, collected his rifle and his mule, and moved to where he could see the cattle camp below. The bustle was winding down. The settlers would soon have their supper and turn in for the night.

"I'm sorry, Owen," Ebidiah said. "I can't keep watching over you. From here on out, you're on your own."

Chapter 27

Owen Burnett hardly ever had trouble sleeping. He usually worked so hard from dawn until dusk that when he turned in, he was out soon after his head hit the pillow. Not this night. He hated to admit it, but he was as excited about the prospect of making a lot of money from the cattle drive as Gareth Kurst. In Gareth's case, his excitement was driven by greed. For Owen, it was being able to provide for his family as never before.

Owen always put his family before all else. His pa had been the same, and his pa before him. Family was everything to the Burnetts. He would do anything for his, anything at all. Including risk his life on a venture few had tried.

When Owen thought of all the things he could do with his share of the money, his head swam. He could add on to their house, expand the barn, buy more livestock. Even better, he could treat Philomena to new dresses and womanly foofaraw. He'd seen how she looked through the catalogue at the general store, seen her wistful longing for things they couldn't afford. Then there was Luke and Sam and Mandy and Estelle. He could help them get a step up in life. Sam had mentioned how he'd like to take some schooling and become a veterinarian. The boy liked working with sick animals more than anything. Estelle dreamed about going off to a college, of all things. She claimed to have heard about one just for females. That seemed far-fetched to Owen, but then again, there was a lot of talk of late about giving women the right to vote, so anything was possible.

Mandy's ambitions weren't as lofty. She wanted, one day, to have a husband and a house of her own, and to give Owen and Philomena grandchildren.

Luke was the wild card in the deck. All he seemed to care about was being quick with his pistol. Not that he wasn't a good worker. But there weren't a lot of jobs for shooters.

After a long while, Owen finally drifted off. It felt as if he'd hardly closed his eyes when a noise woke him and he raised his head to find Lorette kindling a fire for breakfast. The eastern sky was brightening, and once the sun was up, the roundup would commence.

Presently, everyone was up. Not much was said. Usually the Kursts couldn't start the day without a spat but today they were subdued. Reuben Weaver mumbled something about how they should mark the occasion with a toast, but no one ever paid any attention to Reuben.

They did to Gareth Kurst. Their horses were saddled when he stepped out in front of everybody and cleared his throat.

"This is it," Gareth said. "Root, hog or die, as they say where I'm from. We've done all we can to get ready. If there's something we've missed, we'll fix it. Learn as we go." He paused. "This won't be easy. But if a bunch of cowpokes can herd cattle, we can, too. Cowboys aren't no smarter than us. All we have to do is get the longhorns we collect to the railhead, and we'll be rich. When you're worn and hungry, think of that. When you want to give up, think of that. It will keep you going. Any questions?"

No one had any.

"Then let's mount up and get to it."

Owen liked Gareth's speech. Short, yet inspiring.

They'd already decided that working in pairs wouldn't do for the roundup. Two riders might not be able to handle a contrary longhorn. Three should be able to, though. Owen had wanted to be with Luke and Sam but Gareth proposed they draw lots and Jasper agreed. The night before, that's what they did. Owen would work with Wylie Kurst and Reuben. Luke was going out with Gareth and Silsby. Sam, with Harland and Lorette. Jasper Weaver was to ride with Thaxter and Iden.

On reaching the hills, everyone separated. Owen led Wylie and Reuben to the west, uncoiling his rope as he went.

The morning air held a chill, and the earth gave off that rich scent it always did early in the day.

"Are you ready, boys?" Owen said to encourage them.

"I'm not no boy," Wylie Kurst said.

"I don't mind you calling me that, Mr. Burnett," Reuben Weaver said. "My pa still calls me one. And yes, I'm as ready as I can be."

"Aren't you something?" Wylie said.

"We'll be at this for days, so it's best we get along," Owen said. "Wylie, I meant no offense. I call my own sons boys from time to time."

"That's honest enough, I reckon," Wylie said. "I'm not mad about it."

On that uncertain note, they threaded into the thickest of the thickets and soon flushed a couple of cows. Swinging their ropes, they spread out and got the cows between them. With Wylie on one side and Reuben on the other, and Owen herding the cows from behind, they worked the longhorns down the hill. A rope gate had been rigged, and Reuben dismounted and hurriedly untied it, then stood aside as Owen and Wylie drove the cows in. Reuben quickly retied the gate and scrambled onto his horse as if afraid the longhorns would turn on him.

The three of them waited to see what the cows would do. It would be easy as sin for the cows to break through the rope and bring the whole roundup scheme crashing down.

Owen scarcely breathed. Everything depended on what those critters did next. The cows had gone a short way and were gazing about. They showed no fear or alarm. Soon one dipped her head to graze, and the other followed suit.

"We did it, by God!" Reuben exclaimed.

"Not anywhere near," Wylie said.

"Huh?" Reuben said.

"Holdin' two ain't the same as holdin' two thousand," Wylie said.

Reuben appealed to Owen. "It's a good sign, though, isn't it, Mr. Burnett? If the rest prove as tame as these . . ."

"They won't," Wylie said.

"Are you always so sour about things?" Reuben asked.

"I don't put the cart before the horse," Wylie said.

"Gents, gents," Owen interrupted. He was going to say "Boy, boys," but he caught himself. "It's a start, and it's promising. But Wylie is right. We have a lot of long-horns to round up yet, and there's no predicting how it will turn out."

"Let's get to it and see," Wylie said.

They headed back up, Owen in the lead. Hollers and whoops to the northwest let them know that Luke and his partners had caught some longhorns, too.

Owen wondered if they had found cows or a bull, and how contrary the bulls would prove to be. No sooner did the thought enter his head than the underbrush crackled and out lumbered a big male with a horn spread of seven feet, if it was an inch. He drew sharp rein.

Reuben came to a stop next to him. "Oh, my," he said. "That's a big 'un."

"I've seen bigger," Wylie said.

So had Owen, but this one would be trouble enough if it proved reluctant to be driven.

The bull stood chewing and staring at them. A fly landed on an ear and the bull flicked it off.

"I'll swing wide," Wylie said.

Unconcerned, the bull watched him start around.

"I'll go the other way," Reuben said.

Owen was mesmerized. He imagined thousands in a huge herd, and the dust they would raise. He imagined all those deadly horns.

"Get along there, big fella," Reuben shouted, and wagged his coiled rope to provoke the bull into motion.

Which was all well and good, except that Owen was supposed to be behind the bull, not in front of it.

The bull came right at him.

Chapter 28

The buckboard rattled and clattered as Philomena Burnett brought it around the last turn before the Weaver farm. The few occasions she'd been here, it always made Philomena feel good about her own place. The Weaver house and barn were small, and not well-built. Barely ten acres had been tilled, and only one well dug. It made her realize how good a provider her husband was compared to Jasper Weaver and others.

A dog yapped, giving plenty of warning. As they drew near, the front door opened and Wilda Weaver stepped out, an apron around her waist. She was wiping her hands on a towel.

As Philomena slowed the buckboard, she glanced at her girls in the bed. "Remember, be on your best behavior."

"When aren't we, Ma?" Mandy said.

Estelle simply nodded.

Philomena brought the buckboard to a stop and smiled at her neighbor. "Good to see you again, Wilda."

Wilda Weaver stepped to the porch rail. "This is a surprise. It isn't often you come calling." She fussed at her hair and smoothed the apron. "I've been baking and must be a sight."

"Nonsense," Philomena said, laying the reins in the seat. "I should visit more often, but you know how things go. You get so busy, there's never time for social calls."

"Isn't that the truth." Wilda beckoned. "Alight and come in. I'll put tea on. And I have cookies for the young ladies."

"No need to go to that much bother." Philomena took her shotgun and climbed down. She made sure that Mandy remembered to bring the rifle. Estelle had a pocket pistol in a handbag she toted around. They never went anywhere unarmed. Not in Comanche country.

"It's no bother at all," Wilda was saying. "I'm pleased to have visitors. It's lonely with Jasper and Reuben gone."

"I know what you mean. I don't like having my husband and my sons gone, either," Philomena said.

"I didn't say I don't like it," Wilda said. "I only said it's lonely. And I can stand a little loneliness in return for a little peace and quiet."

"You like that they're away from home?"

"I get more rest when they are," Wilda said. "I don't have to do as much cooking or washing, and I can slack off on the cleaning. So yes," she said, and nodded. "I like it a lot."

The comment troubled Philomena. She had come for a specific purpose. It never occurred to her that Wilda might not feel the same way she did. She must pick her words with care. "I miss my Owen a terrible lot."

"I miss Jasper, too," Wilda said, yet she made it sound as if she didn't miss him all that much. "I don't miss him sucking down bug juice every hour of the day. Or the smell of liquor on his breath and on his clothes."

"Do you miss Reuben?" Philomena asked. She almost added "at least."

Wilda shrugged. "Some, I do. Don't take me wrong. He's a good boy. It would help if he grew up, but I'm afraid he'll take after his pa and never amount to much."

"Wilda," Philomena said, aghast. "Your own husband?"

"Well, it's true. What's the use in pretending it's not? We have to see things as they are, not as we'd like them to be. I knew Jasper wasn't a great catch when I married him. But I'm no great catch, either. I'm not a beauty, like your girls, or smart, like you."

"Thank you for the compliment, ma'am," Mandy said. "But you're pretty, too."

"You shouldn't ought to lie, missy," Wilda said. She gestured at the house. "But why are we standing out here talking when we can do it in the comfort of my parlor? Come on in."

Troubled, Philomena followed. The dog, a mongrel with short, bristly hair, came over and sniffed them and growled.

Wilda kicked it. "Shoo, you nuisance."

"Poor thing," Mandy said.

"Don't feel sorry for him," Wilda said. "He's always underfoot. If he wasn't such a good watchdog, I'd have shot him long ago."

"You're a hard woman, Mrs. Weaver," Estelle said.

"I prefer to think of it as being practical," Wilda said.

Philomena went in first. The house did smell of whiskey, as if Jasper Weaver drank so much, the odor seeped into the walls. The parlor was cozy if plain, with a settee and chairs and a rug.

Philomena and Mandy leaned their weapons against the wall.

Wilda bid them take a seat, then excused herself and whisked off to the kitchen for refreshments.

"Should we help her, Ma?" Mandy asked.

"She didn't ask for any." Philomena clasped her hands and settled back in her chair.

"Are you sure you want to do this?" Estelle said.

Philomena never failed to be impressed by how her youngest often picked up on things before her oldest did. "The women are our only hope. If we can persuade them, we might bring it about."

"Not Ariel Kurst," Mandy said. "She doesn't breathe without her husband's say-so."

"That's just gossip," Philomena said, when she knew very well it wasn't. She'd seen it with her own eyes.

A clock on the wall ticked loudly in the silence that followed. Philomena tried to think of small talk to make but she was focused on one thing and one thing only.

When, at last, footsteps sounded on the hardwood hall, she called out, "Do you need help, Wilda?"

"Not at all."

Wilda entered bearing a large tray with cups and saucers and spoons, and a teapot in the middle. She set the tray on a small table, nearly tripping in the process, and gave a light laugh. "Clumsy of me."

The cups were old china, and the spoons had seen a lot of use. The tea was warm but not hot as it should be.

Philomena sipped and smiled. "We're grateful for your hospitality."

Wilda roosted in a rocking chair, her hands in her lap. "Suppose you tell me the reason for your visit."

"It's a social call," Philomena said.

"Please. I'm not stupid. You came for a purpose," Wilda said. "I don't hold that against you. I'd just like to know what it is."

"You don't beat around the bush, do you, Mrs. Weaver?" Mandy said.

"Never saw the use," Wilda answered. "Some women, that's all they do. Prattle polite talk about things that don't matter. That's not me. I like to get right to the point."

"Very well, then," Philomena said, and lowered her cup. "I've come to talk about this cattle-drive business."

"What about it?"

"I'm against it, Wilda. Heart and soul. I tried to talk Owen out of it, but he wouldn't listen. My last hope is that if us wives stand together and tell our men we want them to stop, they'll listen to us."

"What on earth do you have against it?"

"A whole host of things," Philomena said. "The dangers, primarily. From the longhorns, for instance. You're bound to have heard stories about people who have been gored. And what happens if the cattle stampede?" She paused. "Then there are the Comanches to worry about, and who knows what other hostiles between here and Kansas. To say nothing of storms and tornadoes and flash floods."

"Life is full of hardships," Wilda said.

"Why court them when there's no reason to? I'd rather have my man at my side than dead, and I'm hoping you feel the same way."

Wilda Weaver smiled. "I don't."

Chapter 29

Owen Burnett's blood froze in his veins. The bull coming toward him could bowl his horse over and gore him before he got off a shot. He expected it to lower its head and charge. Instead, the animal walked past the chestnut without so much as a glance, the tip of its horn missing the horse by inches.

"You should have waited, boy, until he was out of the way," Wylie growled at Reuben. "That was close."

"Sorry, Mr. Burnett," Reuben said. "I wasn't thinking."

"No harm done," Owen replied, composing himself. "Let's take it down with the others."

The bull proved to have the temperament of a kitten. Given all the accounts he'd heard about how violent longhorns could be, Owen was both relieved and puzzled. Either the accounts were tall tales, or they didn't apply to all longhorns.

Maybe some had gentle dispositions and some didn't.

When they reached the grass, they found that nine more longhorns had been added. Luke, Gareth, and Silsby had just brought several cows and were about to go back out.

"How's it going with you, Pa?" Luke asked.

Before Owen could reply, Reuben Weaver laughed and said, "It's been plumb easy. At this rate, we'll have a hundred or more by the end of the day."

"A hundred is a far cry from two thousand," Gareth Kurst grumbled.

"Problems?" Owen said.

The head of the Kurst clan shook his head. "It's been easy so far. Too easy. Longhorns ain't supposed to be this tame."

"Some are and some aren't," Owen shared his conclusion.

"Then we've been lucky," Gareth said. "And we're due to tangle with one that isn't."

"My pa says we should always look at the bright side of things, Mr. Kurst," Reuben said.

"Your pa's idea of bright is the inside of a flask, boy," Gareth said. "Don't be lecturing me on how to think."

"I'd never!" Reuben exclaimed.

Gareth sighed, lifted his reins, and looked at Owen. "I will say this. Your boy, Luke, there, is a worker. He pitches in and does his part."

"I thank you for the compliment," Owen said.

"What about me, Pa?" Silsby said. "Don't I do good?"

"You'd better, or I'll wallop you." Gareth nodded at Owen, tapped his spurs, and led his partners up into the hills.

"That's my pa," Wylie said. "Do it his way, or else."

"If you don't mind my saying," Reuben said, "he's sort of mean. My pa has never walloped me."

"There's no 'sort of' about it," Wylie said. "My pa lays down the law and we fall into step. It's how he's been my whole life. I learned early to please him so I wouldn't be cuffed, or, worse, taken to the woodshed."

"How about you, Mr. Burnett?" Reuben surprised Owen by asking. "Do you ever beat on your boys?"

"I made them go without supper a few times when they were younger," Owen recalled.

"But do you hit them?"

"No." Owen's own pa had taken a switch to him now and then, and he'd never forgotten the humiliation. He'd spared his sons that by coming up with other punishments.

"I feel sorry for you, Wylie," Reuben said. "Your pa hitting you, and all."

"I don't need your damn pity," Wylie shot back. "He

does what he has to. My brothers aren't weak sisters, like you. When they act up, my pa has to step in quick and stop it. Like the time Thaxter slit a calf's throat to see it bleed. My pa blistered him black and blue." He smirked at Owen. "Making Thaxter go without food wouldn't have done any good. He'd only laugh, and the next time, it might have been a cow or a horse he killed."

That was the most Owen ever heard Wylie say at one time. "I reckon different families call for different ways."

"Why are we talking about this, anyhow?" Wylie said. "We have longhorns to catch."

Over the next several hours, Owen and his helpers brought in six more. Not one cow gave them a lick of trouble. He began to worry Gareth was right, and it was only a matter of time before their luck gave out.

As the day wore on, something became apparent; there were a lot more cows than there were bulls. Either there were fewer males, or the bulls were better at hiding.

Owen fretted that the bulls would take to fighting once they were thrown together, but as yet none had. When he mentioned his worry to the others, Wylie said that he'd heard longhorn bulls were like roosters. A typical barnyard usually had two or three, and there was always one that lorded it over the lesser birds, the cock of the walk who would fight any and all challengers at the drop of a feather. So it must be with longhorns. There were lesser bulls and cocks of the walk. A lot of lesser bulls, evidently, and only a few of the latter.

Owen shuddered to think what would happen if they caught one.

At midday, he and the others switched to fresh horses. They'd brought extras for just that purpose. It was tiring work, for the mounts and the riders alike, and a tired animal was more likely not to respond when it should.

Owen would have liked to change his pants, too. He'd only brought the one pair, and by late afternoon they were torn from the thickets and thorns.

Along about four o'clock, when they went deeper into the hills than they'd gone all day, they climbed to a grassy shelf that wasn't much wider than a Conestoga. Owen started across. He was staring up the hill, looking for longhorns, and happened to glance to his left. His breath caught in his throat and he drew rein and blurted, "Look yonder."

"What's wrong, Mr. Burnett?" Reuben said, coming up. He glanced over and his mouth fell.

Wylie Kurst drew rein last. "God Almighty," he exclaimed.

Beside some tall oak stood a longhorn as massive as a buffalo, a bull with a horn spread more than eight feet, weighing upwards of a ton. From nose to tail, it was as white as a ghost.

"Do you see what I see?" Reuben said in amazement.

Owen nodded. He was too incredulous to talk.

"It must be one of those cocks of the walk," Reuben said.

"And then some," Wylie said quietly.

"Think of the money it will fetch us in Abilene," Reuben said excitedly. "Why, it's a fortune in itself."

"Provided we can get it there," Wylie said.

"What's to stop us?" Reuben said. "We'll treat it the same as the others. Spread out and we'll catch it between us."

"Don't rush things, boy," Wylie said.

Before any of them could move, the bull raised its huge head, shook its long horns, and let out with a rumble of bovine anger.

"Uh-oh," Reuben said.

Chapter 30

"I must not have heard right," Philomena Burnett said to Wilda Weaver. "You don't want your husband back home safe? Where you don't have to worry about him?"

"No," Wilda said.

Philomena glanced at Mandy and then at Estelle. Both appeared as surprised as she was. "How can that be?"

"I'm not you."

"Yes, but—"

Wilda didn't let Philomena finish. "The last thing I'd do is try to talk Jasper out of going after those longhorns. I was so happy when he told me. Happier than I've been since we said our 'I do's.'"

"But the dangers . . ." Philomena tried again.

"He's a grown man. Besides, there's dangers on the farm, too. A horse might kick him and stave in his head. He might fall from the hayloft and break his neck. Or trip on a pitchfork and break his leg. What's the difference if it's that or a longhorn?"

"A horn through the chest will kill a man as quick as anything," Philomena argued.

Wilda sat back. "I'm afraid our opinions differ. And it's not the dangers that matter, anyhow."

"What does, then?"

"The money."

"Oh, Wilda."

"Don't you dare," Wilda said. "You with your fine house and big farm, and a man who doesn't drown himself in a flask every day. You already have a lot going for you. Both Ariel and me envy you to no end."

Philomena was taken aback. "There's nothing to envy. I'm as ordinary as can be."

"You have it good, Philomena Burnett," Wilda said without rancor. "Yet you don't even realize it."

"You have your own farm. Your own house. Your own land."

"Pshaw. Jasper and me are barely above the bottom of the barrel. But now we can change that. If this cattle drive works out, for the first time in my life, I'll have more money than I'll know what to do with. My ma couldn't ever make that claim. Nor her ma before her. Or on back as far as anyone in my family could remember if they tried."

"You value the money more than your husband's skin?"

"I do," Wilda said.

"I don't believe it," Philomena said. "No wife can care so little for her man. Jasper has done right by you, just as Owen has done right by me. We owe it to them not to let them be killed trying to provide for us."

"I can't think of a better reason," Wilda disagreed. "I've stood by Jasper for over twenty years. I've put up with his drinking and his laziness. I've fed him when he was hungry, nursed him when he was sick. I even let him touch me in the bedroom on occasion."

"Mrs. Weaver!" Mandy said.

"That's not proper talk for a lady," Estelle said.

"Child, what would you know?" Wilda countered. To Philomena she said, "This cattle drive is a godsend. At long last my husband can repay me for the years I've devoted myself to him. At long last we'll go from hardscrabble to comfortable, from famine to feast, from barely scraping by to having plenty. If that's not a blessing, I don't know what is."

"Money won't keep you warm at night," Philomena tried.

"I keep myself warm, thank you very much. I make Jasper sleep on his side of the bed and I sleep on mine."

Philomena frowned. This was getting her nowhere.

"In fact," Wilda went on, "if Jasper were to show up and say he's quit the drive, I'd boot him out the door and tell him to finish what he started. I'm not about to let him ruin our chance at happiness."

"His or yours?" Philomena said, unable to keep some of the bitterness out of her tone.

"Mine is the one that counts," Wilda said. "Call me selfish if you want but that's the way it is."

"I never heard a wife talk like you in all my born days."

"I'm being honest with you, Philomena. Would you rather I lied? That I say Jasper matters more to me than the money? He's a means to an end. When you think about it, that's all any husband ever is. A means for a woman to get the things she wants out of life."

"Why, Wilda, that's"—Philomena had to think to come up with the right word—"hideous."

"Oh, please. You're making a mountain of disgrace out of an anthill of yearning. Is it wrong to want the good things in life? To have what a lot of other women have? To live in a nice house? Have pretty things?"

"It's not wrong in and of itself, no," Philomena answered. "But we can take anything to an extreme."

"Listen to you. The woman who has it all, accusing me of being a poor wife for wanting what she has."

"I'm not accusing you of anything," Philomena said defensively.

"Sounds like it to me. Sounds like you'd like it if my life went on as it has been. A life of misery, of working my fingers to the bone for a man who loves his liquor more than he loves me."

"That's harsh."

"But true." Wilda placed her hands on her legs, and sighed. "I can see this isn't getting us anywhere. If all you wanted was to persuade me the cattle drive is a bad idea, you've wasted your time. You might as well leave."

Philomena saw her last hope of persuading Owen to give up the cattle business falling apart. "I was counting on your help."

"You shouldn't have."

"I thought we were friends. Or at least friendly toward each other."

"I'm being friendly now. I've heard you out, haven't I?" Wilda stood. "Our talk is over. There's nothing you can say or do that will change my mind."

Reluctantly, Philomena rose. Her girls did the same. Both Amanda and Estelle looked troubled. "In any event, I thank you for your time. And for the tea."

Wilda took a step, then stopped. "Philomena, listen. This isn't about you. Do you understand that? It's about me and my life and how I can better it. How I can be happier."

"Some people are happy without a lot of money and whatnot."

"They say they are, but are they really?" Wilda shrugged. "Even if that's true, it's only true for those women. Not for all of us. We can't all be as virtuous as you are."

"It's not about virtue, Wilda. It's about living out the rest of my years with the man I married."

"That's important to you. Good. I see that. Why can't you see it's not as important to me? If Jasper can't provide, he's not my helpmate. He's an anchor, dragging me down with him."

On that sobering note, Philomena led her daughters down the hall and out onto the porch. The fresh air didn't seem so fresh, the sunshine didn't seem as bright. "I thank you again for your time."

"I'm sorry, Philomena. I truly am," Wilda said, and shut the front door on them.

"Gosh, Ma," Mandy said. "I never heard anyone talk like her."

"Me either," Estelle said.

They walked to the buckboard and climbed on. As Mandy was settling into the bed, she remarked, "That Wilda Weaver is a terrible woman."

"She's something," Philomena said.

Chapter 31

For something so huge, the white bull could move incredibly fast. On the heels of its bellow, it whirled and plunged into the vegetation.

"There it goes!" Reuben cried.

"Thank goodness," Wylie said.

Raking his spurs, Reuben bawled, "After it!"

"Hold on, boy!" Wylie hollered.

In his enthusiasm, Reuben raced after the giant, yipping and whooping.

Owen would have rather let the bull go. They weren't up to handling a monster like that. They needed more experience. But he couldn't let Rueben Weaver get himself killed. Galloping in pursuit, he shouted for Reuben to stop.

The bull threaded through the trees with an ease that belied its size. It reached an acre of dense thicket and hurtled in, heedless of the thorns. In the blink of an eye it disappeared.

It spooked Owen, a creature that size vanishing like that. It didn't seem possible. "Reuben, don't go in after it!" he yelled, but once again, the Weaver boy must not have heard him.

Reuben barreled into the scrub.

"That damned lunkhead!" Wylie Kurst shouted.

Owen lashed his reins. The swath of crushed vegetation was easy to stick to and spared him from the worst of the needles. The trail angled to the right, and there

Reuben was, not ten feet away. Owen hauled on his reins, praying he could avoid colliding with Reuben's animal. The chestnut dug in its hooves and slid to a stop an arm's length from disaster.

"Reuben, what in the Sam Hill?" Owen said in anger.

Reuben was looking all around in consternation. "Do you see it? Where did it get to?"

"I don't see the bull anywhere," Owen was happy to say.

"One second it was here, and the next it was gone," Reuben said. "How can it do that, as big as it is?"

"Maybe it's for the best."

"All that money on the hoof." Reuben appeared on the verge of tears.

"There will be other bulls," Owen said. "Big ones like him."

"Not that big. He's the biggest, ever."

Wylie Kurst had drawn rein. "Consider yourself lucky, boy. If that thing had turned on you, you'd be worm food."

"Stop calling me boy," Reuben said. "You're not much older than me."

"You rode off without thinking," Wylie said. "That's what a boy does. Not a man."

"Who are you to talk?"

Owen nipped their spat in the bud with, "That bull might take it into its head to circle around. We should light a shuck."

Wylie stiffened. "I didn't think of that. You're right."

"I thought of it," Reuben said.

Owen didn't like the dark look Wylie gave the younger Weaver. He waited for Wylie to rein around, then did the same. Once they were out of the brush and resumed their hunt, he gigged the chestnut alongside Wylie's roan. "Don't take it personal, what he said back there."

"I'll take it any way I want."

"We can't afford hard feelings. We have to get along to make this work. And like you brought up, he's still a boy."

"Don't worry, Mr. Burnett," Wylie said. "Our pa told

us we're to behave until the drive is over. We're not to cause a ruckus. Not to hit anyone or shoot anyone. We do, and we answer to him."

"That's good to hear," Owen said. Although the fact that Gareth had to expressly forbid them to shoot someone was disturbing.

"If we didn't have to work together," Wylie continued, "I'd have pistol-whipped that brat for talking to me the way he did."

"Reuben Weaver is no brat. He has better manners than most, and is always polite to everyone."

"Not to me, he wasn't."

Owen let it drop. But it didn't bode well. Petty bickering could turn into something uglier. He'd have to keep as tight a rein on his partners as he did on the chestnut.

"Tell me something," Wylie said.

Owen looked at him.

"What makes you the way you are?"

"Excuse me?"

"You're always so damned reasonable about things. Always trying to talk things out. Don't you ever lose your temper? Don't you ever get mad?"

"Of course I do. I'm human, aren't I?"

"You don't ever show it. You're not like my pa. He gets mad a lot. And when he's mad, you can be sure he shows it. Once at the supper table Lorette mentioned how she admired that you never lose your temper—"

"She did?" Owen said in surprise.

"—and Pa told her you're the same as everybody else but that you pretend you're not. He said you're like a teapot that keeps the steam in until it's fit to explode."

"That's not true." Owen never had been one for holding grudges and the like. The few occasions he did become mad, he got over it and went on with his life.

Wylie grunted.

"You don't believe me?"

"I believe you pretend. I've never heard you so much as cuss anyone, so you must hold it in, just like my pa says."

Owen never would have imagined he'd be a topic of

discussion at the Kurst table. Or that Gareth held such a low opinion of him. He pondered that over the rest of the afternoon.

By sunset they'd added six more longhorns, which brought the total tally for the first day of the roundup to eighty-three cattle.

Later, as they sat around their campfires, relaxing, Owen did the arithmetic in his head and announced, "If we can keep this up, in four to five weeks we'll have two thousand head or more."

Gareth, who was pouring coffee, remarked, "Three thousand would be better. In case we lose some on the drive."

"Three might be more than we can handle."

"Between two and three, then," Gareth said. "But not less than two."

"We're quibbling over a few hundred," Owen said.

"Ten to twenty thousand dollars more is nothing to sneeze at."

"I suppose it's worth it, then," Owen conceded.

"You *suppose*?" Gareth set the pot down, and glowered. "Are you sure your heart's in this, Burnett?"

"What a thing to say to me," Owen said, feeling offended. "I'm here, aren't I?"

"My heart is sure in it," Jasper Weaver said. Instead of a tin cup, he had his flask. "Wilda told me that if I don't come home with our share, she'd make me sleep on the settee the rest of my life."

"Now there's a woman who knows her mind," Gareth said. "You should listen to her."

"I always do," Jasper said.

Gareth smirked at Owen. "Do you *suppose* Mrs. Weaver would pass up an extra ten to twenty thousand?"

Jasper laughed, but Owen didn't think it was the least bit funny.

Chapter 32

Philomena was nothing if not tenacious. Owen always said that when she set her mind to something, she wouldn't let anything stand in her way. She'd failed to convince Wilda Weaver to side with her. But maybe, just maybe, she could persuade Ariel Kurst to have a talk with Gareth. It was a long shot. Everyone knew who ruled the Kurst roost. She decided to try, anyway; she had nothing to lose except her husband.

Rather than take the buckboard, Philomena rode. She told her girls to stay close to their farmhouse and not go anywhere without a rifle. They were old enough to take care of themselves, and were both passable shots.

Philomena took her shotgun. It was English-made, and had belonged to her grandfather. Her pa gave it to her when she announced Owen and she were leaving for the West. The gift touched her deeply since her pa had been fond of it.

The whole ride to the Kursts', Philomena couldn't help thinking that she was wasting her time. If she had any sense, she'd turn around. But another part of her refused to give up. Without the Kursts, Owen and Jasper would be forced to come home. They couldn't do it themselves.

The trees thinned, and Philomena emerged from the woods into a clearing. Before her stood the Kurst cabin. She had been here once before and been both amazed and appalled. Amazed, because it looked as if the logs had been slapped together by a drunk. Appalled, because the cabin wasn't much bigger than a chicken coop, yet eight people lived there, crammed together like so many eggs in a nest. She'd heard, but she hadn't been able to confirm it, that the five boys slept on the floor in the main room, and that Lorette, in order to have some privacy, slept in the root cellar.

Avoiding stumps that hadn't been removed, Philomena brought her horse to a halt and swung down. A threadbare curtain with holes in it moved in a window.

Cradling her shotgun, she stepped to the door and knocked. No one came. She rapped again, louder, and called out, "Ariel? It's me, Philomena Burnett. I'd like to talk to you."

From the other side of the closed door came a timid, "What do you want?"

"You just heard me say. To talk."

"About what?"

"Open this door and I'll tell you," Philomena said. "It's silly to shout back and forth."

A bolt scraped and the door opened just wide enough for a brown eyeball to peek out. "I wasn't expecting company."

"We're neighbors, aren't we?" Philomena replied. "Can't I come calling?"

"I don't mind, but it's not me who wouldn't like it."

"You're alone. The rest of your family is off with my man. We can talk and they will never know." When Ariel still didn't open the door, Philomena added, "I won't tell anyone I was here. You won't get into any trouble."

The brown eye glanced about the clearing and settled on Philomena again. "I reckon it's safe enough. But if I see any of them coming, I'm ducking back inside. Gareth says I'm not to talk to other ladies when he's not around. He says they try to put notions in my head." Ariel stepped out, as mousy in appearance as a person could be, with a small face and ratty gray hair that had turned that color prematurely. The corners of her eyes had more crow's feet than a legion of the raucous black birds.

Philomena chose what she was about to say with care. "I'm not here to put any notions in your head. Only to ask a favor. I'd like for you and me to sit down with our husbands and impress on them that the cattle drive is a bad idea."

"Gareth says it's a good one."

"No doubt," Philomena said.

"Gareth says the Good Lord is being nice to us for once and has dumped a gold mine in our laps. Gareth's very words."

"What do you think?"

"Pardon?"

"What do *you* think?" Philomena asked a second time.

"I don't," Ariel said. "I generally let Gareth do my thinking for me."

Don't give up, Philomena told herself. "He doesn't decide everything, does he? Aren't there some things you make up your own mind about?"

Ariel's brow sprouted furrows. "Not that I can think of, no. He'd blister my back with a switch if I was to do something without his say-so."

Philomena almost shuddered at the image that popped into her head. "He hits you?"

"Only when I deserve it."

Containing her anger, Philomena said, "Are you his wife or his child?"

"A man has to keep his woman in line," Ariel said. "I'm sure Owen does the same with you."

"Owen has never laid a finger on me once our whole marriage."

"I don't know as I believe that. I'm proud my man keeps me under a tight rein, and I can't imagine a woman who wouldn't feel the same about her man."

"A wife deserves to be treated with respect."

Ariel seemed not to hear her. "Gareth made everything plain to me soon after we were wed. Women are flighty creatures. Men aren't. We're ruled by our feelings and they're ruled by their brains. Men are the smart ones. Men know what to do. That's why God gave Eve to Adam for him to lord over. We have to be kept in our place."

"Oh, Ariel." Philomena had a sense that Ariel was reciting what her husband had told her.

"What?"

"A lot of ladies would disagree. I do. God gave Eve to Adam to be his helper, not to think and do everything he demands. It's all right to have minds of our own."

"Well, we shouldn't talk religion. We're women. We don't know enough about it."

"You worry me, Ariel. No woman should be so subservient to her man. It's not right."

"Right has nothing to do with it," Ariel said. "It's how things are."

"Not at my house. Not at Wilda Weaver's, either. There, she tells Jasper what to do, not the other way around."

"Gareth says the Weavers aren't natural. That Wilda is the man and Jasper is the woman. Gareth says that happens when the husband is weak."

"People are different, is all," Philomena said.

"Is this all you wanted to talk about? The cows, and men and women? You're a mite peculiar, Mrs. Burnett."

"Call me Philomena, please."

"Gareth says to always use the last name. To keep everything proper. So people won't take liberties."

"What sort of liberties?"

"Become too friendly." Ariel gave Philomena a very pointed look. "Ask favors when they shouldn't."

Philomena saw that this was getting her nowhere. But she stubbornly persisted. "It's wrong for a neighbor to ask a favor of another?"

"It's wrong to impose," Ariel replied. "You show up out of the blue. You ask me to side with you against my own husband. You say it's for his own good, as if you know better than him. If that's not imposing, I don't know what is."

Philomena was at a loss what to say. Nothing would break the shackles Gareth had on Ariel's mind.

"Let me be clear, Mrs. Burnett. My husband is my life. He provides for me. He keeps me safe. He looks after our young'uns. I wouldn't turn on him for any reason. Certainly not for a woman I hardly know and who thinks I should trust her more than the man I've lived with for

over twenty years. I'll thank you to go, and not grace my
doorstep again." Ariel glared coldly, backed inside, and
closed the door.

"Wait," Philomena said, too late. She knocked, saying,
"Please. Can't we talk this out some more?"

Minutes went by. No sounds issued from within. The
cabin might as well have been a tomb.

Returning to her horse, Philomena slid the shotgun
into the scabbard and climbed on. She could practically
taste her disappointment. "That went well," she said to
the empty air, and tapped her heels.

Chapter 33

More than two weeks had gone by since Ebidiah Troutman killed the Comanche. He happened to be in the vicinity of Comanche Creek and decided to see how the settlers were doing. He climbed to the crest of the same hill where he'd spied on them before, took his spyglass from a pack on Sarabell, and sat on the same boulder.

Before he even unfolded his telescope, he saw a lot of cattle. At a guess, he would say there were close to a thousand. "My word!" he exclaimed. The cattle were grazing or drinking or lazing in the sun. The rope corral was intact, and a few small fires smoldered around the perimeter.

"It's working the way they'd hoped," Ebidiah marveled. He'd never seen so many longhorns in one place at one time.

On a whim, Ebidiah replaced his spyglass in the pack without using it, took hold of Sarabell's rope, and headed down. With that many cattle, he figured they'd have someone keeping watch, and he was right.

Owen Burnett and one of the Kurst boys were hunkered by a campfire, drinking coffee.

Ebidiah hesitated before showing himself. He couldn't stand those Kursts, but he squared his shoulders and ambled out into the open, Sarabell plodding behind. Plastering a smile on his face, he called out, "Got any of that you can share?"

The Kurst boy jumped to his feet, his hand dropping to his revolver. "Hell," he said. "It's only you, old man."

"Be civil, Wylie," Owen said as he rose. He smiled and offered his hand. "It's good to see you again, Ebidiah. How have you been?"

Ebidiah nodded at the longhorns. "Not as busy as you. It's going well, I take it?"

"Better than we dreamed," Owen said, giving the herd an appreciative glance. "We've got so many, we take turns as herd guards. Reuben Weaver is making a round right now, seeing that the other fires stay lit."

"Have the critters given you any trouble?"

"Once we get them down here, hardly a lick," Owen said. "It surprised me considerably, all the tales I've heard."

"My pa wouldn't like this old goat being here," Wylie Kurst remarked.

"Ebidiah is my friend," Owen said. "What difference does it make, anyhow?"

"They don't get along."

"No, we don't," Ebidiah said. "Not through any fault of mine. It's your pa who acts so high and mighty."

"Watch what you say about him, old man," Wylie warned.

"Enough," Owen said. "Ebidiah, have a seat and I'll pour some coffee for you. It's Arbuckles'. Have you ever had any?"

"Mrs. Weaver gave me some once." Ebidiah had liked the taste. Arbuckles' was relatively new on the frontier, and was already popular. The way he heard tell, a couple of brothers from back east had invented a new way of roasting the beans, and sold them by the pound.

Ignoring the hard stare of Wylie Kurst, Ebidiah got his tin cup out, held it while Owen filled it, and squatted. Taking his first sip, he smiled in contentment. "It's as good as I recollect."

"We're about out," Owen said. "Of coffee and other things. My son Luke went into town with Gareth and Silsby this morning for more supplies."

Ebidiah grunted. That was good news. He'd be long gone before Gareth got back. "I was by your house about a week ago. Your missus and your girls are doing fine."

"Thank God. I worry about them all the time."

"You shouldn't. That wife of yours has a good head on her shoulders. When I showed up, she came out toting a shotgun."

Owen chuckled. "That's my Philomena."

Gazing out over the hills, Ebidiah casually asked, "Had any trouble of any kind?"

"The creek hasn't flooded," Owen joked.

"I was thinking of the Comanches," Ebidiah said. "Word is, one has been seen in these parts." He didn't mention that he'd done the seeing—and killed him.

"We haven't spotted any," Owen said. "If they're around, they've left us alone."

"Good," Ebidiah said, relieved to hear it.

"They'd better leave us be," Wylie said. "We have enough guns, we'll blow those stinking redskins to hell and back."

"The Comanches were here long before us white folks," Ebidiah mentioned.

"So?"

"So they have a right to live here, too."

"Are you addlepated, old man? Those red devils kill every white they come across. They want to drive us out and keep this country for themselves."

"You can't hardly blame them."

Wylie snorted. "You *are* addlepated. There's no getting along with the Comanches. They're not friendly, not even a little bit. It's them or us, and as my pa says, it damn well won't be us."

"You two are at it again," Owen said.

"He started it," Wylie said. "Or are you an Injun lover, too?"

"Simmer down," Owen said. "I'd rather we were at peace, but since we're not, I'll shoot any Comanche who's a threat to me or mine."

"You'd better," Wylie said. "Or they'll kill you."

"All this talk of killing," Owen said. "So long as we mind our own business and don't give them cause to attack, we should be fine."

"Let them try something," Wylie said, and patted his

six-gun. "My pa and my brothers and me will make them regret it."

"The important thing is to not give them cause," Owen stressed.

Ebidiah sipped, and swallowed, and didn't say anything.

Chapter 34

They had been in the brush, searching for longhorns, for half the day, and their horses needed to rest.

Sam Burnett could use a break, himself. The long hours he spent in the saddle, the work, the heat, the dust, were wearying. Sitting on a log, he opened his canteen and tipped it to his mouth to slake his thirst.

Overall, the roundup was going better than his pa had imagined. The longhorns weren't giving them nearly as much trouble as everyone feared. Not that there hadn't been incidents.

Several days ago, Sam came on three young bulls. From what he gathered, young bulls sometimes congregated together. These three had stood tail to tail, brandishing a ring of horns at Sam, Lorette, and Harland.

"We'll each take one," Harland had proposed.

His rope in hand, Sam had singled out one and moved in, waving the rope to provoke the bull to move. Harland and Lorette were doing the same when suddenly the bulls exploded into motion. For a few harrowing moments, Sam thought the one he had picked was charging right at him. But no, it swerved at the last instant and bolted into the scrub. He had to chase the thing for half a mile but eventually he overtook it and drove it down to the herd.

"Mind if I join you?"

The sweetly posed question was followed by Lorette Kurst plopping herself down next to him, so close that their bodies brushed against each other. In doing so, she jarred Sam's elbow, and he almost spilled water from his canteen.

"Watch it, will you?"

Lorette flashed her teeth and took off her hat to fuss with her hair. "Feeling grumpy today, are we?"

Sam shifted so they weren't touching. For over two weeks now he'd had to put up with her constant shenanigans, and it was annoying. "I just want to relax a bit."

Lorette glanced over at where Harland was scanning the hills to the west. "In case you haven't heard," she said so only Sam would hear, "a woman can relax a man better than anything."

"There you go again."

"What?"

"The things you say." Sam capped his canteen. "Don't you have any shame? A lady wouldn't say the things you do."

"Ladies can't have fun?"

Another thing that aggravated Sam was how she turned his own words against him. "Is that what you call it? He was trying to stay mad but it was hard. She looked awful pretty sitting there with the sun in her hair and her green eyes sparkling.

"You're a trial, Sam Burnett," Lorette said, and puckered her lips as if she were upset.

Sam had been thinking of her lips a lot the past few days, and it bothered him. They were just lips. They shouldn't keep creeping into his head. "What did I do?"

"Nothing. And that's the problem. I've made it as plain as plain can be that I'm interested, and you act like I have fleas or something."

Sam's throat seemed to tighten. "Interested how?"

"Oh, please. You're not a dunce. You know darned well."

"Maybe I'm not as smart as you think."

"You were raised on a farm. You must know about mares and stallions and such."

"Lordy, Lorette," Sam said. "How can you be so brazen? And why me? Why not Reuben Weaver?"

"You brought him up before. I'd sooner become a nun and live in a convent than take him for my man."

"What's wrong with Reuben?" Personally, Sam liked him. They got along fine. At night they'd sit around the fire and talk about everything under the son.

"Nothing is wrong with him that a different body and a different brain wouldn't fix," Lorette said. "I'm not Wilda Weaver. I won't settle for less when I can have more."

"And I am more?"

"You surely are, but you're too dumb to see it."

"So which am I?" Sam countered. "Smart or dumb? I can't be both."

"Sure you can. You're male."

"There you go. Poking fun again." Sam had half a notion to ask his pa to be partnered up with someone else. Maybe he could switch with Reuben. That would show her.

Lorette placed her hands on the log and half-turned to look him in the eyes. "How long before you stop dancing around it? I'm patient but I have my limit."

"I don't even know how to dance."

Snorting, Lorette leaned in and kissed him on the cheek. As she was drawing back, she seemed to realize what she had done and appeared as surprised as he was; she gave a slight start, and her eyes widened.

Sam tried to talk but his throat had a lump in it.

Lorette glance over at Harland again, and let out a breath. "Thank God he didn't see. He'd tell Pa." Abruptly, she stood and placed her hands on her hips. "We can't go on like this. I can't do all the work. You need to make up your mind one way or the other."

"About what?"

"You're plumb hopeless," Lorette said, and flounced off.

For the life of him, Sam didn't know what he had done to make her so mad. A suspicion dawned, and he chewed on it a bit, recollecting past comments she'd made, which he hadn't taken entirely serious. He'd thought she was playing. But if she wasn't? The answer struck him like a thunderclap. "Oh my, oh my," he blurted.

A shadow fell over him.

Sam looked up, thinking Lorette had come back. But it was her big brother, and he didn't appear happy.

"She must think I'm blind, deaf, and dumb."

"Harland?" Sam said.

Bending at the waist so they were face-to-face, Harland said, "What are your intentions?"

"I didn't know I had any," Sam said.

"She does. And in case you're the one she's serious about, there's a few things you should know." Harland held up a finger. "One, me and my brothers won't take kindly to her being trifled with." Harland held up another finger. "Two, nor will my pa, and he's worse than all the rest of us put together." Harland held up a third. "Three, I can't stop her from kissing you, but it better go no further than that unless you're as serious as she is. Savvy?"

"Uh," Sam said.

Harland straightened. "Don't play me for a dolt, boy. I'll be keeping my eye on you."

"But . . ." Sam got out.

"Treat her right and I'll stay out of it. Treat her wrong and our entire clan will come down on you like a Comanche war party. Savvy me?" And with that, Harland wheeled and stalked off.

"God help me," Sam said.

Chapter 35

Owen Burnett couldn't be more pleased. It had taken seven weeks, but they had rounded up more than two thousand longhorns. They had so many, the grassland along Comanche Creek was a sea of horns. He was excited for the drive to begin. First, though, there was something they must do.

Collecting a big herd wasn't enough. They must be able to prove the cattle were theirs. Should the animals stampede, anyone could claim them.

The thing to do was brand them—each and every longhorn.

Owen knew next to nothing about branding. Fortunately, Gareth had learned enough, and even brought back a branding iron from his last visit to town. Gareth had the blacksmith make it. The brand consisted of a 'K' in the middle with what Gareth said were the letters 'B' and 'W' to either side. They stood for Kurst, Burnett, and Weaver. But to Owen the B and the W looked like squiggles. Someone who didn't know any better might think the Kursts were the sole owners of the herd.

Owen didn't say anything to Gareth but he did ask Jasper's opinion. Jasper thought the branding iron was fine.

The next day they'd started the branding.

It involved roping the longhorns and holding them so the branding iron could be used. The rope had to be thrown just so, dallied just so. The branding iron had to be kept hot.

They worked in teams of six to reduce the risk. Even so, on the fifth day Jasper didn't keep his rope tight and a cow nearly got loose, almost goring Thaxter. Thaxter wasn't happy; he slapped his hand to his Colt and threatened to put windows in Jasper's skull. If not for Gareth stepping between them and telling his son to simmer down, Wilda might have been a widow.

As new cattle were added, they were branded. They got so good at it, Reuben joked they should all become cowboys.

On a peaceful evening with the sun red on the horizon, Owen and Gareth stood admiring the fruits of their labors.

"Will you look at all those critters?" Gareth said with pride. "We did it, by God."

"Another week and we should have the twenty-five hundred you were aiming for," Owen said.

"I'd be happier with three thousand." Gareth rubbed the stubble on his chin. "But twenty-five might be as many as we can handle. Seeing them all together like this"—he whistled in appreciation—"it's a damn big herd."

"And it's all ours."

Gareth blinked. "Yes," he said. "Ours."

"I hope we don't lose many on the trail to Abilene," Owen said. Especially after all they had gone through rounding them up.

Spurs jingled, and Sam and Harland approached. They had only just come down out of the hills, along with Lorette who was over talking to Iden.

"There you are," Gareth said to his oldest. "What kept you today? You were the last to get back."

It was Sam who answered, saying to Owen, "We found something, Pa. Something peculiar."

"Such as?" Owen said when his son didn't go on.

"A grave."

"Did it have a tombstone?" Gareth said, and laughed.

"We're serious, Pa," Harland said. "I saw it, too. It's the strangest thing. As if someone dug up a body and then dragged it off. We saw the drag marks."

Owen swapped perplexed looks with Gareth.

"Lorette came across it, and hollered for us," Harland went on. "The hole wasn't that deep, but it was man-sized. And there was no mistaking the stink. A body had been there, sure enough."

"Where was this?" Owen asked.

Sam pointed at a hill to the north. "Atop that hill yonder, Pa. Just on the other side."

"There's enough daylight left, we should go have a look-see," Gareth suggested.

Owen agreed. The idea of a grave so close to their camp was disquieting. "It bears investigating."

The four of them mounted and crossed to the hill at a gallop. A swift climb brought them to the crest. The cedar scrub was heavy, and Sam and Harland weren't sure exactly where the hole had been. They spent ten minutes looking, and finally Sam yelled, "Here it is!"

Owen gigged his chestnut over. It wasn't so much a hole as a shallow trench, but it was long enough and wide enough to have held a body.

"I'll be damned," Gareth said.

Owen swung down. The drag marks Harland had alluded to were easy to follow. They led to a cleft halfway down the hill, where torn brush and a pile of rocks suggested the body had been placed in the cleft and covered.

"What the hell?" Harland said. "Whoever it was took the body out of the grave and brought it here to bury again? What was the point?"

"I'd like to see," Owen said, and stooped over the rocks.

"Maybe you shouldn't, Burnett," Gareth Kurst said.

"We have to know," Owen insisted. "This close to our camp, it could be important." As he removed the rocks, a foul odor assailed him. The smell grew stronger the deeper he went. He didn't have to dig far.

The body had been wrapped in a blanket.

"Pa," Sam gasped. "That there is the one Reuben couldn't find."

"What?" Owen said, placing a hand over his nose.

"Don't you remember? Reuben said one of his blankets went missing. Him and his pa were looking all over for it."

"I remember," Gareth said.

"Someone stole a blanket from the Weavers just for this?" Harland said, pointing at the body. "Who'd do such a thing?"

"Someone who didn't have a blanket of their own," Owen guessed. He continued to remove the rocks.

The body had been wedged tight into the cleft. To see it, Owen had to tug and pull at the blanket to loosen it. After a while he exposed an arm. A lot of the flesh was gone from the hand, and white bone gleamed. But the buckskin sleeve was intact. He removed more rocks, revealing part of a shoulder and long black hair.

"An Injun, by God!" Harland exclaimed.

Gareth swore. "I've heard they like to bury their dead in spots like this. Clefts and ravines and such."

"Who does?" Sam said.

"The Comanches."

Owen lifted more rocks, and shuddered.

The face was partially rotted, the eyes gone, the mouth agape. A maggot wriggled in an eye socket.

"What do you think killed him?" Sam said.

"No telling," Owen said.

"Who cares?" Harland said. "It's just a dead Injun. Nothing will come of it."

"I hope to God you're right," Owen said.

Chapter 36

The sun was setting when they got back. Owen had covered the body back over with the rocks, leaving it as they found it. A feeling of unease came over him as he worked, a feeling that grew stronger on the ride down.

The campfire was crackling and the cooking pot was on. Everyone else was relaxing after a hard day's work. After their meal, they would take turns riding herd. The longhorns were settling in for the night, and largely quiet.

Lorette was stirring the stew. She raised the dripping wooden spoon, took a taste, and announced, "Supper will be ready in a couple of minutes."

Raising his arms, Owen said loudly, "Everyone, I need your attention, please." He related the finding of the grave, and the body wrapped in the Weavers' blanket, and ended with, "We need to talk about what to do."

"You're worried over nothing," Harland said.

"Hush, boy," Gareth growled.

Owen continued. "It raises all kinds of questions. How did it get there? Who killed him? Why bury him so close to us? I'm no real judge, but I'd say the body hasn't been in the ground all that long. A few weeks to a month would be my guess."

"Harland is right," Jasper Weaver said. "It has nothing to do with us."

"Didn't you hear the part about the blanket?" Owen said. "Whoever reburied the body snuck down into our camp and helped themselves to one of yours. They took it from right under our very noses."

"Had to be other Comanches," Wylie said. "They're as sneaky as anything."

"So let them keep it," Jasper said. "I don't mind."

"You're missing the point," Owen said.

"They didn't attack any of us," Reuben said. "That shows they're friendly."

"Comanches?" Thaxter said, and laughed.

"All it shows," Owen said, "is that they needed something to wrap the body in, and our blankets wcrc handy. They might not have attacked because there were only a few of them. By now they could have gone to their village for more warriors."

"Might and could have," Harland said. "You don't know for sure."

"Why should they come after us?" Jasper said. "We didn't kill that one you found."

"Thcy don't know that."

"You think they might attack us, Pa?" Luke asked.

"I think it's a very real danger, son," Owen said.

"They haven't bothered us this whole time," Jasper persisted. "Why would they start now?"

"Get your head out of your flask, Weaver," Gareth said. "Burnett is right. This could be serious."

"Don't talk to my pa that way," Reuben said.

"Or what, boy?" Thaxter said. "You'll go for your six-gun?"

Some of the others laughed.

"Enough," Owen stepped in. "Save your bickering. From here on out, we have to be on our guard more than ever. It was luck we found that body. More than luck, I'd say. It was the hand of Providence, warning us."

"Oh, please," Wylie said.

"What's Providence, Pa?" Iden said to Gareth.

"The Almighty."

"I thought that was God," Iden said. "Or is Providence His last name?"

"Shut up, little brother," Lorette said.

"Let's stay focused on the Comanches," Owen said. "They might take it into their heads to stampede our cattle, undoing all the work we've done."

"To say nothing of lifting our scalps," Luke said.

"What can we do?" Silsby Kurst anxiously asked. "Comanches spook me something awful."

"They spook everybody," Sam said.

Owen raised his arms again so they would focus on him. "I propose we stay close to the herd until we're ready to start the drive. Don't go anywhere alone, and keep your guns handy."

"You heard the man," Gareth said, giving each of his brood a sharp glance. "This is no time to get sloppy. Too much is at stake."

"All that money," Harland said.

"All that money," Gareth echoed.

Lorette had been hunkered by the pot, but now she stood and wagged the big spoon. "Seems to me the most important thing is the one question we can't answer."

"Who killed that Comanche," Wylie said, "and buried him up on the hill?"

"Exactly," Lorette said.

"You'd think we'd have heard it if he was shot," Harland said. "It's not that far away."

"Maybe it was another Comanche," Reuben Weaver said.

"Comanches hardly ever kill other Comanches," Gareth said. "And none would have stuck him in that hole, then come back to bury him again."

"An Injun from another tribe, maybe?" Reuben said.

"There aren't any other Injuns hereabouts," Gareth said.

"Apaches?" Jasper said.

Gareth shook his head. "The Comanches drove them out of these parts years ago."

"Kiowas, then?" Jasper wouldn't let it drop. "Aren't they and the Comanches supposed to be friendly?"

"They are," Gareth said. "But I never heard of any Kiowas this far south."

"How is it you know so much about Injuns?" Reuben asked.

"It pays to learn all you can about anyone who might be out to kill you," Gareth said.

The youngest of the Kursts, Iden, looked utterly confused. "Well, if it wasn't another Comanche and it wasn't the Apaches and it wasn't the Kiowas, who in the world was it?"

"A white man, maybe," Harland said.

"You could be right," Luke said. "The grave that was dug is something a white man would do."

Owen followed their line of reasoning aloud. "A white man killed him and buried him, and then other Comanches came looking for the one who was missing, found him in the grave, and reburied him their own way."

"That fits," Gareth said.

"Except that we're the only white folks here," Reuben said. "We haven't seen another soul since — " He abruptly stopped.

"Oh, hell," Harland said.

"Surely not!" Jasper said.

"That old trapper!" Lorette said.

"We don't know it was him," Luke said.

"Surely Ebidiah would have told us if he did it," Owen said. "Something that important, he wouldn't keep to himself."

"Could be he thought the body would never be found," Gareth said. "Could be he didn't think it worth mentioning."

"It had to have been him," Harland said.

"We should go find him," Lorette said. "Ask him to his face."

Gareth shook his head. "No one is going anywhere. The cattle are more important. If that old coot was to blame, we'll wring it out of him the next time we see him."

"I'd give anything to know where Mr. Troutman is right now," Luke remarked.

"So would I," Owen said.

Chapter 37

Ebidiah Troutman was near giddy with delight. It wasn't often fortune favored him with so rare a pelt. He sat cross-legged by his small fire in a gully and fingered the smooth fur, and laughed.

"A white fox, by God!"

Albino foxes were rare. Ebidiah had only ever seen one other albino fox in all his years, and that was back in the early days, and up in the northern Rockies. To trap one here, in the Texas hill country, was tantamount to a miracle. He smoothed the fur and laughed some more.

A white fox was special. People would pay good money. Mrs. Burnett or Mrs. Weaver might be interested, but he doubted they could afford the price he'd ask. He wasn't letting this one go cheap.

Placing the pelt across his legs, Ebidiah carefully rolled it up, then rose and just as carefully placed it in a pack on Sarabell.

The sun had been up an hour. Normally, Ebidiah would have been on his way by now, but he'd been savoring the miracle. He hadn't been this excited about a pelt in ages. In the old days, every pelt brought a flush of accomplishment. Not so much, anymore. Maybe he had just gotten used to it.

Back then he'd felt more pride in his work. The trapping was hard. Then came the skinning. It had to be done just right or a fur would be ruined. No one wanted a shabby or stiff fur, or a fur with holes in it. Truth be told, preparing the hide was more important than the actual laying of the trap. And he was good at it. One of the best, folks always said.

Grinning at the memories, Ebidiah kicked dirt onto the fire until only a few plumes of smoke rose. Taking hold of Sarabell's rope, he climbed out of the gully and made to the southeast.

"Yes, sir, old girl," Ebidiah declared. "When I sell the fox, I might even put you up at the stable for a night. How would that be? You could have your own stall and a feed bag."

Sarabell plodded along with her head down, showing no interest in his prattle.

"You deserve a treat for putting up with me for so long," Ebidiah praised her. They'd been together pretty near thirty years. Longer than many marriages. He only hoped she lived another ten, which was about as long as he could count on lasting. He'd heard of a mule, once, that lived forty-one years, so it was possible.

Although, now that he thought about it, Ebidiah wouldn't want Sarabell to outlast him. She'd be at the mercy of strangers. No one might take her in, and she'd be forced to fend for herself. At her age, she wouldn't last long.

Cradling his Sharps, Ebidiah took note of the landmarks. That was how a frontiersman got around so well in the wild—the landmarks. A hill with a split in the middle told him he wasn't more than a day from the Weaver place. He considered stopping. Mrs. Weaver was a snooty hen, but she made good coffee.

Dreaming of the money he would make from his new pelt, Ebidiah hiked for half the morning. He was winding along a dry wash when, out of the blue, a feeling came over him that he was being watched. Stopping short, Ebidiah turned. He saw no one behind him, saw no one on the hills that flanked the wash.

"Must be nerves," Ebidiah joked to Sarabell, and walked on.

The sun was warm on his face, the sky as blue as a high country lake. A few pillowy clouds drifted lazily along. It was a gorgeous day, the kind the Texas hill country was famous for.

Ebidiah took to humming his favorite song, "Rock of Ages." His ma used to drag him to church when he was a sprout, and the only thing about going that he liked, the only thing that stuck with him, was the music. He didn't remember much about the sermons except mention of the Ten Commandments, and specifically Thou Shalt Not Kill.

The recollection reminded Ebidiah of the Comanche he'd slain. And as if that were an omen, the same feeling came over him again, stronger than before, that unseen eyes were on him.

Ebidiah stopped. "Surely not," he said to Sarabell. He'd killed the Comanche weeks ago. And he'd come a far piece from the cattle camp, and that hill. No one could connect him to the grave, even if by some chance someone stumbled onto it. He was perfectly safe.

"Consarn me, anyhow." Ebidiah tried to make light of his worries, but he didn't succeed.

He'd only gone a short way when another troubling notion took hold. He'd been smart enough to bury the young warrior where no one would find him. But it hadn't occurred to him at the time to do something else just as important: erase the tracks.

The ground had been rock hard, but what with the scuffle and all, there were bound to have been prints. Maybe not a lot, but there didn't need to be. Comanches were superb trackers. They could read sign better than any white man.

"Wait," Ebidiah said out loud. "So what if they do find some?" He wore moccasins. The Comanches would think an Indian was to blame.

"I'm safe, I tell you," Ebidiah addressed his own doubts.

Then the nagging voice in his head reminded him that some trackers could tell if a white man or a red man left a set of prints by the gait and the positions of their feet. In fact, some trackers could tell one individual's tracks from another's as easily as, say, a sheepherder could tell one of his sheep from another. So it was possible the Comanches did know a white man was responsible.

Even worse, if they came across his trail later, they'd recognize his tracks and be out for his hide.

"Think of the odds, though," Ebidiah said, to dampen his concern. There weren't any Comanches within fifty miles. He must stop his fretting.

Early afternoon found him perched on a sawtooth rise studying his back trail. No one was after him. Or if they were, they stayed well hidden.

Ebidiah tried to will himself to relax, and couldn't. He thought of Mrs. Weaver, of her coffee and cakes. A visit with her would relax him.

All he had to do was get there.

Chapter 38

Wilda Weaver wished her husband had heard about cattle drives years ago. The peace and quiet were wonderful.

Wilda loved having the farm all to herself. She slept in later than she did when Jasper was there, would eat a leisurely breakfast, then go to the barn to milk the cows and to the coop to feed the chickens and collect their eggs.

Her mornings were spent sewing or knitting or cleaning. In the afternoons she'd take a stroll. After supper she'd sit in the rocking chair on the porch and enjoy the setting of the sun and the blossoming of the stars.

This was the life, Wilda happily told herself. No men around. No husband or son to feed and clean up after and nag about doing things they should do without her having to remind them.

On this particular evening, the sunset was spectacular. Wilda had always liked sunsets more than sunrises; they were more colorful. All those reds and yellows and other bright hues.

Slowly rocking, Wilda enjoyed the spectacle, grateful her husband wasn't home because she'd be inside cooking his supper.

As slowly as a turtle sinking in a pond, the sun sank from view and the gray of twilight spread. A single star sparkled, a harbinger of the multitude to come.

The serenity of it all made Wilda drowsy. Her eyelids grew heavy and she closed them and must have dozed off, because the next thing she knew, her eyes snapped open and that one star had become fifty. With a contented sigh, Wilda stretched. She was about to get out of the rocking chair and go inside when she noticed something strange.

Over by the barn was a . . . figure.

Wilda gave a mild start. It looked like a man. "Jasper?" she called, and rose. In doing so she glanced down, and when she looked up again, the figure was gone. "What on earth?" she said, wondering if her imagination was to blame. "Jasper?" she called again. "Reuben? Is that you?"

No one answered.

Wilda stepped to the rail and peered into the gathering darkness. A stillness had fallen, a quiet so complete, she could hear herself breathe. She saw no one. Shaking her head in bemusement, she went inside. Out of habit she bolted the door, then laughed and threw the bolt open. There was nothing to be afraid of.

Wilda decided a cup of tea was in order. She walked down the hall to the kitchen, rekindled the stove, and got the tea tin down from the cupboard. The tea came from England. It was her opinion that if anyone knew good tea, it was the British. They'd been drinking tea for ages. Her grandmother, who came over from England on a ship when in her teens, used to say that Brits had special times for "taking" tea, as they called it. There was low tea, which was taken in the early afternoon, and high tea, which was taken in the evening. Wilda always thought that was classy, having two times for tea.

Her pitcher only had half a cup of water left, so Wilda carried it out the back door and over to the pump. She worked the handle several times and a trickle appeared. A few more and she got a steady flow. When the pitcher was full, she stopped pumping. She turned to go back in, happened to glance across the way, and stiffened.

About thirty feet off in the darkness were two more figures, watching her.

Wilda blinked, but they didn't disappear. "Who's there?" she demanded. "Jasper? Reuben? Are you two playing games?"

Neither answered her.

Wilda started toward them. She only took a couple of steps, and stopped in consternation. They were gone. She looked for sign of them, but they had melted away as if they were ghosts. "Well, I never," she said.

A seed of fear took root. Her husband and son never played pranks on her. They knew she wouldn't like it. It must be someone else. But all the menfolk were away, and she couldn't see Philomena Burnett or Ariel Kurst coming all the way to her place and acting so silly.

Smothering a spike of fear Wilda hurried inside. She set the pitcher on the counter, stared at the back door while gnawing her bottom lip, then quickly bolted it and hastened to the front to bolt that door, as well.

"It can't be," Wilda said as she returned to the kitchen. She refused to countenance the notion that the figures might be the very ones she had dreaded encountering ever since they came to Texas. "Not now."

Wilda set to making the tea. After filling the teapot and setting it on the stove, she sat in a chair to wait for the water to come to a boil. Crossing her legs, she resisted an impulse to run to the barn, jump on her horse, and flee. She could be at the Burnett place before midnight.

"No," Wilda said out loud. That would be childish. Adults didn't let their fears get the better of them. Besides, no one had tried to harm her. It could be they were curious.

Impatient to have her tea, Wilda drummed her fingers. People liked to say that a watched pot never boils, and apparently they were right. She tore her gaze from the stove and looked over at the side window, and all the blood in her veins changed to ice.

A face was staring back at her. A swarthy face, with paint on the cheeks and the forehead, and eyes that glittered like black coals.

Wilda gasped and placed a hand to her throat.

The face vanished.

Overcoming her fright, Wilda ran to the window. The warrior was nowhere to be seen. "Just curious," she said aloud, and closed the curtains.

Her mouth had gone dry. She needed that tea more

than ever. Taking her seat, she licked her lips, but there was no spittle to wet them. "I refuse to be afraid," she said. But she was.

The water took forever to heat. Now and then she glanced at the window, but the face didn't reappear.

"Gone, I'd wager," she reassured herself.

Her teapot let out a hiss. She got a cup and saucer down from the cupboard, and a spoon from the drawer, and opened the tin. As she always did, Wilda raised it to her nose and inhaled. She loved the scent. Not bothering with the strainer, she put tea in the cup, added water, and stirred. The tiny *tink* of the spoon against the china was unusually loud.

Taking her seat, Wilda raised the cup in both hands, closed her eyes, and sipped. Warmth spread through her but not the relaxation she sought. She was so tense, her body might as well be made of nothing but bone.

"Cut this out," Wilda chided herself. She was a grown woman. She must behave as such. She kept her eyes closed and sipped. So long as she kept her eyes shut, she told herself, nothing would happen. They were passing by, was all. They were passing by and were merely curious, and in a while they would go their way and let the white woman be.

She sipped, and swallowed, and said bitterly, "Where are you when I need you, you worthless man?"

She shouldn't blame Jasper. She was the one who'd convinced him to go. Forced him, was more like it. He hadn't wanted to. She'd made him go for their own good. For the money they stood to make.

A soft scrape caused Wilda to break out in gooseflesh. She didn't open her eyes, though. Not until she'd swallowed the last drop of her tea and set the cup down. Girding herself, she looked up.

"Lord, no."

Somehow they had gotten in. Not two or even three but eight or nine, with more in the hallway. The nearest had his knife out.

Forcing a smile, Wilda motioned at the stove. "Would you gentlemen care for some tea? I have plenty."

They might have been carved from granite. Their faces resembled so much stone.

"What did I do?" Wilda said.

They neither spoke nor moved.

"Why do this to me? I've never hurt any of you."

Wilda remembered hearing about a Comanche village to the north that was wiped out not long ago. Most of the warriors were away, after buffalo, so it was mostly women and children. They were cut down; some were mutilated, and some were scalped. She remembered saying that it served them right for all the whites their kind had killed. Maybe that was the reason they were here.

Now three of them had drawn their knives, and a fourth had produced a tomahawk.

"Please," Wilda said. "Don't."

More entered the kitchen.

Behind her, the back door crashed open.

Quaking uncontrollably, Wilda closed her eyes. So long as she kept them closed, she would be all right.

She would be all right.

She would be . . .

Chapter 39

Ebidiah Troutman came within sight of the Weaver farm when the sun was at its zenith. He hoped Mrs. Weaver was in a good mood. She could be shrewish, that woman. She treated her husband and her son as if they both were ten years old. With his own ears, he'd heard her boss them around as if they were privates in the army and she was their general.

She usually treated Ebidiah nice, though. Probably because she liked the furs he brought.

Ebidiah was almost to the Weavers' pasture when he noticed something strange. The barn door was wide open. He'd once seen Mrs. Weaver take Reuben to task for not closing it. She'd been worried their cows might wander out. Odd that she'd leave it open herself when they weren't around.

Then Ebidiah noticed that the door to the chicken coop was wide open, too. That in itself wasn't unusual since coop doors were usually left open during the day so the chickens could wander about. Most farmers only closed their coops at night to keep the foxes and coyotes out. But now there were feathers all over the place, strewn around the door as if there had been some sort of chicken massacre.

Ebidiah slowed and said to Sarabell, "This ain't right."

A few more yards and Ebidiah stopped in his tracks.

The front door to the farmhouse was the same as the others.

Ebidiah felt the skin on the back of his neck prickle.

Wilda Weaver would never leave the door to her house open, not when bugs and who knew what else could get in. She was a stickler for keeping her house clean.

Going over to a tree near the house, Ebidiah tied off Sarabell's rope, and patted her.

"Stay put, girl."

Hefting his Sharps, Ebidiah went up the steps. The rocking chair was gone. That puzzled him until he saw it lying on its side in the grass. Someone had apparently tossed it over the rail.

"What in the world?"

Leveling his Sharps, Ebidiah cocked it. He hadn't thought to check the ground for tracks, but now he did. At the base of the steps, where the grass had been worn away leaving only bare earth, were moccasin prints, some coming and some going.

Ebidiah's breath caught in his throat. An icy dread came over him, and he almost backed away. But no, he owed it to Mrs. Weaver to find out.

The farmhouse was as silent as a cemetery, and there wasn't any movement at the windows.

Every nerve taut, Ebidiah crept to the doorway. He could see the length of the hall, clear back to the kitchen. Just inside, pieces of a broken vase were strewn about. Further in lay a quilt, ripped to ribbons. The kitchen floor appeared to be a shambles.

Ebidiah entered. He stayed close to the wall to avoid the pieces of vase, which might crunch underfoot and give him away.

The parlor was a mess. Mrs. Weaver's china cabinet had been pushed over and her prized china busted. Her settee had been overturned, her drapes slashed.

Ebidiah edged to the kitchen. Broken dishes were everywhere, chairs upended, the table on its side. But it was the other thing that horrified him; pools and smears of dried blood. More was splattered on the walls. There were even scarlet drops on the ceiling.

A foot poked from behind the table.

Taking a breath, he poked his head around. Bile rose in his gorge, and he felt light-headed. He could take the sight of a butchered animal without flinching. But this had been a human being. A woman, no less.

The things they'd done to her were hideous.

"Comanches," Ebidiah gasped the obvious. Sagging against the table, he bowed his head. He would like to think it had been a quick death, but he knew better. She had taken a long time to die.

The smell of the blood made him want to gag. Holding his breath, he collected himself and hurried out.

All the tales he'd heard came back to him. Stories of Comanche atrocities. Not that the Comanches had a monopoly on butchery. Other tribes, and plenty of whites, were capable of the same vile deeds.

Even so, the manner of Wilda Weaver's death seemed excessive. As was the destruction of her chickens, and possibly the cows. It was almost as if the Comanches were leaving a message for the whites. Or as if—and Ebidiah froze in midstride—this attack was more personal than most.

More vengeful.

"Lord, no," Ebidiah breathed. That young warrior had been trying to kill him. . . . What else was he to do?

Ebidiah got out of there. The fresh air and sunlight were a tonic. He breathed deeply, then set to searching for sign. A good distance behind the farmhouse he found what he was looking for: the tracks of unshod horses.

The tracks of a large war party.

Ebidiah had a decision to make. Town was to the southeast. Comanche Creek and the cattle camp, to the northwest. The smart thing was to head southeast. Report the attack to the marshal. The lawman would get word to the army, and soldiers would come.

Ebidiah went over to the oak. He untied Sarabell, gave the house a last look, and started back the way he had come. Owen Burnett and Jasper Weaver needed to be warned. Thanks to him, they were about to be massacred.

Ebidiah stopped again. "What am I thinking?" He must warn Philomena Burnett and her girls, and the Kurst woman, before he warned their menfolk. Their homesteads were closer.

And the Comanches were heading their way.

Chapter 40

Philomena Burnett was peeling potatoes for supper when her youngest came in and informed her that Blue was acting up. "How so?" Philomena asked without taking her eyes from a potato. A flick of her wrist, and the knife sent another peel to the floor.

"He's growling off at the woods," Estelle said.

"Growling?" Philomena stopped peeling. Blue would bark at strangers and he'd howl on occasion, usually if he heard coyotes yipping, but he rarely growled.

"He'd have run off except Mandy got hold of him and put him on his rope," Estelle said. "He's still growling."

"Peculiar," Philomena said. Setting the potato and the knife on the table, she rose, smoothed her apron, and went out the back and around to where Blue was tied.

A big mongrel they had acquired when he was a pup from a man giving a litter away, Blue was so named because he had one brown eye and one blue eye.

At the moment, the hackles of his short, bristly hair were raised, and he was half-crouched, staring at a tract of woodland about a hundred yards away, and growling.

Mandy was next to him, her arms crossed, quizzically studying the same patch of woods.

"What has his dander up?" Philomena asked.

"The devil if I know," Mandy said. "He's been this way for about ten minutes now. I was weeding the garden when he started in. I've shushed him, but it does no good."

Philomena moved past Blue and scanned the woods. Everything appeared normal.

"What do you think, Ma?" Mandy said. "A bear, maybe? Or a mountain lion?"

"It could be anything," Philomena said. "The wind must be blowing just right, and Blue has picked up the scent." She tested her notion by licking the tip of her index finger and holding it up. Sure enough, the breeze was blowing from the woods toward them.

"I don't like it," Estelle said.

"Relax, little sister," Mandy teased. "No bear or mountain lion will attack us in broad daylight."

"A bear might," Philomena said, although bear attacks were rare these days. In early times there had been a few.

"What if it's not an animal?" Estelle said. "What if it's Indians?"

"Unlikely," Philomena said. "The last report of hostiles hereabouts was years ago."

"One of us should go have a look-see," Mandy suggested.

Philomena shook her head. "Not on your life. Neither of you is to go anywhere. Stay close to the house, you hear me?"

"I won't go anywhere, Ma," Estelle said.

"Amanda?"

"What?"

"Don't act dumb. You're not to go look. Whatever is out there, we leave it be and it will leave us be. Understood?"

"Yes, Ma," Mandy said with little enthusiasm.

"I mean it," Philomena impressed on her. "I know that independent streak of yours. You might take it into your head to go anyway."

"I won't go if you don't want us to."

"Promise me," Philomena said.

"Oh, Ma."

"Promise."

Mandy frowned. "All right. I promise. Happy now?"

"You promise what?"

"Must you make such an issue of this?" Mandy said indignantly.

"Let me hear the words," Philomena insisted. Ever since Amanda was little, she'd always kept her promises. Which was why she was sometimes reluctant to make them.

Exhaling and fluttering her lips, Mandy said, "I promise not to go off to those woods. Happy now?"

"Don't take that tone with me, young lady," Philomena said. "And yes, I'm happy."

"But what if it is Indians?" Estelle brought up again. "Wouldn't you want to know?"

"What can I do if it is?" Philomena said. "They're not going to run from a woman." She shook her head. "No, we're better off here. Be ready to rush inside if you have to. In fact"—she came to an abrupt decision—"both of you come in right now." They would stay there until she was sure it was safe.

"Oh, Ma," Mandy said. "All Blue is doing is growling."

"I wont brook any sass," Philomena said. "In you go." She motioned and waited for them to precede her. Estelle did so without complaining, but Mandy grumbled under her breath.

Philomena didn't care that Mandy was upset. Their lives came first. Beasts and Indians weren't the only things they had to worry about. A lot of hard cases prowled the Texas frontier, outlaws and whatnot who might regard a mother and her two girls as plum pudding. Once they were inside, she threw the bolt.

"Estelle, go bolt the back door. Then you and your sister go from room to room and make sure all the windows are latched."

"Pa always says you're too cautious by half," Mandy said.

"One of us has to be." Philomena smiled and patted Mandy's arm and returned to the potatoes. She got so involved with preparing their meal that she forgot about Blue and the woods until Estelle hurried in.

"Ma! You have to come see."

"What is it?"

"Come. Quick."

Estelle led her up to the girls' bedroom. Mandy was at the window when Philomena walked in, and beckoned.

"I take back what I said, Ma. You were right."

A knot in the pit of her stomach, Philomena went over. The window overlooked the barn and the corral, and the woods beyond. At first all seemed to be normal.

"I don't see . . ." Philomena began, and stopped. Well back in the trees, in the shadows where they couldn't be seen from the yard, were horses. She couldn't count how many, but there had to be a dozen, at least. All she could tell was that they didn't have saddles.

"Ma?" Mandy said.

A cold finger rippled down Philomena's spine, and she almost trembled. Struggling to keep her voice calm, she said, "I see them."

"Are they what I think they are? Injun horses?"

"They appear to be," Philomena said.

"Are they friendly, do you think?" Estelle asked.

"Use your head," Mandy said. "If they were, would they be hiding?"

"If they mean us harm, what are they waiting for?" Estelle said.

Philomena knew the answer to that. The Indians were waiting for night to fall. Under the cover of darkness, they could slip in close.

"Do you reckon they know that Pa and Luke and Sam aren't here?" Estelle asked.

"I don't see how they would," Philomena said. Not that it mattered. "Mandy, I want you to fetch that old revolver out of the top drawer in our bedroom. And Estelle, you go find Sam's squirrel rifle."

"What do you aim to do, Ma?" Mandy said.

"Fight for our lives," Philomena said.

Chapter 41

The branding was going well. There had been no sign of any Comanches, and as Reuben Weaver put it, "Looks like we were worried over nothing."

Hostiles or not, they needed to eat, and they were almost out of meat. Gareth proposed to Owen that he would take his two oldest and go off into the hills after deer or whatever else they could bring down.

"We should be back by dark. There's plenty of game hereabouts."

"Be careful," Owen said. "If Comanches are around, you'll need eyes in the backs of your heads. We don't want anything to happen to you."

Gareth led Harland and Thaxter off to the west. Once the forest closed around them, Harland let out a hard laugh.

"Did you hear that jackass, Pa? He doesn't want anything to happen to us."

"I'd call that right neighborly," Thaxter said, and grinned.

"It was," Gareth said. He had taken his rifle from the scabbard and was holding it across his saddle. When they spooked a deer, they'd have to shoot quick to drop it.

"Listen to you," Harland said. "As if you give a damn about Owen Burnett."

"As if any of us do," Thaxter said.

The trees teemed with bird life. A squirrel scampered

from limb to limb. Bees buzzed, and a butterfly flitted in search of flowers.

"Thanks for reminding me," Gareth said, and wheeled his horse side-on to his sons.

"About what?" Harland said.

"The talk I've been meaning to have with the two of you," Gareth said. "I should have Wylie here so he knows, too."

"When are you fixing to tell Lorette, Silsby, and Iden?" Thaxter wanted to know.

"Your sister is too fond of Sam Burnett. I'm not sure I can trust her to keep it secret. As for your brothers, they're too young yet. They might not understand it's for their own good."

"They're not *that* dumb," Harland said.

"They're not as hard as they need to be, either," Gareth said. "I doubt either of them would shoot Owen Burnett in the back if I asked them to."

"I would," Thaxter said.

"You'd shoot anybody," Gareth said. "Harland, there, too. Which is why I can trust the both of you."

"Speaking of which, you should turn us loose on them," Harland said. "We don't need the Burnetts or the Weavers any longer."

Gareth gazed back toward their camp and glimpsed their campfire through the trees. "That's your problem, son. You're too impatient."

"We're more likely to be caught if we wait until after Abilene," Harland said. "By then too many folks will have seen them. The buyers, too."

Thaxter nodded. "We should do it soon. We don't need their help on the drive. Longhorns aren't as fearsome as we were told they'd be."

"Just the seven of us to herd twenty-five hundred cattle?" Gareth said. "The cowboy I talked to told me there should be at least ten tending a herd that size. No, we need Owen and Jasper a while yet."

"I don't agree," Harland said.

"It's my opinion that counts," Gareth reminded him.

"Don't you worry they'll catch on somewhere along the way?" Thaxter asked. "It's a far piece from Texas to Kansas."

"Why should they?" Gareth said. We've worked as hard as them, and treated them more decent than we've ever treated anybody. Owen Burnett trusts me. I can see it in his eyes, and in how he acts. He has no cause at all to be suspicious."

Harland chortled. "Won't he be surprised when you splatter his brains?"

"He'll reckon I've gone loco," Gareth said. "A man like him, an honorable man, sees honor in others even when there is none. It would never occur to Owen that I'd betray his trust and turn on him, because it's something he would never do."

"I never have understood folks like him," Harland said.

"All of them sheep, waiting to be sheared." Gareth rested the stock of his rifle on his thigh. "I almost feel sorry for them."

"I still think we should kill them now, Pa," Harland said. "We could use the Comanches as scapegoats. We'll say the war party killed the Burnetts and the Weavers, and everyone will believe us."

"When I said no I meant no," Gareth said. "Not until we have the money. We'll claim outlaws jumped us and tried to take it. Folks will believe that as much as Comanches. Once we make it back, we should put tombstones in the graveyard in town in honor of our dear, departed friends."

"Waste money on tombstones?" Thaxter said. "You're joshing, Pa, aren't you?"

"I sure as hell am."

They laughed and rode on.

Gareth found it hard to concentrate on the hunt. He couldn't stop thinking about the money. Twenty-five hundred head at forty dollars each came to one hundred thousand dollars. More than he'd ever dreamed he'd have. *One hundred thousand.* Gareth rolled the sum in his mind and then on his tongue under his breath. They'd be rich. Or, rather, he would.

Once he had the money, the question became how much to give to his sons. He got the impression Harland and Thaxter were expecting a lot. Five to ten thousand apiece, maybe. Fat chance. He was their pa. The lion's share went to him. And by lion's share, he was thinking ninety eight thousand was the right amount. The other two thousand he'd pass out to his sons and Lorette.

As for Ariel, she didn't deserve a cent. She hadn't done anything to earn it. He might give her shopping money now and then, but she, like the money, was his to do with as he pleased.

The only hitch might be the Comanches. But as time went by and the hostiles didn't show, Gareth became convinced they weren't going to. Soon the drive could commence, and in a couple of months or so, he could claim his fortune.

Gareth went to laugh and caught himself. His boys might wonder. They didn't realize that everything they did was for his good, not theirs. They'd get mad if they knew the truth. But that was part of being a parent.

You had to be tough with your kids whether they liked it or not.

Chapter 42

Sam Burnett wasn't fond of branding. It was dangerous work. Longhorns were unpredictable, and now and then one would break free and turn on them. He also didn't like the burning smell when the hot brand was pressed to the hides. It made him want to sneeze.

Sam had been at it with some of the others for over an hour, branding the last of the unmarked cattle. He was grateful when his pa came over and told him he could take a break. He was tired and sweaty, and his throat was parched. Instead of treating himself to water from his canteen, he went to the creek, dropped to his knees, cupped both hands, and wet his face and his neck. Then he cupped more, and drank.

"Look at you, kneeling there," said a familiar voice behind him.

"You've never seen anyone kneel before?" Sam said.

Lorette came around, and hunkered. "Not anyone as handsome as you."

"Keep it up," Sam said.

Lorette laughed. "Admit it. You like that I pay so much attention to you."

No, Sam definitely did not. "We have been through this before. Have your fun, if you must."

"When will you get it into that head of yours that I'm serious?"

"There are times when I think you are and times when I think you're not," Sam admitted. "I can't wait until after the drive so I don't have to put up with your shenanigans anymore."

"What a mean thing to say," Lorette said, scrunching her face into an exaggerated pout.

Just then a cow came to the creek to drink. The longhorn ignored them and lowered her muzzle.

To Sam, it was a wonderment. All the tales he'd heard of how fierce longhorns were, and a lot of them were as gentle as kittens. A cow protecting a calf could be a problem, and the bigger bulls made trouble now and then, but overall, once they were caught and branded and thrown in with the rest, the longhorns gave them little trouble.

"A gold eagle for your thoughts," Lorette said.

"Isn't it supposed to be a penny?"

"You're worth more."

Sam gazed skyward. "Lord, save us from her kind."

"Which kind is that?"

"Females."

Sam loved to hear her laugh. It was like music, so light and airy, it was pleasant to the ears. But he couldn't let her know. "Don't you have someone else to annoy?"

"Is that what I'm doing? Annoying you?"

"What else?" Rising, Sam wiped his hands on his shirt and started toward their campfire. She fell into step, sashaying along, her hands clasped behind her back, that infernal smile on her face. "You're enough to drive a man to drink."

"I haven't seen you ask Jasper for a swill from his flask."

"You know what I mean."

"I doubt even you do," Lorette said. "Fortunately for you, I'm patient. You'll stop fighting it eventually."

"Fighting what?"

"Yourself."

Sam snickered. "Has anyone ever told you that you hardly ever make a lick of sense?"

"Has anyone ever told you that you have the prettiest eyes?"

"Men aren't pretty. Women are."

"The handsomest eyes, then." Lorette bit her bottom lip, then cocked her head at him. "Do you think I'm pretty, Sam?"

"I'd rather talk about something else," Sam said. Anything else, actually.

"No. Do you? I'm told I am. My brothers tease me that I'm ugly, but Ma says I'm pretty as can be. And the boys in town seem to think the same. Not that they matter. Only you do."

Sam halted and turned. "Will you stop?"

"Stop what?" Lorette said innocently.

"Stop pretending you care for me. Stop pretending I'm special. You could have any boy in town you wanted. Or any boy in the territory, for that matter. Playacting with me only makes me mad."

Lorette brightened. "Why, Sam. That's the sweetest thing you've ever said to me."

"What was sweet about it?"

"That I could have any boy in the whole territory," Lorette said. "And the boy I want is you."

"I could just scream," Sam said. "If I was older, I'd take you over my knee and spank you."

"You still can," Lorette said, and giggled.

So annoyed he could spit tacks, Sam wheeled and went to the fire. If he thought he'd be shed of her, he was mistaken.

Lorette poured herself coffee and followed him to a grassy spot and sat. "This is nice," she said. "Just you and me."

"It's supposed to be just me."

"You don't mean that," Lorette said. "Secretly you like that I'm interested in you. Secretly you like that you and me are going to be man and wife."

"Where do you get these notions of yours?" Sam went to swallow, and jerked his cup down. "Wait. What?"

"You should ask me. Right here and now. I'll say yes. I promise I will."

Flushing with embarrassment, Sam said, "You're taking this too far. You'd no more marry me than you would a Comanche."

"I'm beginning to wonder if you should have the saw-bones check your hearing," Lorette teased.

"I've no hankering to marry you or anyone else. Hell-fire, I haven't even kissed a girl yet. Not that way, any-how."

"Which way would that be, Sam?"

"You know damn well."

Lorette grinned. "I like it when you talk manly. That's the first time I've heard you cuss."

"I give up," Sam said in exasperation, and put on a show of ignoring her while he drank his coffee. He hoped she'd get up and leave, but no. When he was done, he set the cup in his lap and noticed she was looking at him. "What now?"

"I like how you drink."

"Oh, for crying out loud. I drink the same as every-body."

"That's not true. People don't drink the same. My brother Harland swallows in big gulps. Thax always takes little sips. Your pa always holds his cup in both hands. And you, you curl your lip over the edge. I never saw anybody do that. It's adorable."

"First I'm pretty and now I'm adorable," Sam said. "Shoot me and put me out of my misery."

Lorette laughed. "I'd never harm a hair on your head."

"What will it take to get you to leave me alone?" Sam asked.

"Being dead," Lorette said.

"Well, I have news for you," Sam said. "I'm going to go on living to spite you."

"I didn't mean you being dead, Sam. I meant me."

"Honestly, girl," Sam said.

A dreamy look came over her. "I'm always honest with you, Sam. And I always will be. Would you like me to tell you what I like best about you? Honest and true?"

"No, I wouldn't, but you'll tell me anyway, so go ahead."

"What I like best," Lorette said, "is that you're noth-ing like my pa or my brothers."

"No two people are ever the same."

Lorette shook her head. "It goes deeper than that. You're nice, Sam. Nice down to your bones. Or to put it another way, you have a nice heart."

"Silly as silly can be," Sam said. "Is that important?"

"To me," Lorette said, that dreamy expression coming over her again, "it's the most important thing in the world."

Chapter 43

Philomena stared with trepidation out the parlor window at the setting sun. "We have to go out and close the shutters," she announced. She had been putting it off, but it had to be done before dark set in.

"All three of us?" Mandy said.

Philomena nodded. "So we can cover each other. You'll hold my shotgun. Estelle, you keep that squirrel rifle ready."

"I've never shot anyone, Ma," her youngest said.

"Who of us has?" Philomena replied. Not that she doubted she could. When it came to protecting her family, she'd do whatever she had to. Moving to the door, she quietly threw the latch, then cracked the door and peered out. The porch was clear, the yard empty save for Blue, who was sitting and staring off at the woods. He'd stopped growling, but his ears were pricked. "There's no sign of them."

"We're right behind you," Mandy said.

Philomena stepped out. If the Comanches were watching, they'd see her. But it couldn't be helped.

The shutters had been Owen's idea. An old-timer had told him it was a wise precaution to ward off arrows and the like. A lot of houses and cabins also had loopholes in the walls, to fire through. Owen had wanted loopholes in theirs, but she had balked. A house shouldn't have holes in it, she'd told him. Looking back, she saw that Owen had been right and she had been wrong. Loopholes would come in handy right now.

As for the shutters, they'd made a mistake putting theirs on. Back east, shutters were always on the outside. Here in the Texas hill country, the shutters were on the inside, so they could be opened and closed without exposing the occupants to danger. Owen had offered to take the shutters off and put them inside, but once again she had balked. "It can't make that much of a difference," was how she'd put it. Now she realized it did.

Philomena worked quickly. The sun was half-gone. It wouldn't be long before the Comanches made their intentions known.

"We should take Blue in with us," Estelle suggested.

"We leave him out here so he can bark and warn us," Philomena said as she swung a shutter shut.

"And be skewered with arrows?" Mandy said. "Please, Ma. I've heard the Comanches even eat them."

"That's not true, daughter," Philomena said. "I know for a fact Comanches don't eat dog or fish. A scout we met told us that. The Sioux do, though. The Cheyenne, too."

"So can we bring Blue in?" Estelle said. "I'll be sad as anything if you let him be killed."

Philomena gave in. "As soon as we're done with the shutters, we'll get him." Now that she gave it more thought, they'd be better off with the dog inside. Should the Indians try to break in, Blue would fight them tooth and claw.

The deepening darkness spurred her to go faster. So did the unnatural silence. Usually birds were warbling their last songs of the day and the chickens would be clucking in the coop, but everything had gone quiet.

"Hurry, Ma," Mandy urged.

"Did you see something?"

"No. Just hurry. Please."

"Calm yourself. We're perfectly fine," Philomena lied. They were in dire straits, but she refused to show it. She must inspire her girls to be brave. They would need all the courage they could muster.

None too soon, they'd made a circuit of the house, and Philomena had shut the last shutter. She took her shotgun and they hastened out to Blue and untied him. Thankfully, Mandy held on to his collar, because no sooner was the rope untied than he strained to run off toward the woods. He whined when Mandy wouldn't let him, and twisted in her grip.

"He wants to go after them," Estelle said.

"They'd kill him dead," Mandy said. Using both hands, she had to practically drag Blue toward the house.

Philomena went last, the shotgun to her shoulder. She'd only fired it a few times, and reminded herself that she needed to brace herself. It had quite a kick.

"I thought I saw something," Estelle suddenly whispered.

"Where?"

"Over by the barn."

Dreading that an arrow would flash out of nowhere or a war whoop would rend the air, Philomena shooed them along. Her nerves jangled fiercely until she had closed and bolted the front door. "There. We're safe for the time being."

"Should I tie Blue or give him the run of the house?" Mandy asked.

"The run," Philomena said. He would hear the Comanches before they did, and give them warning of where the Indians were about to break in.

Blue moved off down the hall, his claws clacking on the hardwood floor.

"I'll set out a bowl with water for him," Estelle said.

"You do that." Philomena was racking her brain for a means of thwarting their besiegers. A lit lantern or lamp in every room would help. So would putting kitchen knives near each of the ground-floor windows. She contemplated heating water on the stove to throw in their faces, but lugging the heavy pot would slow her.

"Do you think we'll live out the night?" Mandy unexpectedly asked.

"What a thing to say," Philomena chided. "Of course we will."

"You don't need to sugarcoat it, Ma," Mandy said. "I'm not a little girl anymore."

Memories washed over Philomena, of her daughters when they were younger, of Amanda with curls in her hair, laughing gaily, of Estelle playing with a raggedy doll, of them playing hide and seek, and tag. Precious memories, they tugged at her heartstrings and brought a lump to her throat. "None of us are dying tonight. I won't let that happen."

"Sure, Ma," Mandy said.

Philomena put a hand on her eldest's shoulder. "Don't ever give up. You hear me?"

"I've always admired that about you," Mandy said. "Pa says that when you start something, you always see it through, come hell or high water."

"Your father said that? And don't swear."

"Sorry. But he's right. I've always looked up to how you never let anything keep you down. Pa says you're a scrapper, and you are. If I've learned anything from you, it's that a person should never let life trample them down."

Welling with affection, Philomena gave Mandy a hug. "I keep forgetting you're almost full-grown."

"Almost?" Mandy said, and grinned.

Their tender moment was brought to an end by the patter of feet as Estelle rushed up, her eyes wide.

"Ma! Come quick!"

"What is it?"

"Blue is growling again. I think someone is prowling around the back of the house."

It's starting, Philomena thought, and hurried to the kitchen.

Blue was by the back door, his nose to the jamb, sniffing and rumbling in his barrel chest.

"See?" Estelle whispered.

Philomena went over. She put her ear to the door but didn't hear anything. Moving to the window, she put her ear to it. Again, nothing.

"I wish Pa and Luke and Sam were here," Estelle said.

"They're not. It's just us, but we're not helpless," Philomena said more harshly than she intended.

"I didn't mean . . ." Estelle said, but she didn't finish.

"Ma!" Mandy whispered. "Look!" And she pointed.

The latch was moving. Slowly, quietly, as someone outside tried to open the door.

Blue let out a *whuff* and a loud growl. He pawed at the bottom of the door, his claws digging into the wood.

Philomena was about to tell him to stop; she didn't want her door scratched. The absurdity of it made her grin.

The latch became still. Then the door itself moved slightly as pressure was applied to the outside.

"They're pushing on it!" Mandy whispered.

"If they get in, shoot at their heads," Philomena instructed. A head shot to man or beast, her grandfather always told her, was the surest way to put something down. "We'll retreat down the hall, and if we have to, barricade ourselves in an upstairs bedroom."

"Listen," Estelle whispered.

Now there was a scratching sound, as if a fingernail were being run over the outside of the door.

"What are they up to?" Mandy whispered.

"If they want in, they'll have to batter it down," Philomena said grimly.

The next moment, the door shook violently.

Chapter 44

Ebidiah Troutman hadn't gone far into the woods after he left the Weaver place when he spotted something in the trees ahead. Halting, he raised his Sharps but held his fire. When he saw it was a horse he dropped into a crouch, thinking the Comanches must be nearby. As the minutes passed and the horse didn't move and no warriors appeared, Ebidiah made bold to move forward with Sarabell's rope in his left hand. He wasn't about to leave her untended and have her stolen.

The horse was a sorrel that looked to be on in years and stood with its head hung low. On its flank was a scarlet slash. Around its neck was a rope, the loose end tangled in some brush, which explained why it wasn't moving.

Ebidiah stopped and squatted. He reasoned that the horse must belong to the Weavers, that maybe it was Wilda's animal, and that the Comanches had let it run loose. They probably didn't take it because it was so old.

Whatever the case, Ebidiah could use it. Wary of a trick, he edged closer. The sorrel heard him and looked over. It didn't whinny or try to run off.

Ebidiah felt safe in straightening. He patted the sorrel, which nuzzled him, and spent a minute untangling the rope. Using his bowie, he cut a length suitable for a halter, and swung up.

The lack of a saddle didn't bother him. He was used to riding bareback. Leading Sarabell by her rope, he rode in a beeline for the Kurst place. He wanted to go to the Burnett farm first but he knew that Ariel Kurst was alone. Her husband and all her brood were at Comanche Creek.

Ebidiah had only ever seen the woman twice. The first time was when he paid the Kursts' cabin a visit to see if they were interested in buying any of his hides. That they'd practically laughed in his face, saying they were perfectly capable of skinning and curing their own, and telling him to peddle his wares somewhere else, had rankled.

The second time Ebidiah saw Ariel Kurst was in town. She was there with her husband. Or, rather, behind him, for Ebidiah had noticed that everywhere they went, Ariel stayed a step or two behind Gareth. She never walked at his side. When Gareth stopped, she'd stopped. When Gareth talked to people, she'd barely said a word.

Ebidiah never had cottoned to men who treated their womenfolk as if the women were their personal property. That whole lords-and-masters business seemed to him to be nothing more than a man keeping his boot heel on a woman's neck. That some females stood for it never ceased to amaze him. But then, sometimes folks didn't have much choice.

Yet another reason Ebidiah avoided civilization as if it were a plague. In a sense, it was. A plague of people imposing their will on others and making people do things they didn't want to do. That wasn't for him. Give him freedom any day. True freedom, which in his mind was the right to make his own decisions and do as he pleased without anyone telling him different.

Ebidiah gave his head a shake. With a war party on the loose, he couldn't afford to be distracted. He stayed vigilant for sign of the Comanches, but Providence was kind to him and in due course he came to the top of a hill overlooking the clearing where the Kurst cabin lay.

Right away, Ebidiah could tell he was too late. The cabin door hung from one hinge, and articles from within were scattered about the clearing. The corral was open, the horses all gone. A pair of hogs lay in pools of blood in their pen.

Against his better judgment, Ebidiah went down. He knew what he would find but he had to be sure. At the edge of the clearing he dismounted and tied the sorrel and Sarabell.

A lot of the scattered items had been broken. A chair was busted to pieces. Blankets had been cut up. That surprised Ebidiah a little. Indian gals were fond of blankets. Apparently this war party had no interest in plunder. They were out to count coup on their enemies.

Flies buzzed about the doorway. The smell of blood was strong.

Ebidiah found out why when he dared to step inside.

Ariel Kurst had gone to her reward in about as grisly a fashion as a person could.

Ebidiah felt his gorge rise, and backed out. Gulping in air, he leaned his brow against the cabin and closed his eyes. That was a sight he'd take with him to his grave.

Two homesteads attacked, two women slain. The war party was making a sweep of the outmost settlers. Which meant the next on their list would be the family he liked best.

Ebidiah hurried to Sarabell and the horse. He doubted he would be in time, but he had to try.

As he rode, Ebidiah wondered, yet again, if he was responsible for the spreading slaughter. He'd killed that warrior, after all. It could be what brought the war party. It could be the Comanches were out for revenge.

Ebidiah hoped not. He'd thought he was doing the settlers a favor when he confronted the warrior spying on them. How was he to predict this would be the result? He'd hidden the body the best he could.

The ride to the Burnett place was the longest ride of his life. Every minute was an hour. He prayed he would be in time to warn Mrs. Burnett and escort her and her daughters into town. They'd be safe there.

It occurred to him that Mrs. Burnett might insist on going to the cattle camp to be with her husband. He'd try to talk her out of it, although she had struck him as the kind who didn't take no for an answer.

The issue became moot once Ebidiah reached the

hills that fringed the Burnett farm. Everything was un-naturally still.

Fortunately, Ebidiah saw the Indians before they saw him. They were in a stand of trees not far from the farm-house. Some were sitting, some milling about. They appeared in no rush to attack. Then it hit him. They were waiting for dark.

Beyond the woods, past a corral, were the two Burnett girls, Amanda and Estelle, going about their daily chores.

Ebidiah withdrew until he was out of sight. He had to warn the women. He secured both animals, whispered in Sarabell's ear that he would be back, and began to circle wide of the Comanches. He didn't have a lot of time. The sun was low to the west. Within the hour it would set, and the warriors would close in.

A part of Ebidiah wanted to get out of there. Part of him felt he should climb on the sorrel and ride hell-bent for leather. He didn't owe the Burnetts anything. Certainly not his life.

Another part of him said that wasn't so. That women were in peril, and no man worthy of the name would run out on them when they needed his help. It wasn't because of pride that he kept going. Nor was it out of any sense of honor. It was simply the right thing to do.

Ebidiah almost chuckled at the irony. He'd spent most of his life avoiding human contact. Now he was risking everything to save a few he did have contact with, on occasion.

It was his intention to reach the farmhouse before the sun went down, but he was still a hundred yards from it when he glimpsed furtive figures coming out of the woods.

Flattening, Ebidiah anxiously licked his lips, and crawled. He wasn't about to stop. He had to do it.

Come what may.

Chapter 45

Philomena Burnett pointed her shotgun at the kitchen door, prepared to fire the instant the Comanches broke it in. She must prevent the warriors from overwhelming them and buy time for her and the girls to make it down the hall to the stairs.

"Ma?" Mandy whispered. "Don't you hear that?"

Philomena had been so intent on shooting that she hadn't realized someone else was whispering—outside the door.

"Mrs. Burnett? Let me in."

Startled, Philomena blurted loudly, "Who in the world?"

"It's Ebidiah Troutman, ma'am. I've come to help. Please be quick, or I'm a goner."

"Hold on to Blue," Philomena said to Estelle. Swiftly working the bolt, she jerked on the handle and the old trapper spilled inside, nearly tripping over his own feet. Righting himself, he shoved the door shut and threw the bolt himself.

"Thank goodness. They knew I was there and were closing in."

"Mr. Troutman?" Estelle said, struggling to retain her grip on Blue's collar. The dog recognized the trapper from his previous visits, and whined for her to let go. "What on earth are you doing here?"

"Is that any way to greet someone out to save your hides, girl?" Ebidiah said, cradling his Sharps. "I about scraped my elbows and knees raw crawling to your house."

Philomena was glad to see the old man. But given his years, and the fact he was armed with a single-shot buffalo gun, she didn't see how he'd be of much use.

Nonetheless, she said, "I thank you, Mr. Troutman. We had no idea you were in the vicinity."

"Save your thanks for if we make it out alive," Ebidiah said. "The Injuns have your place surrounded. They mean to exterminate you."

Motioning with her eyes toward her daughters, Philomena said, "Mr. Troutman, if you please." He would upset her girls with talk like that.

"Well, they do," Ebidiah said. "They aim to do you in, the same as they've done to Mrs. Weaver and Mrs. Kurst."

"What's that, you say?" Philomena asked, aghast.

"Wilda Weaver and Ariel Kurst. The Comanches paid them a visit before coming here."

"Both of them are gone?" Mandy said, incredulous. "We were at their places not long ago."

"If our menfolk were here this wouldn't be happening," Philomena declared. It proved she had been right about the cattle drive. Owen should never have gotten involved.

"Don't kid yourself, ma'am," Ebidiah said, brushing at grass and dirt on the front of his buckskins. "Those red devils would attack, regardless."

"You don't know that for a fact."

A strange look came over him. "Yes, ma'am, I do."

"What do we do, Mr. Troutman?" Mandy asked. "How can we make it out of this alive?"

"Do you have a root cellar?" Ebidiah asked, scanning the floor. "We can fort up in there and shoot them as they come down the steps."

"No," Philomena disagreed. "We'd be trapped. There's only the one way in or out. They could swarm us so even four guns aren't enough. Or set fire to the house and do us in that way."

"How about an attic, then?" Ebidiah asked. "With a rope we can pull up so they can't get at us?"

"Again, we'd be trapped," Philomena said. "And they could burn us out as easy as anything."

"Then we fight them tooth and nail," Mandy said, "and take as many of them with us as we can."

"You're awful young to be so fierce," Ebidiah remarked.

"Are you here to help or criticize?" Philomena said.

Estelle suddenly pointed at the window. "Look!" she cried.

Whirling, Philomena trained the shotgun but no one was there. "Nothing," she said. "You need to get control of yourself, daughter."

"There was a face, Ma," Estelle said. "I saw it."

A thump on the side of the house caused them all to stiffen. "What was that?" Mandy said breathlessly.

"Are all the windows latched?" Ebidiah asked.

"Of course," Philomena said. Not that it would stop the hostiles if they got a shutter open. They could just bust the glass out. The breaking glass would give some warning, though.

Ebidiah gnawed his lip. "To be honest, ma'am, I don't much like the notion of making a stand, either. We're at their mercy so long as we stay in this house."

"Out there wouldn't be any better," Mandy said.

"If we can slip out without being seen it would," Ebidiah said. "It's dark. We could slip away. I have a horse and my mule back in the trees. If we can reach them, I can get you to town."

"To my husband," Philomena corrected him. "And my sons."

"An iffy proposition," Ebidiah said. "The redskins will be after us at first light. Some of them are bound to be good trackers. They'll catch us before we reach Comanche Creek. The town is closer. We might make it there."

"Might," Philomena said.

"Think of your girls."

"Don't you dare," Philomena said. "My family is all I ever think about."

"I want to be with Pa and Luke and Sam, too," Mandy said.

Estelle nodded.

"Womenfolk," Ebidiah muttered, and scratched his chin. "All right. You have your minds made up. We'll make the best of it. The question is how to sneak out without being caught. They're on all sides of the house."

"They'll be watching the doors," Philomena guessed. "We'd have to distract them somehow."

The old trapper snapped his fingers and grinned. "I know just how to do it, ma'am."

"You do?"

Ebidiah nodded. "All that talk of them burning you out gave me a brainstorm. We'll distract them by setting your house on fire."

Chapter 46

Luke Burnett was troubled. As he rode night herd with his hand resting on the butt of his Remington, he recollected things said to him by the Kursts over the past week or so, and some of the looks he'd been given.

The longhorns were bedded down, many of them on the ground. They were as still as gravestones except for an occasional grunt or snort. Across the way, the huge white bull they called the Ghost was silhouetted against their campfire.

Luke came to a decision. When another rider loomed out of the darkness, he drew rein and quietly said, "We need to talk, Pa."

His father drew rein and smothered a yawn. "This night herd work makes me sleepy. We've only just started and I'm ready to turn in."

"It's about the Kursts," Luke said.

"Not that again."

Luke let his misgivings spill out. "The other day, when Reuben mentioned what he aimed to do with his share of the money, Harland looked at him and said he was putting the cart before the horse. Thaxter keeps acting as if he can't wait to slap leather on me. Then there's Lorette. She told Sam she would hate for anything to happen to him, and when he said that he wasn't aiming to be gored, she said it wasn't the cattle he should be worried about. When he asked what she meant, she said she dare not say and turned and walked away."

Leaning on his saddle horn, his father gestured at the herd. "You see all those cattle? The Kursts can't get all them to market on their own. They need help. They need *us*. They're not about to risk losing the herd. Trust me, son."

Luke would like to. He'd always held his pa in the highest regard. In this instance, though, Luke felt sure, clear down to his marrow, that his pa was making a mistake. "If you say so."

"I know that tone. You don't believe me."

"I don't believe the Kursts, Pa. I don't believe they intend to share the money. They want it all for themselves."

"I haven't seen any evidence of that."

A lost cause, Luke decided. His pa wouldn't believe him until the Kursts jerked their pistols. It was up to him to look out for his father and Sam. Jasper and Reuben, too, while he was at it. "I won't bring it up again, then," he said, and reined around. He heard his father sigh.

The thing to do, Luke reckoned, was to force one of the Kursts to reveal what they were up to. But how could he, short of shooting one? He was puzzling it over as he circled the herd and came within a stone's throw of the sleeping figures in camp.

Everyone should have been asleep, but voices fluttered out of the woods on his left. Whispers, some spoken in anger.

Luke drew rein and dropped his hand to his revolver.

The brush crackled and someone strode out, hatless, muttering. Someone else came after the first one and clutched at an arm.

"Leave me be. This has gone too far. I shouldn't have let you, but I couldn't help myself."

"Sam?" Luke said quietly so as not to awaken any of the sleepers.

His younger brother drew up short. So did Lorette Kurst, also hatless, her hair in a wild mane.

"What the dickens?" Luke said.

Sam was rooted in surprise. "Luke," he said, and turned to Lorette. "Look, it's my brother."

"I have eyes," Lorette said.

"What are you two doing out here by yourselves?" Luke asked, and felt foolish the moment the words were out of his mouth. Lorette's interest in Sam had been obvious to everyone.

"Uhhh," Sam said.

"Oh, Samuel," Luke said.

"I can explain."

"No," Luke said. "You can't."

Lorette brazenly clasped Sam's hand and stood shoulder-to-shoulder with him. "We don't have to account to you, Luke Burnett. What we do is no one's affair but our own."

"Consarn you," Sam said to her. "He's my brother. Don't treat him that way."

"What would Ma say?" Luke said.

Lorette placed her other hand on Sam's chest and leaned in close. "Don't listen to him. Listen to your heart. To how it feels. If we don't follow through, we'll regret it the rest of our days." She kissed Sam on the cheek, glared at Luke, and marched toward their camp, her head high.

"Ain't she something?" Sam said.

"Your heart?" Luke said.

His younger brother stared after her. "I've done some things I shouldn't ought to have done."

Luke didn't say anything.

"She's been after me for weeks now. Follows me like a puppy. But I suppose you know that."

"Everyone does," Luke said. "She followed you out here tonight, did she?"

"No," Sam said quietly. "She led me by the hand and I couldn't stop myself. I wanted to, as much as she did." He paused. "What's happening to me?" He didn't give Luke time to answer. "She says she loves me. That I'm the one for her. That if I can't see it, she can."

"Do you feel the same?"

Sam raised a face twisted with confusion. "I don't know what I feel. Some days I'm mad at her. Other days . . ." He didn't go on. He didn't need to.

"Have you told Pa?"

"No. He might send me home. Or say something to Mr. Kurst and he'll take a switch to Lorette. He does, you know. Beats on her now and then."

"It would stop her from pestering you."

"To tell the truth," Sam said, his mouth splitting in a lopsided smile, "I've come to sort of like being pestered."

"That answers my question."

"I've stepped into her loop, haven't I?"

"With both feet," Luke said.

Chapter 47

Ebidiah Troutman thought he had come up with a brilliant idea. He was taken aback when the lady of the house thought differently.

"I've heard some addlepated notions in my time, but this beats all," Philomena Burnett declared. "We're not burning our house down, and that's that."

Ebidiah Burnett could have pointed out that the Comanches might do it themselves. Instead he said, "Not actually burn it. We'll only pretend."

"Make sense," Philomena demanded.

"We light a small fire near the front door," Ebidiah proposed, thinking furiously, making it up as he went. "Then we throw a wet blanket on it to make a lot of smoke and throw the door open. The Comanches will see the smoke and think there's a fire. They should all come around to the front for a look-see, and when they do, we'll slip out the back door and be gone before they know it."

"Why not go out a window?" Mandy asked.

"Those shutters," Ebidiah said. "It would make too much noise. That's why I came in the back."

"I don't know," Philomena said. "A lot of things could go wrong with that plan."

"If you have a better one, let me hear it," Ebidiah said gruffly. He'd come all this way to help, snuck into the farmhouse under the Comanches' very noses, and she was giving him a hard time.

"I don't," Philomena admitted.

"Let's try it, Ma," Mandy said. "We have to get to Pa and the others."

Estelle, holding on to Blue, nodded. "I don't want to be trapped in here. We wouldn't stand a chance."

Ebidiah was pleased to see that the girls were having an effect.

"All right, then," Philomena said, reluctantly.

"We have to hurry," Ebidiah stressed. The Comanches could attack at any moment. "Find me some towels or blankets."

"Mandy, come with me," Philomena said, and bustled into the hall.

Ebidiah glanced at the window and then put his ear to the back door to listen. Outside, all was quiet. *The lull before the storm.* When the war party struck, they would come from all sides in a rush, whooping and hollering and killing everyone they saw.

"Thank you for coming for us, Mr. Troutman," Estelle said.

Ebidiah had almost forgotten she was there. "Least I could do, girl. You folks have been kind to me."

"You're very brave."

"I just don't know any better," Ebidiah made light of it.

"My pa says you're a good man."

"He said that?"

"The last time you were here, as you were leaving with your mule. My ma said that you're a bit strange and Pa looked at her and said you're a good one, and he trusts you."

"Well, now," Ebidiah said, and coughed. Many folks were like the wife and regarded him as peculiar for sticking with a way of life most had given up. Trappers were becoming rare, even in the Rockies where they once thrived. It was the death of the beaver trade that started the decline. Once beaver hats went out of fashion, interest in beaver pelts waned. There was still a demand for other furs, but not nearly as much as before. Store-bought clothes were the thing these days. Except for the rich, who liked to dress fancy, and who were fond of fur trim and fur coats and the like.

Estelle brought him out of his reverie with, "What's keeping them?"

As if they had heard her, Philomena and Mandy hustled into the kitchen bearing folded blankets. "These should do," the former said.

"Wet one really good," Ebidiah said.

Mandy moved to the pitcher on the counter and proceeded to pour the water over a blanket until it was soaked. She used every last drop. "That's all there is unless we go out and get more from the pump."

"With the Indians out there?" Philomena said.

Ebidiah stepped to the stove and touched the side. It was barely warm. "When was the last time you used this?"

"About noon," Philomena answered. "We had soup."

Opening it, Ebidiah poked around inside for an ember they could use. He didn't find a single one. "Damn."

"I'll thank you not to use that sort of language in front of my girls," Philomena said.

"Your husband never cusses?"

"Not in my presence he doesn't, no."

Ebidiah didn't doubt it. Some women ruled their roosts with an iron will. Others, like Ariel Kurst, were ruled over by their men.

"We have some parlor matches," Philomena was saying. She crossed to a drawer, opened it, and brought back a metal tin. "These should do."

"Why didn't you say so sooner?"

"You didn't ask."

Ebidiah took them and led the females down the hall to the front door. "Keep an eye on the windows," he cautioned. It wouldn't do for the Comanches to see what they were up to.

The dog sniffed at the bottom of the door, and growled.

"Keep Blue quiet," Philomena told her youngest. "And move back out of the way."

Hunkering, Ebidiah unfolded two blankets and fluffed them, then placed one on top of the other on the floor. With his fingernails, he pried at the tin and opened it. He seldom used matches. A fire steel and flint had sufficed for him his whole life. But he knew how to use matches, and struck one. It caught and flared, the acrid odor almost making him sneeze. He applied the tiny flame to the edge of a blanket, but the flame went out.

"It didn't work," Mandy said the obvious.

"There's a heap more matches." Ebidiah struck another and tried again. The flame licked at the blanket, growing brighter. Smoke rose, but only a little. Craning down, he puffed lightly until the flames grew. Slowly they began to engulf the pile.

"Starting a fire in my own house," Philomena said. "I never thought I'd see the day."

"It's been my experience, missus," Ebidiah said, "that we see a lot of things in life we never thought we would."

"Aren't you the philosopher?" Philomena said, not unkindly.

"No," Ebidiah said. "I've just lived long." He stood and moved back a step. "Hand me the wet blanket."

Mandy did, then wiped her hands on her dress.

"How do we keep Blue from barking and giving us away once we're outside?" Estelle wanted to know.

"Put your hand over his muzzle," Philomena said. "He usually listens good, so we can only hope."

The flames were high now, and smoke began to fill the hall. It stung Ebidiah's eyes and was getting up his nose. Holding the wet blanket wide in both hands, he announced, "The time has come."

Chapter 48

Amanda Burnett had never been so scared in her life. Not even that time she almost stepped on a rattlesnake. Fortunately, it had rattled its tail, giving her enough warning to spring back before it struck.

Mandy had long harbored a fear of hostiles. So did most everyone who lived on the frontier. Since coming to Texas, and thanks to all the horrible stories she'd heard, the mere mention of Comanches was worrisome. They were the terrors of the territory, the bogeymen who came in the dead of night to massacre and mutilate.

And now a war party of those bogeymen had their house surrounded and were fixing to wipe them out.

Mandy was trying to be brave but it was hard. Fear clawed at her insides, much as the Comanches' knives would. Unless a warrior took her for his wife. It didn't happen often, but it *did* happen. Sometimes the women were returned in trades for Comanche prisoners. One woman, Mandy had heard tell, refused; she preferred to stay with the Indians. To Mandy, that was beyond the pale of reason. Only a lunatic would do such a thing.

Ebidiah Troutman picked that moment to fling the wet blanket onto the burning pile. He covered them entirely, extinguishing the flames and causing a copious amount of smoke to rise.

Mandy coughed.

Darting around the blankets, the old trapper worked the bolt and opened the front door. As if pulled by invisible hands, the smoke streamed out and up in a thick column, spreading rapidly.

"Quick, now," Ebidiah urged, and raced down the hall.

Outside there were yells. The Comanches had seen the smoke. They sounded surprised. Mandy prayed all of them would go to see.

She let her ma and sister go ahead of her and watched over her shoulder, half-expecting Comanches to come bursting in.

Ebidiah reached the kitchen and raced to the back door. He threw the bolt and pulled the door open just wide enough to poke his head out.

"What do you see?" her mother whispered.

"Shhhh," Ebidiah said.

"Don't shush me. Are they there or are they not?"

"*Please*, ma'am," Ebidiah whispered, and went on looking.

Mandy nervously fidgeted. Her sister had both hands around Blue's muzzle and was saying something softly in his ear to calm him.

"The coast looks clear," Ebidiah said, pulling his head in. "I think they've all gone around front like we wanted."

"They better have," her mother said.

Ebidiah opened the door wide, and moved aside. "After you, ladies. Be quick. Stay close to the house and go to the right, clear to the corner. Stay low and try not to make much noise."

Her mother didn't argue. "Estelle, you first, with Blue. Mandy, right after her. Hurry now." She had a grim look on her face, the likes of which Mandy had never seen before.

Estelle nodded and went out without any hesitation.

Mandy stepped to the doorway, then had to force her legs to keep moving. The cool air, or her fear, made her break out in gooseflesh. Tucking at the knees, she followed her sister and stopped when Estelle did.

Her mother was close behind, gripping her shotgun in both hands.

Mandy searched the night for Comanches. The old

trapper's ruse appeared to have worked, and none were near. But they were masters at hiding, and one could spring up at any second.

She suddenly realized she had broken out in a sweat and was perspiring from every pore.

With an alacrity his years belied, Ebidiah Troutman glided past them to the corner, his Sharps leveled. "Stay close," he whispered. "Move when I move, stop when I stop. If I say to flatten, you drop fast. If I give a holler, run like hell."

"Mr. Troutman, your language," Philomena said.

Mandy swore she heard the old man sigh. Any other time, it would have been funny.

"There's more important things to worry about," Ebidiah said. He nodded toward their barn. "We'll head there first." He glanced at Estelle. "Hold on to that dog of yours, young miss. One bark, and our goose is cooked."

Mandy was worried about that, too. When Ebidiah whispered "Now!" they broke into motion.

Blue tried to twist toward the front of the house but Estelle held firm, propelling him along. Blue struggled. To help Estelle, Mandy darted up and slipped her fingers under the collar.

No war cries rang out. No arrows whizzed out of the dark.

To Mandy's amazement, they reached the barn safely and ducked inside. Blue growled and Estelle whispered, quieting him.

Mandy peered out.

A lot of shadowy shapes were at the front of the house, watching the smoke that still poured from the doorway.

"My trick worked, by heaven," Ebidiah said, sounding proud of himself.

"Why haven't they rushed in?" Mandy wondered.

"They're not stupid," Ebidiah said. "They suspect it's a trick, and they'll be shot if they do."

"We're not out of the woods yet," Philomena said.

"Speaking of which," the old trapper replied, and moved toward the rear of the barn. "Come on, ladies."

Mandy considered suggesting they hide up in the loft, but that would be folly. Sooner or later the Comanches would get around to searching the barn from top to bottom, and they'd be caught.

"I wish Pa and Luke and Sam were here," Estelle whispered.

"Makes two of us," Mandy said.

"We get out of this, I'm never complaining about Pa's and Ma's rules ever again."

Mandy either. When they first settled there, her parents had laid down certain rules. They were never to go anywhere alone. They were always to be in the house by dark. They were never to ride anywhere without letting their folks know where they were going. And more. All to keep them from being waylaid by Comanches. At the time, she'd thought some of the rules were silly. Not anymore.

The rear door opened into the corral. To their left was a gate. Their mother opened it, shooed them through, and closed it again.

Ebidiah stopped and motioned for them to do the same. Hunkered down, he stared hard into the night.

"What are we waiting for?" Philomena said. "Where's that horse and mule of yours?"

"Off a ways."

"Let's go, then."

They ran, just as Comanche war whoops shattered the air, followed by the crash of breaking glass.

"They're breaking in," Ebidiah said over his shoulder. "It won't take them long to discover we're not there."

Mandy pumped her legs, pacing her sister. Estelle had let go of Blue and the dog loped between them. The ground was uneven, with clumps of weeds, and ruts. She prayed she wouldn't trip. A sprained ankle, or worse, would be a calamity.

She hadn't let go of her rifle all evening. Her hands were sore from holding it so tight, and the stock brushed her leg with every stride. She wondered if she would be able to shoot it if she had to. She'd never killed before. Not a human being.

A black wall of vegetation loomed. They were almost to the woods.

Ebidiah reached the trees and plunged right in. "We'll be there soon," he said.

Mandy was glad. She was growing winded. "I can't believe we got away."

She spoke too soon.

Behind them, fierce howls rose and feet drummed the earth. The Comanches were in pursuit.

Chapter 49

"You're the luckiest gent alive," Reuben Weaver said, and chuckled. "I'd give anything to be in your boots."

Sam Burnett didn't feel lucky. He felt confused. He summed up his feelings with, "Why did she pick me?"

They were riding night herd. They were each supposed to take one side of the herd and ride back and forth until they were relieved. But they liked to ride together so they could talk.

As two of the youngest, they had a lot in common. Iden Kurst was about their age but he was standoffish, like all the Kurst boys, and wanted nothing to do with either of them.

"She has to have a reason?" Reuben said.

Sam had made the mistake of mentioning that Lorette Kurst was dropping hints about the two of them getting hitched, which had shocked him considerably. "I'm young yet. I'm in no hurry to tie the knot."

"Seems to me you're looking a gift horse in the mouth," Reuben said. "Besides, I know of some who have done it a lot younger. I have a cousin who married at thirteen. In some parts of the country, that's considered an old maid."

Sam had a cousin of his own who had married at fourteen and been a pa by fifteen. "Even so," he said.

"A girl as pretty as Lorette," Reuben said. "If she showed any interest in me, I'd eat it up with a spoon."

"You wouldn't wonder why?"

Overhead, a host of stars sparkled. Far off in the hills a coyote keened and was answered by another. There was little wind, and the longhorns were quiet.

"I'm not much for wondering," Reuben said. "When things happen, they happen. What's the use of complicating things?"

"This isn't just any old thing," Sam said. "Marriage is forever. I say 'I do,' I'll be with her the rest of my life."

"And that's bad?"

Sam hesitated. Just the other day, Lorette had come up to him when no one was around, pressed herself against him, and kissed him full on the mouth. He'd just stood there and let her run the tip of her tongue over his lips and her hands over his chest. His body had grown so hot, it was a wonder he hadn't caught on fire. And he'd liked that she'd done that. What came next, though, rekindled his worries. She'd stood back, cocked her head, and said, "I am tired of waiting. Admit you're as fond of me as I am of you and I will do for you as Eve did for Adam." With that, she had smiled, touched the tip of a finger to his chin, and strolled off.

Reuben brought him back to the here and now with, "You reckon she's playing some kind of female game?"

No, Sam didn't, but he said, "You must have heard the stories about her. She's a tease and a flirt and has no shame."

"I don't claim to know a lot about women," Reuben said. "But you've held her off for weeks now, and she keeps it up. Seems to me that if she were only teasing, she'd have tired of the game."

Sam had come to the same conclusion. Lorette was sincere. Which scared him worse than her flirting. He'd come out to Comanche Creek with his pa to round up cattle, not find himself a wife.

"You have a heap more willpower than I do," Reuben was saying. "If it was me, I'd let her sweep me off my feet."

Sam decided to change the subject. All this talk about Lorette was making him uncomfortably warm, like her kisses. "What do you make of those moccasin tracks Silsby found?"

Just that morning, Silsby Kurst had discovered foot-prints in the soft earth along the creek. Only a few, and only partials, but enough to tell they were made by moc-casins. Gareth Kurst said they were made within the last few days, and he should know, all the tracking and hunt-ing he did.

"The truth?" Reuben said. "We're asking for trouble if we stay here much longer. Mr. Kurst told my pa that there must be Comanches about, spying on us. That maybe they've been spying on us for a while now."

"If that's so," Sam said, "why don't they attack?"

"Who knows? Could be it's just a few, and we have too many guns. Could be they're waiting for more to show up. Or it could be a lot are out there, and they'll strike when they're good and ready."

"Lord, I hope not," Sam said. The only thing that scared him worse than Comanches was Lorette.

"Pa says maybe they're puzzled by what we're up to. By why we're rounding up so many cattle, and what we plan to do with them."

"I doubt that matters much to Comanches."

"Who knows with Injuns? I'm just glad the roundup is over and the drive will commence soon."

Sam was glad, too. They had more than enough cattle, and the herd-tending had grown tedious. The plan was for each of the married men to pay a last visit to their wives, and then the trek to Kansas would get under way. The men were to take turns, and had drawn straws to see who went first. Jasper Weaver had won the honor, and would leave in the morning for his farm. When he got back, Sam's pa would go see his ma. Last to have a turn would be Gareth Kurst.

Apparently Reuben was thinking about the same thing because he said, "I might ask pa if I can go with him. He wants me to stay, but I'd like to see Ma one more time before we head out."

"I'd like to see my ma, too," Sam said. He'd like to see his sisters even more. They were close, Mandy and Es-telle and he.

He glanced at the longhorns and saw that a score were

up and staring intently at a wooded hill to the north. They
didn't normally do that, and he drew rein. "Look there."

"At what?" Reuben said. He stopped and shifted in
his saddle. "They must smell something. My pa says they
have real good noses."

More than a few had their ears pricked.

Sam listened, but all he heard was the distant hoot of
an owl.

"It's not anything to worry about," Reuben said. "They
don't act agitated or anything."

"Still," Sam said. Combined with the moccasin tracks,
it filled him with unease. A feeling that something terrible
was about to crash down over them with all the violence
of a thunderstorm. "Maybe we should tell someone."

"What for?" Reuben said, and nodded at the herd. "A
lot of them are lying back down."

Whatever had caused the stir, most of the longhorns
had lost interest and were settling in again.

"I guess it was nothing," Sam conceded.

"Good," Reuben said, and grinned. "Now, then, about
Lorette . . ."

Sam groaned.

Chapter 50

Ebidiah Troutman wasn't half the man he'd once taken such pride in being. Hardship used to roll off him like water off a duck's back. Wading in ice-cold streams and ponds to set beaver traps? No problem. Toting those heavy bodies back to camp to skin them? No strain at all. Endless hours spent hiking over some of the most rugged country on the continent? He took it all in stride.

Nowadays, Ebidiah's body objected when he pushed too hard. His joints creaked. His muscles ached. His stamina wasn't what it used to be, as his pounding heart and aching legs now reminded him.

They had been running for minutes, Ebidiah and the Burnett women, plunging pell-mell through the forest. Mired in shadow, with only patches of starlight to relieve the blackness, the woods presented almost as much danger as their pursuers. A misstep could bring them down, or they might collide with a tree. It took all of Ebidiah's concentration to avoid disaster.

They wouldn't be running if the horse and Sarabell had been where Ebidiah left them. But when they got to the spot, he'd been horrified to find the animals were gone. Either they had pulled loose and wandered, which was unlikely, or the Comanches had found them.

Now Ebidiah and the women were flying for their lives, the women at his heels. So far they were holding up well.

Ebidiah was surprised the Comanches hadn't caught

them yet. He figured the warriors were hanging back, waiting for him and the ladies to tire and slow. Then the Comanches would swoop in and overwhelm them.

The women were breathing heavily. Especially Philomena, who wasn't accustomed to so much exercise.

Ebidiah encouraged her with a smile. "You're doing fine, missus," he puffed.

"See to yourself, old man."

The dog was the only one not showing the strain. He loped between the girls, almost invisible thanks to his dark coat.

Ebidiah's knees were hurting something awful. The left was the worst. It had been giving him fits for years, ever since he broke it when he slipped on some talus and tumbled into a boulder. Gritting his teeth against the pain, he did his best to ignore it.

His Sharps seemed to weigh ten pounds more than usual, but he would be damned if he'd let go of it. When the Comanches came in for the kill, it would buy them precious moments of life. That, and his bowie.

More than ever, Ebidiah regretted killing that warrior on the hill by the cattle camp. Maybe he was just curious. By sneaking up on him, Ebidiah had set this whole mess in motion. Wilda Weaver, dead. Ariel Kurst, dead. And now Mrs. Burnett and her daughters might suffer the same fate. All because he didn't leave well enough alone.

A stump appeared out of nowhere. Ebidiah tried to avoid it but he was moving too fast. He slammed into it hard. Upended, he spilled head over heels. Pain flooded through him. He came to rest on his back, the stars spinning as if caught in a whirlwind, and was vaguely aware of a hand plucking at his buckskin shirt.

"Mr. Troutman?" Mandy Burnett said. "Are you all right?"

"Fine, girl," Ebidiah gasped, when the truth was that he hurt all over.

Mandy pulled on his shirt. "You've got to get up. We have to keep going. They're not far behind."

"Sure, girl, sure." Ebidiah made it to his feet, and swayed. His legs felt like butter. He took a step and would have fallen if not for Mandy's support. "I need a second to clear my head."

"We don't have a second," Mandy said.

Ebidiah realized the mother and the other daughter had stopped and were waiting for him. "Go on, all of you."

"Not without you," Philomena said, taking deep breaths.

Ebidiah forced his legs to work. He refused to be to blamed for them being caught. Gaining strength, he shrugged free of Mandy. "I'm all right. Get up there with your ma and your sis."

The sounds behind them had momentarily faded. The warriors had stopped when they did.

Ebidiah had been right about the Comanches waiting for them to tire. "Go, ladies, go!" he urged.

Grimly, they raced on.

Ebidiah was in agony. His shins, from striking the stump, were welters of pain. But that was good, in a way. The pain kept him alert.

Still, they were only delaying the inevitable. As much noise as they were making, they couldn't possibly shake the Comanches.

An idea took root. An act of desperation that might save the women. It would probably cost him his own life but he was on in years, and didn't have long to live, anyway.

Ebidiah would sacrifice himself for the ladies. He owed them that, for bringing this ordeal down on their heads. But he must do it without them catching on. He began to slow—not much, but enough that Philomena and her girls pulled further ahead. None of them noticed.

Dropping even further behind, Ebidiah deliberately made a lot of noise, brushing against limbs and pounding his feet harder to drown out the sounds the women made. He must trick the Comanches into thinking that he and the ladies were still together.

A branch barred his way and he broke it with a swing of the Sharps. The loud crack was like a shot.

And he slowed even more.

Behind him, so did the Comanches.

Grinning at how he was fooling them, Ebidiah changed direction. Instead of north he ran to the west, continuing to make as much racket as he could. Tilting his good ear, his grin widened when it became apparent the Comanches were following him and not the ladies.

Ebidiah gamely sped on. Once he went far enough that the women should be safe, he would turn and make his stand.

"Come and get me, you red devils."

Chapter 51

Philomena Burnett's lungs were burning and every muscle in her legs hurt. She had run for a considerable distance and didn't know how much farther she could go. She glanced back, saw to her dismay that Ebidiah Troutman was no longer behind them, and stopped. Doubling over, she gasped for breath as quietly as she could.

Her girls stopped, too.

"What's wrong, Ma?" Mandy said.

"Are you all in?" Estelle asked.

Her sides were hurting and it was an effort to breathe, but Philomena pointed and got out, "Eb . . ."

Mandy looked, and understood. "Where's Mr. Troutman? If the Comanches got him, wouldn't we have heard?"

"Maybe he got confused in the dark and ran a different way than us," Estelle said.

The truth hit Philomena like a kick to the gut. "No, not confused," she gasped. "On purpose."

"Ma?" Mandy said.

"He drew them away from us," Philomena guessed, "to give us a chance to get away."

"But that would put him in more danger, wouldn't it?" Estelle said.

"Yes."

"Oh." Estelle looked back the way they'd come. "Why would he do that for us? We're not his family or anything."

"Why do you think, daughter?" Philomena said. "He's sacrificing himself for us. Your father was right about him. Ebidiah Troutman is as noble as they come."

"You wouldn't know it to look at him."

"Yes, well." Sucking in air, Philomena straightened. "We can't let him give his life in vain. We have to get out of here."

"And go where?" Mandy said.

"Where else? To your father."

"It will take days on foot," Mandy said, "and the Comanches are swarming over the countryside."

Estelle cupped a hand to her ear. "I don't hear a thing."

"Maybe we've gotten away," Philomena said. It seemed too good to be true, but the woods were perfectly still.

"I wouldn't count on that," Mandy said. "I wouldn't count on anything. Mrs. Kurst and Mrs. Weaver are both dead, and who knows how many more? We need to keep moving, and not toward Comanche Creek."

"How's that?" Philomena said.

"Ma, it's too far. Town is closer. We stand a better chance of making it there. Once we do, they'll send men to warn Pa and the others."

"Wouldn't the Comanches expect that?" Estelle said. "Won't they have warriors between here and town to stop us?"

"I can't say how Indians think," Mandy said. "I only know it's a mistake for us to go find Pa. As much as I want to, I fear it would get us killed."

Estelle turned. "Ma, what do you say? Do we head for town or not?"

Philomena both hated and liked the idea. She'd be abandoning the man she loved. But once in town, her girls would be safe. And if none of the menfolk would ride to warn Owen and the others, she'd go herself, and leave the girls with friends.

"Ma?" Estelle said once more.

"I'm thinking." Philomena stared into the distance, her heart sinking in her chest. *Oh, Owen*, she thought. His cattle venture had put them in the direst peril of their lives. As much as she would rather be at his side, she had their daughters to think of. Owen would want her to keep them safe above all else.

Just then Blue growled low in his chest. He was looking back, his spine and legs rigid with tension.

"They must still be after us," Estelle whispered in dismay.

"Hush that dog," Philomena commanded.

Years ago, Owen had taught her that to tell direction at night, all she needed was to find the Big Dipper. The Dipper always pointed at the North Star. She peered up through the trees, said, "Follow me," and headed east.

"It's town, then?" Mandy whispered.

"It is," Philomena said.

Crouching, she led them through a belt of cedar. She tried not to make noise but it was hopeless. There were too many leaves and twigs on the ground. The brush snagged her dress. She did the best she could, and presently they came to a plain. Beyond, barely visible in the black, were more hills.

Wearily kneeling, Philomena announced, "We'll rest here a minute."

"Are you sure that's wise?" Mandy said.

"I need to."

"Blue's hair is up," Estelle whispered. "He hears them, I think."

Philomena debated whether to cross the plain or go around. Out in the open, they'd be exposed. But straight across was shorter. And if she remembered right, about a mile past those hills they would come to the rutted excuse for a road that they used when they took the buckboard into town.

"How much longer, Ma?" Mandy anxiously asked. "I'm ready to go now if you are."

Grunting, Philomena stood. "Stay low." She heeded her own advice, parting the high grass with her shotgun. Her dress swished much too loudly.

"God, I hate this," Mandy whispered.

"Don't blaspheme, daughter. It's not respectful." If there was one thing Philomena had taught her daughters, it was to never take the Lord's name in vain. That included treating "God" as if it were just like any other word.

They were well out on the plain, about halfway by Philomena's estimation, when Estelle whispered in alarm.

"Ma! I think they're right behind us!"

Philomena stopped and flattened. "On the ground, both of you. Estelle, keep your hand on Blue's muzzle. Don't let him growl if you can help it."

Her girls were quick to comply.

Rising on her elbows, Philomena craned her neck as high as she could. At first she thought Estelle was imagining things. Then movement caught her eye. Someone was coming toward them.

"Stay down," Philomena hissed in warning, and hugged the earth. If she could, she would have dug down into it. She dreaded hearing a war cry, dreaded iron hands would seize them, or tomahawks and knives descend.

Footfalls fell loudly.

"Ma?" Mandy whispered, a strange note to her voice.

"Quiet," Philomena said, amazed her oldest would be so careless.

"Ma, you have to look."

Philomena raised her head.

Out of the dark plodded a longhorn. An old cow, by the looks of her, more skin and bone than anything. One of her horns was broken. She paid them no mind whatsoever, but walked right on by.

Philomena knew a godsend when she saw one. Pushing to her feet, she said, "Come on. We'll follow her." The cow was headed in the right direction. And should the Comanches come after them, they would drop flat, and maybe, just maybe, the Comanches would think it was the cow they'd heard.

A body could only hope.

Chapter 52

Ebidiah Troutman was at the limit of his endurance. His chest was a bellows, his legs quaked and shook. His blood was roaring in his ears, and he was close to collapsing.

Even so, Ebidiah smiled. He'd given the Comanches a run for their bloodlust. Several times he would have sworn they were about to overtake him but somehow he'd slipped away. He'd lost count of the number of times he'd changed direction. He didn't even know if he was going north, south, east, or west.

They were still after him, though. Comanches didn't give up easily. They wanted him dead and they'd have him dead if they had to chase him clear to sunrise.

"Won't be long now," Ebidiah said under his breath. He veered past some scrub, tripped over a root or a rock, and pitched to a knee. Exhausted, he would have collapsed then and there except that somewhere to his rear a coyote that wasn't a coyote yipped.

They knew where he was, Ebidiah reckoned, or they had a good idea, and they were converging for the kill. He tried to stand and couldn't. He tried to raise his Sharps but his arms were leaden.

He was all in.

Ebidiah never thought he'd see the day when he'd give up. But he had nothing left in him, nothing at all. With a low groan, he let his body fall forward and closed his eyes as his cheek struck the ground. Great relief washed over him. He didn't have to run anymore. He would lie there and rest, and when they found him, that would be that. He was too weak to lift a finger to defend himself. Let them do as they would.

Ebidiah had never been so tired. He wanted to sleep. To drift off and not feel the pain and fatigue. But even though his body had given out, his senses still worked. He heard stealthy movement and furtive whispers.

The Comanches were close.

Any moment, Ebidiah expected an outcry and the terrible sensation of an arrow or a lance piercing him. He would try not to scream, try not to beg for mercy. He had his dignity, if nothing else, and he would die as he had lived: on his own terms.

The suspense ate at his nerves. The Comanches were taking their sweet time finishing him off. He wondered if it was deliberate, if they were toying with him as cats might play with a mouse.

Something crunched, lightly, very near.

Ebidiah opened his eyes. Through a gap in the brush he glimpsed a dark form about ten feet off.

The warrior went by without seeing him.

If he wasn't so exhausted, Ebidiah would have laughed. The next Comanche would spot him, he was sure.

Another figure appeared, but like the first, it glided past without spotting him.

Ebidiah didn't know what to make of it. He was lying in plain sight. Or was it that his buckskins blended so well into the undergrowth? Rolling onto his back, he looked for others. There were none. There had been the two and that was it.

Providence again, Ebidiah thought. The Almighty was looking out for him.

He didn't know how else to account for having lasted so long.

Ebidiah closed his eyes again. He might as well rest while he could. He thought of Philomena and the girls and was glad they had gotten away. He'd done that much, at least. It didn't make up for Wilda Weaver and Ariel Kurst, but it was something.

The hills were quiet. It had a calming effect. He felt himself drifting off and fought it. He should stay awake and watch out for the Comanches. But his body wouldn't be denied.

Ebidiah blinked, and gave a start. He'd fallen asleep. Not for a few minutes, either. The position of the stars told him he'd been out for an hour or more.

The rest had done him good. He had enough strength to slowly sit up and take stock of his surroundings.

Bathed in the pale glow of starlight, the cedars were undisturbed. There wasn't a single Comanche anywhere.

Ebidiah refused to believe he had eluded them. They must be nearby, waiting for him to give himself away.

He'd outfox the devils. Lying back down, he made himself comfortable. He'd stay there until daylight. Once the sun was up, he stood a better chance of eluding the warriors.

He lay listening for he knew not how long. Finally he succumbed, and slept the sleep of the dead, a slumber so deep, it would have taken a lance through the chest to awaken him.

Awareness came abruptly. One instant he was out to the world, the next he blinked at a brightening sky. In a little while dawn would break and he could get his bearings. He cautiously rose onto an elbow.

He saw no one.

Ebidiah waited until a golden arch crowned the world before he pushed to his feet and gazed about in wonderment. He had done the impossible. He had gotten away.

He shuffled a few steps, his body protesting. He was sore all over, and his shoulder throbbed.

The smart thing was to head for town. Ebidiah headed for the Burnett homestead. He wouldn't go anywhere without Sarabell. The horse he didn't care about, but he couldn't do without his mule. She was more than an animal. She was his lone companion.

It might get him killed, but he didn't care.

"I'm coming, old girl," Ebidiah said, and started off.

Chapter 53

Owen Burnett never tired of the sight. Over twenty-five hundred longhorns. Two thousand five hundred and sixty-three head, to be exact. As he sat his saddle surveying the bovine fruits of their long weeks of labor, he whistled in appreciation. "We did it, by heaven."

Beside him, astride his own mount, Gareth Kurst nodded. "We drive them all to Kansas, that's over one hundred thousand dollars."

Owen whistled again.

It was early morning, and the sun was bright. Everyone had only been up a short while.

"Jasper leaves in a bit for home," Gareth mentioned. "When he gets back, you head right out. Take your boy if you want. My brood and me will watch the herd. As soon as you get back, we'll start the drive."

"Hold on," Owen said. "What about Ariel?"

"What about her?"

"Don't you want to take a few days to visit her? It will be months before you see her again."

"So?"

"She's your wife."

"So?" Gareth said again.

Owen turned back to the longhorns. He spied the Ghost moving among them like a sultan among his harem. The huge bull was magnificent. Owen considered it a shame that they would sell him for his meat.

"I like that you don't pry, Burnett," Gareth said.

"Oh?" Owen said, with little interest. He had worked with the man for almost two months now, and knew as little about him as he did at the start.

"I mean that," Gareth said. "Some would want to know why I don't think more highly of my missus. You do. Admit it."

Owen shrugged. "You don't have to answer to me."

"A man never has to answer to anyone," Gareth said. "But I'll tell you, anyway. It might help you." He leaned on his saddle horn. "You recollect me telling you a man has to rule his own roost?"

"I seem to remember something about that, yes."

"There's more to it than who wears the britches. It's a matter of not letting our feelings get the better of us. I've seen too many men go around with a nag on their backs because they think they have to be softhearted to get along. That's not how it should be. A wife should be like a hound dog, seen but not heard unless the husband wants her to be."

Owen couldn't keep silent. "What about love, Gareth? Where does that enter into things?"

"There's no such thing."

"I wasn't born yesterday," Owen said flatly. "I know for a fact you love your boys and your girl. Don't deny it."

"I care for them, sure," Gareth said. "And I've taught them that a family should always stick together. A family that does is strong. A family that doesn't is weak, and a weak family doesn't last long in a world where folks are killed for the money in their pokes." He stopped and gave an odd sort of grin, then said, "As for my missus, I care for her, some. I'll admit that much. But not in the way you care for yours. Your so-called love is a chain that shackles you to her."

"I almost believe you're serious."

"No almost about it." Gareth raised his reins.

"Hold on," Owen said. "If you feel that way about your own family, how do you feel about friends?"

"They serve their purpose."

"That's all?"

"What else is there?" Gareth rejoined. "Take us. I

partnered with you to round up a herd to take to Kansas. Would you say we're friends?"

"I would like to think we are, yes."

"We're friendly, yes," Gareth said, "because it suits us to be. We couldn't do the roundup if we didn't get along."

"That's all you see it as?"

"A money proposition." Gareth nodded. "Don't let it hurt your feelings. I don't treat you any different than I do that weak sister Jasper." He reined around. "I need to go talk to my boys." A tap of his spurs, and he was gone.

Owen sat watching Kurst ride off. He was so deep in thought, he didn't know Luke had come up until Luke said his name. "What was that, son?"

"What were you and Mr. Kurst jawing about? You looked so serious."

"You know how you've been saying for a while now that we shouldn't trust the Kursts?"

Luke frowned. "You're not going to scold me about that again, are you? You wouldn't trust them either if you'd heard some of the things Harland has said."

"No," Owen said, "I'm beginning to think you're right. Gareth just about admitted that he doesn't give a hoot about us. When it comes to the cattle, all he sees is the money. It worries me some."

Luke smiled with genuine affection. "Thank you. It bothered me considerably that you didn't believe me. Now that you've come around, what do we do about it?"

"I don't know," Owen admitted. They couldn't very well just up and leave. Not after all the work they'd put in. They had a right to their share of the profits, the same as the Kursts.

"Do I warn Sam?"

Owen mulled that a bit. "No. He's caught up with that Lorette. He might take it into his head to tell her, and she might take it into hers to tell Gareth."

"We keep quiet and keep our eyes peeled for trouble?"

"For now."

"What if they decide to do us in and take all the money for themselves?"

"We'll cross that bridge when we come to it."

"Provided they don't shoot us in the back without any warning."

Owen hadn't considered that a possibility, until now. Probably because it was something he'd never do. Philomena had often said that he had a habit of thinking people thought the same way he did, when they didn't. "We'll have to grow eyes in the backs of our heads," he said lightheartedly to relieve the gloom he was feeling.

"Or use these," Luke said, and patted his Remington.

Chapter 54

A wind out of the west had picked up and swayed the tops of the trees. The cattle were fidgety, as if they sensed a storm might spring up.

Lorette was riding night herd. It bored her. She was tempted to ride back to camp and sneak over to Sam Burnett and sit and stare at him while he slept. She liked to do that. But if she was caught, her pa would be mad as a wet rooster.

Sam Burnett. These days, he was all she lived for. It surprised her. Since she could recollect, she'd liked to flaunt herself around boys. She'd tease and taunt and use her "female power," as she liked to call it, to make them squirm.

Things were different with Sam. It had started the same, with Lorette teasing him as she would any other boy. Then something happened. She began to grow fond of him. She told herself it was nothing. She couldn't possibly fall for someone so ordinary. Someone so . . . pure. For if ever there was a boy who was an innocent at heart, it was Sam. You wouldn't know he had two sisters, as little as he knew about girls.

The first time Lorette kissed him on the cheek, he'd blushed a deep red. Normally, she'd have laughed and teased him. But a strange feeling had come over her. She'd become all warm inside.

The warm feeling returned whenever she was around him. It got so she hankered to kiss him as she'd never hankered after anybody. Against all odds, against her own nature, she felt feelings she'd never had before. She could have her pick of any male in Texas, and she'd fallen for a boy no older than she was, a babe in the woods, as it were, who was thunderstruck when she eventually got around to kissing him full on the mouth.

Just then Lorette caught sight of the Ghost. The bull was so huge that even at night, he stood out from all the rest.

Lorette should have a man like that bull. Her pa always told her that when it came time for her to pick the man she'd hitch herself to, she should be smart about it. Pick a man with money. A man who knew what he was about. A man who would shower her with all the female foofaraw she hankered after.

Instead, she had her heart set on a penniless boy.

Disgusted and confused by her betrayal of her principles, Lorette straightened and stretched. Because of the wind, she almost didn't hear the pad of a foot behind her. Slipping her hand to her revolver, she twisted in the saddle and went to jerk it from its holster.

"Hold on, sis," Silsby said. "It's just me."

"I almost shot you," Lorette snapped. "What are you doing here? You're supposed to be sleeping." She realized something else. "And where's your horse? You came out on foot?"

"Harland said to," Silsby said. "It's quieter."

Of all her brothers, Lorette liked Silsby and Iden the best. Which was only natural since they were the closest in age. Harland was too bossy. Thaxter treated her the same way their pa treated their ma, and she didn't like that one bit. Wylie was all right but he hardly ever said anything. "Is our big brother afraid the cows will spook if they heard you riding up?" she joked.

"He's called a meeting."

"Who?"

"Who are we talking about?" Silsby said. "Harland wants us all together. The others are already there. He sent me to fetch you."

"I'm riding herd with Iden."

"I already let Iden know, and he'll be there, too."

"Then no one will be on herd," Lorette said in confusion. "What if something spooks them?"

"They'll be all right. Harland says you're to come. This is more important." Silsby turned and beckoned. "It's not far. There's a clearing in the woods where Pa and the Burnetts and the Weavers won't hear us. Follow me."

Lorette gigged her mare and went along. She didn't understand why Harland would call a meeting so secret, even their pa wasn't to know about it. If their pa found out, he'd beat Harland to within an inch of his life.

Starlight lit the clearing. Harland and Thaxter were standing with their heads together. Wylie sat cross-legged, his elbows on his knees, his chin in his hands. Iden was squatting and plucking at grass. Silsby went over to him and hunkered.

Alighting, Lorette let her reins dangle. "What's this about, Harland? Why'd you pull me from night herd?"

"Sit down and you'll find out," Harland said gruffly.

Lorette stayed standing to spite him. She hated being told what to do. Hated it more than anything. With her pa she had no choice. She did what he told her or he'd take a switch to her. He'd been doing that since she could remember. The bigger she'd grown, the bigger the switch. But she would be darned if she'd take it off her older brother. So she stood.

Harland and Thaxter drew apart and faced them—Thaxter, as was his wont, with his hand resting on his Colt.

"Get to it," Wylie said. "Pa could wake up and see we're gone and come looking."

"This won't take long," Harland said curtly. Then he did a strange thing for Harland. He smiled at them. "I've called you together because it's time we stood up for ourselves. Time we showed we have grit and won't be bullied by Pa anymore."

"Pa's not no bully," Iden said. "He's just Pa."

"Does that give him the right to boss us around? To make us do whatever he wants us to do?" Harland countered. "How many times has he tanned your backside or hit you with his fist, little brother? I bet you've lost count. The same as the rest of us."

"He only does it when I don't behave or mess up," Iden said.

"Will you listen to yourself?" Harland said. "You're making excuses for him. For a man who, as I recollect, knocked out one of your teeth that time you let the dog into the cabin and it wet the floor."

"The dog's not allowed in," Iden said.

"You're doing it again. You were only, what, ten at the time? It wasn't your fault the dog snuck in."

"I felt bad that Pa shot it."

Lorette had felt bad, too. She'd liked that hound. It used to lick her face and make her giggle.

"We're not here to talk about the damn dog," Wylie said. He was being talkative for Wylie. "Get on with it."

Harland glared at him, but only for a moment. "All right. I suppose I better." He straightened and held his hands out like a parson about to give a sermon. "It's time we stood on our own two feet. Time we did what we want and not what Pa wants. Take this cattle drive. Pa had us partner with the Weavers and the Burnetts, and when we get the herd to Kansas, we'll split the money three ways."

"What's wrong with that?" Lorette said. "They've done their part in this."

"We could have done it ourselves. It would have taken longer but so what?" Harland paused. "I say enough is enough. Let's get rid of them. Soon instead of later on"

"Pa won't go for that," Iden interrupted.

"Pa is too soft," Harland said. "My way is better. I say we get shed of them and do it all on our own."

"You're loco," Lorette said.

"Don't start on me, girl."

"What are you proposing, exactly?" Silsby said. "You haven't made that clear."

"I'm proposing two things," Harland said. "First, that we stand up to Pa and tell him we'll drive the cattle ourselves." He waggled a hand at Iden when Iden went to speak. "I know what you're thinking. Pa won't take kindly to that. Let Thax and me deal with him."

"How?" Lorette asked, but he ignored her.

"The second thing is that we stop working with the Weavers and the Burnetts. I'll tell them to their faces that we don't want them around anymore."

"They won't go for that," Lorette said.

"They better," Harland said, "or we'll settle it with lead."

Chapter 55

Luke Burnett was glad his pa had finally come around to his way of thinking. The Kursts were up to no good. He felt it in his bones. So when a slight sound awakened him in the middle of the night and he saw the five Kurst boys come slinking out of the darkness toward their blankets, his first reaction was to slide his hand to his Remington. He was covered to his shoulders with his blanket, so they didn't see. Cracking his eyelids to give the impression he was still sleeping, he watched them turn in. Their pa, who was sound asleep over by the horses, never stirred.

Luke wondered where they had been. Lorette wasn't with them, but then, she wouldn't be; she was riding herd. He had half a mind to get up and demand to know what they were doing going off by themselves, but that wouldn't get him anywhere. They'd deny it, or claim they were taking a walk, or some other nonsense. They stuck together, those Kursts.

Thaxter had lain on his back but now he rose on an elbow and stared at Luke as if he suspected Luke were awake. Luke stayed still. Not that he was scared. He'd seen Thaxter practice and Thaxter was quick, but so was he. They were pretty evenly matched. Should it come to that, he couldn't predict the outcome.

His ma, more than once, had asked why he liked to draw and shoot so much. He honestly couldn't say, except that he'd taken to the six-gun like a fish to water.

There was something about it—the motion, the feel. He would practice all day if he could.

His ma also remarked more than once that handling a six-shooter well was a useless talent. Being quick on the shoot, she said, didn't put food on the table. She'd defied him to name one person who ever amounted to much because they could shoot quick. Naturally, he'd answered, "Wild Bill Hickok."

Thanks to *Harper's New Monthly Magazine*, practically everyone on the frontier had heard about Hickok's duel with a man called Davis Tutt in the public square in Springfield, Missouri. For a while it had been all anybody talked about.

Hickok and Tutt had gotten into a dispute over a watch or a woman or both, and had faced off in the square and gone for their six-guns. At a range of seventy-five yards, Hickok put a slug through Tutt's heart. It was an incredible shot, and made Hickok the idol of thousands.

Luke was one of them. He practiced his draw every chance he got, practiced shooting at targets whenever he could afford the ammunition. He wasn't Hickok, but he wasn't a turtle, either, and he'd back down for no man.

Certainly not for the likes of Thaxter Kurst.

His ma didn't like it that he always went around with the revolver on his hip. She did concede that west of the Mississippi River it was a common practice. And she did see the need. Where there was no law, or precious little, a man—or a woman, for that matter—needed a weapon for protection. Carrying a rifle or shotgun around all day was impractical. They were heavy, and only left one hand free. A six-gun was the smart thing.

His pa's only remark had been that he hoped Luke wouldn't resort to his six-shooter without cause. Luke had the impression his father understood but was worried that he might have to use it someday. As a common saying had it, those who lived by the gun died by the gun. Luke had pointed out that thousands of men wore firearms, and relatively few were ever shot. His ma was there at the time, and she spoke up, saying if that were the case, why did he have to wear his all the time? A man had to be ready, Luke told her, because trouble could come at any time.

That was where they'd left it. His mother wasn't happy, though. He'd lost count of the times he'd caught her staring at his holster, and frowning.

Luke focused on the Kursts. They were all lying still, on either their sides or their backs. He wondered where they had gone and what they had been up to. That they snuck off without their father knowing added to the puzzle.

Luke considered mentioning it to Gareth. Harland and the others would probably deny it, and it would be his word against theirs. Whose word was Gareth Kurst going to believe?

Luke wondered if he should ask Sam to ask Lorette. She might know. And as sweet as she was on Sam, she might tell him. Then again, another saying had it that blood was thicker than water. And the Kursts were tight-knit.

Luke's eyelids were growing heavy. With everything peaceful, he figured he might as well fall back asleep. He needed the rest. He was about to close his eyes and let himself drift off when he caught movement at the edge of the trees. Something had moved almost too quickly for the eye to follow. His sleepiness vanished in a twinkling.

Luke almost sat up. Catching himself, he waited. He reckoned it must be an animal. A deer, maybe. They sometimes strayed close to camp. Or a longhorn, drawn out of the brush by the smell of the herd. Now and then one would drift in and they'd add it to the rest.

The minutes dragged, and nothing appeared. Luke was about to try to get back to sleep when he noticed their horses. Nearly every animal had its head up and its ears pricked and was staring into the woods.

The scent of a predator would do that. A mountain lion, for instance. Or a bear. Whatever it was, he doubted it posed a threat. No bear or mountain lion would attack the horses with so many men around.

The horses went on staring. One nickered. Another stomped a hoof.

Luke wrapped his hand around his Remington and waited, just in case he was wrong. No snarls or growls broke the serenity of the night, and after a while some of the horses lowered their heads and went back to dozing. When all of them had, he made himself comfortable and closed his eyes.

He thought about his mother and his sisters, safe and sound at their homestead. As much as he cared for them, and as much as he missed them, he was glad they weren't at the camp. He didn't want his sisters anywhere near the Kursts. He'd seen how Harland looked at Mandy in town. It had taken all his self-control not to pistol-whip the son of a bitch. Harland's mere look was an insult, the way he undressed a woman with his eyes.

Luke needed to think about something else. He wouldn't get to sleep otherwise. He thought about how well the roundup had gone, and how they would soon start the drive north.

Provided nothing happened.

The next day nothing did. They went about their routine, and all was peaceful.

Luke was glad but perplexed. A new night fell, and he turned in, like the rest.

He had trouble falling asleep. He couldn't shake the feeling that something terrible was about to happen.

Chapter 56

Sam Burnett knew he was breaking one of the rules his pa laid down, but hour after tedious hour of riding back and forth on the north side of the herd had made him restless. He'd sing and hum to the cattle to keep them calm, as he'd been told cowboys did. But there was only so much he could take.

He'd rather ride with Reuben Weaver and talk. The time passed faster.

So it was that an hour or so before sunrise, Sam rode around to Reuben's side of the herd. Reuben was glad to see him.

They were coming around the east end of the grassland and Reuben was saying he hoped a girl as pretty as Lorette took an interest in him someday when he straightened in his saddle and pointed. "Will you look at that? Why do they do that every now and then?"

The longhorns had long since bedded down for the night. Usually they didn't stir until near sunrise. But fully a score or more were up and staring intently at the nearest hill and the woodland that covered the slope.

"What do you make of it?" Reuben said.

Sam shrugged. "A bobcat or a coyote or something. It's not worth bothering about."

"I reckon," Reuben said. "Now where were we?"

"We're dropping the subject," Sam said.

"You were the one who brought her up," Reuben reminded him. "Seems to me, the way things are going, pretty soon you'll have to get down on your knee and propose."

Recently Sam had taken to confiding in Reuben. They'd become close friends, and Reuben could keep a secret. He sure couldn't confide in his brother. Luke didn't like his interest in Lorette. "I couldn't help myself," he said quietly even though there was no one else around to hear. "She kissed me, and the next thing I knew, I was kissing her back."

"Women will do that to a man."

Sam snorted. "Says the gent who's never kissed a girl his whole life. As if you're an expert."

"I've kissed my ma."

"That hardly counts," Sam said. "This is serious. If Lorette keeps on as she has, she might well snare me."

"Sounds to me like she already has."

The trouble was, Sam felt the same. He'd fought it and fought it, but day by day he grew more and more fond of her. It had reached the point where he looked forward to her company and to admiring her when she wasn't looking.

"You ask me, you're the luckiest hombre alive," Reuben said wistfully. "I'll probably end my days a bachelor."

"You never know."

"I'm not much to look at, and my family is on the poor side. There's nothing about me that would make a girl sit up and take notice. If one ever does, I'll be on her like a bear on honey and have her say she will before she comes to her senses. I won't care if she only has one ear or two noses."

Sam laughed.

"Some of us don't get to be choosy. We take what comes our way and are thankful for it."

"You're saying I should leap into her arms?"

"From what I hear, the woman is supposed to leap into yours. Me, it wouldn't matter if she tripped and stumbled into mine. Once I've got my arms around her, I'm not letting go."

Sam smiled. He enjoyed Reuben's company. Some of the others, his own brother among them, thought that

Reuben was slow between the ears, but that wasn't true. Reuben was shy more than slow, and didn't open up, didn't show his true self, until he knew someone well.

"I just hope my dream gal comes along before I'm too old to appreciate her," Reuben was saying. "As it is, I'm almost middle-aged."

Sam was well aware that most men lived to about fifty. Sixty and higher was rare, which was why everyone marveled at old Ebidiah Troutman. The geezer had lived long enough for two men. "You have a ways to go yet."

"If I'm not hitched by twenty-five, I doubt I ever will be. I'll end up a lonely old man, sitting in a rocking chair with a dog at my feet. The whole world will have passed me by."

"You're being ridiculous," Sam said. "None of us can predict what will be." If someone had told him a couple of months ago he'd fall for Lorette Kurst, he'd have laughed himself silly.

Reuben abruptly drew rein and stared at the woods. "Did you just hear something?"

Sam brought his dun to a halt. "No."

"I thought . . ." Reuben said, and didn't finish.

"Thought what?" Sam said.

An arrow streaked out of the night and embedded itself in the center of Reuben's chest. The impact jolted Reuben. He looked down at the feathers and then at Sam and bleated, "No!" He reached for the shaft but his hand never made it. His whole body went limp, and he fell in slow motion, his eyes and mouth wide, blood oozing from a corner of his mouth.

For all of five seconds Sam sat riveted with horror. A rush of footfalls galvanized him into grabbing for the Walker Colt in his saddle holster. But he didn't quite have hold of it when rough hands seized him and he was flung violently to the ground. A foot caught him in the ribs. Another clipped his temple. He opened his mouth to scream but a blow to the back of his head rendered him nearly senseless.

He felt hands on his arms and legs, felt himself lifted. Struggling to stay conscious, Sam fought a wave of nausea. He heard whispers in an Indian tongue. He hadn't gotten a clear look at his attackers yet but he didn't need to.

They were Comanches.

Sam didn't resist. He couldn't. His head swam and he was weak all over. Four of them were carrying him by his arms and legs. All he could see were the tops of trees, and stars. He turned his head and almost blacked out. More warriors were all around him. They moved like so many panthers.

Sam's mouth went dry. The tales he'd heard of Comanche atrocities were enough to curdle the blood. He could imagine what they aimed to do to him.

Reuben had been the lucky one.

Sam shuddered. "Oh Lord," he said, not meaning to. It slipped out.

The warrior holding his right arm cuffed him and barked something that might have been Comanche for "Quiet!"

The cuff didn't help Sam's head any. He had an urge to cry but didn't. He wasn't a boy anymore. He was a man. He must face what came as Luke or his pa would. But heavens, he was scared.

He became aware of sounds behind them and twisted his head enough to make out the dark outline of a horse. A Comanche was leading his dun by the reins. He didn't see Reuben's animal.

At the top of the hill was a clearing. Several Comanches were waiting, with a lot of horses. Not one of the Indians said a thing. It was as if they had done this so many times, they didn't need to. They knew just what to do.

Sam was thrown over a horse, belly-down. A saddle was under him, and he realized the horse was his own dun. His hands and feet were grasped, and the Indians bound him, wrists and ankles.

The Comanches swung onto their mounts, and the war party was under way. A stocky warrior led the dun.

Sam tried not to think of what was in store for him, but how could he not? They were taking him to his doom.

Chapter 57

Lorette didn't trust her older brothers. For as far back as she could recollect, Harland had always been up to no good. He was a wily fox, that Harland, always scheming, always thinking of ways to do this or that.

Thaxter wasn't wily but he was deadly. Ungodly quick with that six-shooter of his, he had no qualms about killing anything under the sun. For all his deadliness, though, he didn't have a mind of his own. He did whatever Harland wanted. If Harland told him to jump, he'd ask how high. Thaxter was Harland's shadow. As dark a shadow as there could be.

When Harland announced at the secret meeting that he and Thaxter would deal with their pa over Harland's decision to be shed of the Burnetts and the Weavers, she immediately suspected the worst. She wouldn't put anything past the pair.

More than a few times she'd heard them remark that their lives would be so much better with their pa out of the way.

The notion was obscene, sons killing their own pa. It sickened her to think about it.

Lorette was different from her big brothers. She wasn't as heartless. She wasn't brutal.

She'd always been a willful girl. She liked to get her own way. What female didn't?

She'd also be the first to admit she was uncommonly playful with the menfolk. A regular vixen, an aunt once called her, and it stuck in her head. She liked the sound of it. *Vixen*. It rolled on the tongue, sort of like chocolate. To her, playing with males was a grand entertainment.

Most men were simpleminded. Like oxen with a ring in their nose, she could lead them around however she liked. All she had to do was flaunt herself and they'd start drooling.

She'd discovered her power over them when she was quite young.

They were living back east then. One day her folks took her to town. She moseyed over to the general store and saw a boy she knew sucking on hard candy. He had a whole bag. She asked for a piece but the boy said no. Going up to him, she smiled sweetly and touched her finger to his chin and said, "Pretty please."

The boy couldn't give her candy fast enough.

That was her first clue that females had power over males. She thought it only fair.

Men were forever lording over women. Bossing them around. Wanting food, or to have their clothes stitched, and whatnot.

A woman's power balanced the scales. It let her wrap a man around her little finger, and get him to do things in return.

Lorette had used her power right and left, giddy with delight at how boys bowed and scraped for her. It was marvelous. They took her so serious when all she was doing was playing with them.

Until now.

Until the lone exception came along.

Never in a million years would Lorette have imagined she'd fall for someone as she had for Sam. Not when she was still so young. Later, yes, after she'd sown a few oats. But not now.

In her daydreams, she'd always imagined falling for a dashing, strapping gent who would sweep her off her feet with his good looks and charm and sheer manliness.

Sam was boyish. He wasn't strapping. He was polite, and nice, but she wouldn't call him charming. Yet almost from the moment they were thrown together, she was drawn to him, like a female moth to a male flame. She experienced feelings she'd never felt before. Powerful feelings that mightily stirred her heart.

Now, Lorette wanted him with her day and night. She couldn't stand to be apart. She moped and pouted.

Lorette was in love. It took a lot for her to admit it. She loved Sam Burnett and she was using her power on him to make him her very own.

On this particular morning, Lorette had been up a short while and was at the fire, drinking coffee. She was thinking about the secret meeting, and Harland's comment.

Her pa was across from her, gulping the black brew. He was usually surly until he'd had a few.

"Morning, Pa," Lorette said.

Her pa grunted.

Harland and Thaxter came to the fire, Harland smiling that sly smile of his. "That coffee sure smells good."

"Better than you do," Lorette said.

Harland acted as if he were hurt. "Why say a thing like that? What did I do to you?"

"You were born," Lorette said.

"That'll be enough, daughter," their pa said.

"If you only knew," Lorette said.

Before her pa could respond, Harland turned to him and said, "We'd like to have a talk with you, Pa, Thax and me."

"So talk."

"Not here." Harland glanced pointedly at the other fire, where Owen and Luke Burnett and Jasper Weaver were seated. "Off a ways, if you don't mind."

"There's nothing so important you can't tell me here and now," his pa said grumpily.

"This is," Harland insisted.

His pa gave him a sour look and was about to say something when a riderless lathered horse came cantering in and stopped and shook itself.

"What the hell?" Thaxter blurted.

"Ain't that the Weaver boy's animal?" Silsby said.

Lorette sprang to her feet with the rest. She reached the horse at the same moment as Jasper Weaver.

Jasper touched his fingertips to the saddle, and paled. He held his fingers for them to see the scarlet smears, and said, aghast, "This is blood."

"Injuns, I bet," her pa said.

"Oh, God," Jasper said, staring at the saddle in pure horror.

"Wait a minute," Owen Burnett said. "Where's Sam? The two of them were riding herd. They usually stick together even though they're not supposed to."

At the mention of her true love, Lorette felt a piercing pain in her chest, as if her heart had been cleaved in two. "Sam?" she said breathlessly, and was running toward the horse string before she realized what she was doing.

"Hold on, girl," her father bellowed. "You can't go riding off by your lonesome."

Lorette wasn't about to stop for him or anyone. She picked up her saddle blanket, but before she could throw it on, Silsby and Iden were on either side of her and took her by the arms. "What do you think you're doing?" she demanded, so furious she almost sank her teeth into Silsby's wrist.

"Pa told us to stop you," Iden said.

"Hold still, you she-cat," Silsby said, struggling to restrain her.

The rest were hurrying over, all with their rifles, Jasper Weaver strapping on the six-shooter he never used.

Her pa assumed command. "Hold on. We can't all go. Someone has to stay and watch the camp. Silsby and Iden, that will be you. Keep your guns handy and your eyes peeled." He paused. "Daughter, you should stay, too."

"Like blazes I will," Lorette said.

"It should be the men," her pa said. "These are Comanches we're talking about."

"Oh, God," Jasper Weaver said.

"I can shoot as straight as any of you," Lorette argued, "and can ride a damn sight better than most. I'm coming unless you tie me up, and I'll scratch the eyes out of anyone who tries." To emphasize her point, she tore free of Silsby and Iden and moved to her mare.

"We don't have time for this squabbling," Jasper Weaver said, his voice breaking with emotion.

"You Kursts hash it out," Owen Burnett said, and he and Luke stepped to their mounts.

"Damn it all," her pa said. "All right, girl. You can come. But you do as you're told, you hear me?"

"Whatever you say, pa," Lorette replied, and just to spite him, she smiled sweetly.

Chapter 58

Owen Burnett was never so worried in his life. As he rode alongside Jasper Weaver, he broke out in a cold sweat. He loved Samuel. Loved the boy dearly. And he greatly feared they would find the mutilated and scalped bodies of their sons.

It was always there, that fear. It came from living in the wilds of the Texas hill country, where hostiles roamed and outlaws prowled and beasts ripped their prey with fang and claw.

Fortunately, massacres were rare, outlaws few, and bear and mountain lion attacks infrequent.

Living in the wilds was always a gamble, but when Owen weighed the risks against the pride of having his own farm and not being beholden to anyone, his pride won.

His family was willing to accept the risks because they believed as he did.

Which was small comfort in the still hours of the night when he'd lie in bed listening to Philomena breathe and a howl off in the hills reminded him where they were.

Now, with the image of the blood on Jasper's fingertips vivid in his mind, Owen prayed he hadn't made a mistake he would forever regret. "Samuel," he said under his breath. "Please, not my Samuel."

They were going much too slowly to suit him.

Gareth was out in front, scouring for sign as they went, his oldest sons flanking him. They were good trackers, what with their years of hunting.

They were backtracking the dun. Or trying to. The ground was hard and the dun's prints were mixed with the many made before.

Owen couldn't make sense of it. Which was why he didn't complain, but he chafed at the delay. They needed to reach the boys quickly.

"God in heaven," Jasper said loudly to be heard over the pounding of hooves. "I hope we're wrong. I hope that blood doesn't mean what I think it means."

"Maybe they tussled with a longhorn," Owen said, not taking his eyes off the Kursts. "Or he hurt himself somehow."

"Wilda will be crushed if anything happens to that boy," Jasper said plaintively. "She adores him."

"Don't give up hope."

Gareth picked up the pace. Now and then he rose in the stirrups to scan the hills. They were nearing the east end of the grassland when he rose yet again, and thrust out an arm. "There!" he bellowed, and used his spurs.

Owen brought his chestnut to a gallop. The sight of a body sprawled in the grass made him gasp.

The body was on its belly and the barbed tip of an arrow stuck from between the shoulder blades.

Luke flew past Owen. His horse was the fastest in the family, and he was lashing his reins like a madman. He caught up to Gareth just as Gareth drew rein, and was out of the saddle before his horse came to a stop. Running to the body, he bent and rolled it over.

Jasper Weaver groaned so loudly, it was almost a wail. Swinging down, Jasper started toward the body, tripped, and caught himself. He swayed, stumbled, and sank to his knees. Raising his face to the heavens, he let out a shriek such as Owen never thought a human throat could make.

"No! No! No!"

Owen dismounted. Everyone else stayed in their saddles, Lorette as pale as a sheet, her father and her brothers glancing all around, Gareth and Harland with their rifles out.

"Jasper, I'm so sorry," Owen said, placing his hand on his friend's shoulder.

"Reuben," Jasper gurgled as if his throat were filled with water. Tears poured from his eyes and he feebly clutched at his son's shirt.

No words would suffice so Owen said nothing.

"We can't waste time here," Gareth Kurst said.

"Gareth, please," Owen said.

"Aren't you forgetting someone, Burnett?" Gareth said curtly. "Or don't you give a damn about your own flesh and blood?"

A red-hot flame seared Owen from head to toe. "Oh, God."

"Mr. Kurst is right, Pa," Luke said. "Sam's not here. They must have taken Sam. His horse, too. We have to go after them right this minute."

"Of course," Owen said, feeling like the fool of all fools. He let go of Jasper and moved to his chestnut.

"You should come with us, Weaver," Gareth said.

"No," Jasper said, his cheeks and chin wet, his nose running. He shook his head. "I'll take my son back. I don't want to leave him like this. Animals might . . ." He didn't finish.

"Suit yourself," Gareth said.

Harland and Thaxter were by the trees. "Here, Pa," Harland said, gesturing. "They went this way."

Gareth gigged his big roan over and looked down. "Good eyes, boy." He turned to all of them. "From here on out we go as quiet as we can. Be set to shoot. They might hear us or spot us coming."

Thaxter patted his Colt. "I'd love to kill me some redskins."

"These are Comanches," Gareth said. "They don't die easy."

Luke was back in the saddle and spurred his horse past them. "You talked about wasting time," he snapped, and headed up the hill.

"What's his problem?" Wylie said.

"It's his brother, you lunkhead," Lorette said, and jabbed her own spurs to overtake Luke.

Owen followed. He felt guilty at leaving Jasper, but Sam came first. There was a chance his son was still alive;

sometimes the Comanches played with their victims a while.

The slope was steep. Owen was glad when he broke out of the brush at the summit into a clearing.

Luke and Lorette had already sprung down and drawn, and Lorette was scouring the ground. Apparently she could track, too.

"There were a heap of them," she said, turning in small circles. "They have Sam's horse. See there? The shod one?"

Gareth gigged his animal over to her. "A dozen, at least. They left their horses here and snuck down on foot." He bent low and rubbed his chin. "When they came back they were carrying someone. I saw the tracks on my way up."

"Sam," Owen said, his heart sinking.

"They can't have gotten far, Burnett," Gareth said. "This happened maybe two hours ago."

"What are we waiting for?" Luke said, moving to his mount. "Let's light a shuck."

Owen couldn't give chase fast enough. Every minute of delay increased the likelihood of finding Sam dead.

Gareth reined around. "Stay behind me and ride in single file. We'll raise less dust that way."

"Hold on, Pa," Harland said, and glanced at Thaxter, who nodded.

"What is it, boy?" Gareth asked impatiently.

"Why should we risk our skins for Sam Burnett? He's not any kin of ours. Let the Burnetts go on by themselves."

"Harland!" Lorette said.

"Don't give me that look, sis," Harland said. "You want to help them, fine. We all know why."

"Damn you boy," Gareth said.

"We don't want any part of it," Harland said. "Thaxter and Wylie and me."

"I'll do whatever Pa says," Wylie said.

Owen was practically beside himself. "My son's life is in danger and you do *this*?"

Gareth motioned at Owen. "Go on ahead with your

oldest and Lorette and Wylie. We'll catch up as soon as I have a little talk with my oldest."

"Don't take too long," Owen said. "We'll need your help." There weren't enough of them, otherwise, to effect a rescue.

"I won't be but a couple of minutes behind you," Gareth assured him.

"Maybe longer, Pa," Harland said.

"Lots longer," Thaxter said.

Luke and Lorette were making for the other side of the clearing.

Owen trailed after them, with Wylie behind him. He looked back as the woods closed around them.

Gareth and Harland and Thaxter had climbed down, and Gareth was walking toward them with his fists balled.

Owen wouldn't want to be in their boots, as mad as Gareth looked.

Harland, strangely enough, was grinning an odd sort of grin.

Chapter 59

If anyone were to ask, Jasper Weaver would tell them that the most awful feeling in the world was to be on a horse with the body of your only son thrown over the saddle in front of you. He had one hand on the body to keep it from sliding off.

Jasper wasn't aware of much else. Tears blurred his vision. His nose was clogged. And all he could hear was the pounding of his own heart, beating a dirge in his ears. His chest hurt, and he wondered if his heart might be about to give out.

Jasper didn't care if he keeled over. He'd lost the person he loved most in the world. Sure, he cared for Wilda. She was his wife. She was also a nag and more than a bit of a bitch. But he didn't care for her as he'd cared for Reuben.

From the moment his son was born, Jasper had done the best he could to be a good father. He never beat the boy, like Gareth Kurst beat his, or treated his son as if he was of little account, as Gareth often did. He didn't demand that his son treat his every word as if it was the word of God Almighty, as Gareth was known to do.

No, Jasper had treated Reuben with respect. Reuben had been his pride and his joy of joys.

And now Reuben was dead.

The tears wouldn't stop.

Jasper blinked and sniffled and took his hand off the body to grope behind him at his saddlebag. He got it open, slid his hand inside, and found his flask. Eagerly opening it, he took a gulp and shivered with pleasure as the whiskey warmed his throat and then his belly. It helped to relieve the hurt.

"Oh, Reuben," Jasper said softly. "My sweet son."

Jasper swiped at his eyes with his sleeve. He swiped at his nose, too. He tipped his flask again, and once more, and wished he could stop and climb down and crawl into a ball and cry himself dry.

"God, I am in misery," Jasper said to the air. "How could you do this to me? He was everything."

Jasper hardly noticed the longhorns on one side and the wooded hills on the other. He did glance over once and thought he saw a figure way back in the trees. But when he looked again, it wasn't there. A trick of his tears, he reckoned, and quietly sobbed.

The camp came into sight, smoke rising from a fire. *The damned camp,* Jasper thought. His son was dead because of this cattle business. Because his wife had made him take part. Because she wanted them to be rich, or as close to rich as they'd ever come.

"May she rot in hell," Jasper said, and sucked on his flask. It was her fault, not his. She had cost them the one truly good thing that had come out of their marriage. Gentle, kind Reuben.

Figures were coming toward him.

Jasper wiped away more tears and saw it was Silsby and Iden. He'd forgotten their pa left them to watch the herd. "Boys," he said hoarsely by way of greeting, and drew rein.

"Mr. Weaver," Iden said, but he wasn't looking at Jasper.

"Is that Reuben?" Silsby said.

"What happened?" Iden asked.

"Is he dead?" Silsby said.

"Do you see him moving?" Jasper said harshly, not intending to sound mean. "Do you see the blood?"

"What happened?" Iden asked again.

"Injuns." Carefully climbing down, Jasper wrapped his arms around the body and began to lower it. Both boys leaped to help, and he felt bad for snapping at them. Together, they carried Reuben over near the fire and laid him on his back.

Jasper folded both arms across Reuben's chest and squatted there, gazing down on the face of his precious, dead boy.

"Was it the Comanches?" Iden said.

"Who else?" Silsby said.

Jasper tried to speak but his throat wouldn't work. Instead, he coughed and nodded and more tears trickled.

"I'm awful sorry, Mr. Weaver," Iden said. "I liked Reuben. A lot. Him and me got along fine."

"He was always so friendly," Silsby said.

"I know," Jasper was able to say. Of all the Kursts, these two had been the only ones to treat Reuben halfway nice. The older ones treated him as if he were brainless. Jasper would never forgive them for that, not as long as he lived.

Iden hunkered next to him. "They killed him with an arrow."

Jasper nodded.

"What about Sam? Were they together?"

Jasper nodded a second time.

"Did they kill Sam, too?"

"Took him," Jasper said with an effort.

"The Comanches got hold of Sam?" Iden said.

"He's a goner then," Silsby said.

"Where's Pa and everyone else?" Iden asked.

"Went after Sam," Jasper said. He realized he was still holding his flask and raised it to his lips. It was empty.

"Pa and them went after Sam?" Iden said.

"He just told us they did," Silsby said. "Quit saying everything he does."

"It's just . . ." Iden touched Reuben's shoulder. "He made me smile. And never spoke ill of anybody."

"Thank you," Jasper said.

"For what?"

"For that," Jasper said.

"We should bury him," Silsby said.

"I'm taking him home to bury," Jasper said. So he could visit the grave every day.

"At least cover him with a blanket," Silsby said. "We have more important things to worry about."

"There was nothing on this earth more important to me than my son," Jasper said.

"How about breathing?" Silsby said.

"What are you on about?" Iden said.

"The Comanches, little brother." Silsby hefted his rifle. "They might still be hereabouts looking to kill more whites."

Iden stood and anxiously gazed about. "I didn't think of that. You could be right. And us out in the open like this."

"The Comanches are long gone," Jasper said. "Their tracks led off to the north."

"They can circle around, can't they?" Silsby said. "Or there could be more spread over the countryside. You don't know."

Jasper didn't like his tone. "I know I'm not sticking around. In fact, I'm leaving right this minute. I'm taking my son and going home, and I don't care if I see another longhorn, or any of you, for as long as I live."

"Why, you miserable drunk," Silsby said. "Is that any way to treat us?"

"Sil, don't," Iden said.

"You heard him."

"He's just lost his son," Iden said.

"Who cares?" Silsby said, and smirked at Jasper. He was still smirking when an arrow sheared into his left cheek, tore clear through his face, and burst out his right cheek in a shower of blood and bits of teeth. Silsby staggered, and a scarlet river poured from his mouth.

"Sil!" Iden cried, and there were two swift thunks, one after the other. He staggered, too, and gaped at a pair of arrows that had transfixed him from front to back. Turning on a boot heel, he said, "No!" and collapsed.

Jasper saw it all as if in a haze. He saw Silsby swing toward the hill and raise his rifle, saw a lance catch him in the neck and jut out the other side. Silsby clutched at it, and crashed down.

Belatedly, Jasper grabbed for his six-gun but he couldn't

draw. He was still holding his empty flask. He threw the flask down and got his fingers around his revolver just as shadows fell across him. He looked up.

Painted faces surrounded him, the sun glinting off of their knives and tomahawks.

"Lord, no," Jasper said, and tried to throw himself back.

A rain of weapons fell. He was stabbed, cut, clubbed. So much pain, yet he barely felt it. All he could think of was Reuben. He fell to his hands and knees but the rain didn't stop. He was being chopped and hacked to pieces. Through a haze he saw his son lying just past a pair of moccasins, and thrust his hand between them. He got hold of Reuben's arm, Reuben's hand. Clasping it, he closed his eyes. He didn't mind dying. He would be with Reuben again.

I'm coming, son.

Chapter 60

Gareth Kurst was mad. It always made him mad when his sons refused to listen. When he told them to do something, he expected them to do it. No sass. No fuss. He'd ingrained that into them at an early age with a belt and the back of his hand.

Now, Gareth stared at his two oldest and simmered. "I can't believe my ears."

"Believe them," Harland said.

Gareth came close to punching him in the face; but they would need his help saving the Burnett boy. "I told you we're going to go after Sam Burnett, and we are."

"We don't want to, Pa," Harland replied, "and we're old enough that we should be able to make up our own minds."

Gareth looked at Thaxter, who nodded. "I don't know what's gotten into you two, talking to me like this. We do as I say. What you want doesn't enter into it."

"It does now," Harland said.

"What are you up to?" Gareth demanded.

"Something that is long overdue," Harland said. "We should have done this years ago."

"Is that so?" Gareth was going to thrash his oldest to within an inch of his life. But first he would hear him out. There was something going on here he didn't quite savvy.

"We've put up with you beating on us for far too long. We're grown-up now, Pa. We're not little boys. We're none of us ten anymore. It's about time you treated us how we deserve to be treated."

"And how is that?"

"As men," Harland said. "As equal with you."

"So that's what this is."

"Harland speaks for both of us," Thaxter threw in.

"I know you're full grown," Gareth said.

"You don't treat us as if we are," Harland replied. "You don't let us make up our minds about anything."

"You make all our decisions for us," Thaxter complained.

Gareth was mildly amused at them being so foolish. "That's not true. You pick the clothes you wear. You go into town and drink on your own."

"Only when you say we can," Harland said. "Everything is you, you, you, Pa. You've lorded it over us, and over Ma, since I can remember. And you'll never change."

"Not ever," Thaxter said.

Gareth's amusement faded. They had never come at him together like this, and it troubled him. The last time any of them stood up to him was a couple of years ago when Harland balked at being told he wasn't to bring any liquor home from town. Gareth had found a bottle in Harland's saddlebags and didn't want the stuff around his younger boys.

Harland astounded him by saying he would bring whiskey home if he pleased, and there was nothing Gareth could do about it. Gareth proved him wrong by beating him senseless with his bare fists. No one had dared mouth off to him since.

"Where do your brothers and sister stand in this?" Gareth wanted to know.

"Sis didn't want any part of it," Harland said.

"She always had more brains than you," Gareth said.

"Wylie and Silsby and Iden agree with us, but they're letting us do the talking," Harland said.

"Silsby and Iden are afraid of you," Thaxter said.

"They have brains, too," Gareth said.

"Now you see?" Harland said. "Talk like that doesn't

help. You treat us with no more respect than you do the Comanches."

"That's not true," Gareth said. "I have respect for them."

Thaxter swore and scowled. "There you go again. Treating us like we're lumps of coal."

"What did you expect?" Harland said.

"Do you know what I think, Harland?" Gareth said, his simmer starting to rise to a boil. "I think this is all your doing. You've always been the troublemaker in our family. The one who wouldn't listen. The one I had to punish the most."

"You beat me and slapped me and kicked me more times than I can count," Harland said.

"Whose fault was that? Who wouldn't do his chores unless I made him? Who wouldn't clean up after himself? Who would rather lie around all day doing nothing?"

"A man has that right if he wants," Harland growled.

"You weren't a man then and you're not a man now," Gareth told him. "And sure, I hit you when you deserved it. But I never broke your bones. You don't have any scars from it." He sneered in disgust. "Hell, a little cuff now and then was good for you. It taught you to mind your elders."

Harland looked at Thaxter. "See?"

"We knew how he'd take it," Thaxter said.

Squaring his shoulders, Harland stepped up to Gareth. "From this day on, Pa, we go our own way. We do as we please and not as you want. We make our own decisions. Agree to that and we'll get along fine."

"Is that so?"

Harland nodded. "Our first decision is that we don't need anyone to help us get the cattle to market. We've told you before, but you wouldn't listen."

"No, you wouldn't," Thaxter echoed.

"If they survive the Comanches, we're going to be shed of the Burnetts and Jasper Weaver."

"You blamed jackass."

"Talk like that doesn't help you any."

"You're the one who will need help." Gareth tensed to strike. "The pair of you, for bucking me like this."

Harland paid no heed to the threat. "We don't give a good damn about them."

"How about your sister? Do you give a damn about her? She's with them, and she'll need our help."

"That's on her head," Harland said. "She's the one panting after Sam Burnett. Let her save him."

"That's right," Thaxter said.

"We're going after them whether you like it or not."

"We're staying put, Pa."

"Over my dead body," Gareth said. He had talked enough. It was time to commence pounding.

"If that's how it has to be," Harland said, and his left hand swept out and around.

Gareth caught the gleam of steel. He started to bring his fists up, and felt a searing sensation in his vitals. He looked down at a knife buried to the hilt. "You . . ." he blurted.

"I did," Harland said.

Gareth's legs were like water. Clutching himself, he pitched to his knees.

Harland and Thaxter were staring at him as calmly as if they were butchering a hog.

"Boys . . ." Gareth said. He was stunned into bewilderment. His own sons had done this to him. *His own sons.*

"We run the family now, Pa," Harland said. "You're not the king of the roost anymore."

"Long live the king," Thaxter said.

Gareth felt himself slipping away. He reached out for them as if from the end of a long, dark tunnel.

The last thing he heard was Harland's laughter.

Chapter 61

Lorette Kurst was beside herself with worry. Sam—in the clutches of the Comanches. It was hard to concentrate on the tracks she was following, she was so worried.

Owen and Luke Burnett were behind her, Wylie behind them. She had the impression he wasn't pushing his horse quite as hard as he could. It made her furious that he didn't seem to care if they saved Sam, but now wasn't the time to take him to task.

They had been riding for more than a mile, the morning sun warm on her back. The war party had made no effort to hide their trail, which made it easy. Too easy, she thought. Either they were sure no one would come after them, or they wanted to lure their pursuers into an ambush.

When she drew rein on a crest to scour the land below, she mentioned that to the Burnetts and her brother.

"I don't care if it is a trap," Owen said. "They have my son."

"Sam is all that matters," Luke said.

"We shouldn't be reckless," Wylie cautioned. "I don't care to be killed on his account."

Lorette simmered.

"You don't have to do this if you don't want to," Owen said to Wylie. "He's not your family."

"Pa said to come, and here I am," Wylie replied.

Owen turned to Lorette. "The same holds for you. I

know you like my son, but you being a girl and all . . ."
He shrugged.

"I can ride and shoot as well as any man," Lorette said
flatly. "I'm coming whether you like it or not."

"No need to take offense, Miss Kurst," Owen said.

"All this babble," Luke said. "Let's get after them."

"Maybe we should wait for my pa and my brothers,"
Wylie said. "They can't be far behind us."

Lorette was a little concerned that her pa hadn't
caught up to them yet. She hadn't liked the look on Harland's face when she rode off. He could be downright
sinister at times.

She rode on, down a long grade and around several
hills to a ridge that overlooked a valley. She smelled
smoke and thought, *Surely not.* But there they were. The
Comanches had made camp. A small fire had been kindled and what looked to be a skinned rabbit was roasting
on a spit. The warriors were clustered around it, talking.

"Sam!" Owen whispered.

Lorette had already seen him, bound hand and foot
and lying on his side. He was still alive, then. Her eyes
moistened with tears of pure joy.

"I count fourteen," Wylie said. "Too many for us
alone. We'll have to wait for Pa and the others."

"What if they take too long?" Owen said. "What if the
Comanches start in on Sam before Gareth gets here?"

"There's that," Luke said.

"It'd be foolish, just the four of us," Wylie said.

Lorette had made up her mind. "I'm not waiting. I'm
sneaking down and getting him out of there."

"Be sensible, sis," Wylie said. "They're out in the open.
You can't get anywhere near him without being seen."

"I will think of a way. Stay here if you want. I don't
need your help. Or Pa's. Or anyone's." To forestall an
argument, Lorette reined to the west and rode in a loop
that brought her up on the Indians through a patch of
woods. The cedars and the oaks hid her well enough that
she could get pretty close.

The Burnetts went with her.

Wylie didn't.

Lorette palmed her Colt, checked the cylinder, and shoved the Colt back in her holster. She must make every shot count. With luck she might drop six, but the other eight would be on her before she could reload. She needed to distract them somehow. She saw the fire, and slowed.

Owen brought his chestnut alongside her mare. "I wish you would reconsider. Leave this to Luke and me."

"Go to hell."

"That's harsh talk, young woman."

"You haven't seen harsh yet." Lorette glared at him. "You better get one thing straight here and now, Mr. Burnett. Sam and me are going to be hitched. He's your son, but he's my man. And he'll be my man as long as I draw breath."

"Well, now," Owen said, looking considerably astounded. "You're laying your cards on the table."

"Not cards," Lorette said. "My heart. I'm tired of hiding how I feel from you and everyone else. I want Sam and he wants me even if he doesn't entirely know it yet. So I'll thank you to shut up about leaving this to you and Luke. I'm saving Sam or I'll die trying, and that's all there is to it."

Owen's mouth curled in a grin.

"What?"

"For a second there, you sounded just like Philomena."

Lorette took that as a compliment, although she didn't think she was anything like her. "What can we do to keep those redskins busy long enough for us to get in and get out with Sam?"

"I have no idea."

"Think about it," Lorette said. "Not about me."

Owen smiled. "You're a remarkable young lady."

"Oh, hell."

"It's nothing to be mad about."

"If I was a man, you wouldn't think I was remarkable. A female does what you males do and suddenly she's special. I'm not a lady. I'm a girl. Or a woman, I reckon, now that I'm hankering after your son."

"You don't hold anything back, do you?"

"I learned not to. My ma has no gumption, and my pa bosses her around and beats her if she doesn't please him. It's taught me a female has to stand up for herself or men will run roughshod over her. It's taught me to speak my own mind, and to hell with anyone who thinks different."

"Good heavens."

They were close enough to the Comanche camp that Lorette had to draw rein or the warriors might hear them. Luke and Wylie came up on the other side of her.

"How do we do this?" Luke said.

"We don't know yet," Owen said.

Lorette fidgeted with impatience. "We can't take all day. Once their bellies are full, they'll begin in on Sam with their knives and tomahawks. Wylie, do you have any ideas?"

"Wait for Pa and Harland and Thaxter. We can use their guns."

"They're taking too damn long," Lorette said, and drew her Colt. "It's time to do or die."

Chapter 62

Sam Burnett lay tense with fear. His throat was parched, his body ached. The suspense ate at him like a horde of bugs with tiny teeth, not knowing when the Comanches would come over and start in on him.

To be so helpless compounded his fear. Bound as he was, all he could do was lie there and wait for the horror to commence. He was so scared, he shook, but stopped through sheer force of will.

If he was going to die, Sam decided, he'd do it with some degree of dignity. He remembered a friend of his grandfather's who had died screaming and blubbering and acting so pathetically, everyone in the room turned their heads in shame. Sam had only been seven at the time, but the memory stuck with him. As they were leaving, his ma had said to his pa, "I'm sorry the children saw that." And his pa had nodded and said quietly so no one else heard, "He had no dignity."

Dignity. It meant to have respect for yourself. Sam liked that notion. So if his time had come, he'd do his best to die with dignity.

Just then a pair of warriors rose and strode toward him.

Sam braced for the worst. His moment had come. He met their stares and tried not to show fear.

They were much alike. Their black hair was parted in the middle and hung down in braids on either side of their head. They had high foreheads, and long noses, and oval faces. In a way they were almost handsome. They showed no emotion, no hatred or contempt. They hunkered and looked at him flatly, and then one reached out, cupped his chin, and turned his head from side to side, studying him.

Sam didn't resist. What good would it do? He'd heard tell that Indians respected bravery, so he put on as brave a front as he could. When the warrior let go, he said, "I never harmed any of you in my life." He didn't know if they understood. Some Comanches were supposed to know English.

The warriors stared, their arms folded across their knees.

"I'm not your enemy," Sam said. He almost added *Please, don't hurt me.* "You have no cause to do this."

By their expressions, Sam judged they didn't savvy.

The warrior on the left grunted and said something in their tongue to the one who had cupped Sam's chin. The one who had cupped him replied, then said, "Whites kill his son."

"What?" Sam said. "I didn't kill anyone."

"Whites kill," the warrior said. "So we kill whites."

Sam pushed up onto his elbow. Here was his chance. He must convince them he wasn't to blame. "It wasn't me, I tell you. I've never killed one of you, or any Indians, for that matter."

"You white."

"I can't help how I was born," Sam said. "You should find the one who killed his boy, and kill him."

"All whites die."

"That's not fair."

"You white."

"What kind of logic is that? You can't blame every white for what one did. That's wrong."

The pair stood.

"Please," Sam said. "Be reasonable. I don't want to die for something I didn't do."

The warrior who had lost his son said something to the other one.

"What did he say? Will he spare me or not?"

"Not," the other one said.

They turned and headed back to the fire.

"Wait!" Sam cried. They ignored him. Several of the others looked over and laughed. "I didn't do anything!" he shouted in anger, and some of them laughed louder.

Sam sagged in despair, his cheek on the hard ground. They didn't care that he hadn't killed that warrior's son. A white man had, and he was white, and that was enough.

"Lord, help me," Sam said.

His only hope lay in getting away. The rabbit wasn't quite cooked yet, so he had a little time. Rousing, he glared at his captors. They weren't so smart. They hadn't searched him when they jumped him. They didn't know he had a clasp knife in his front pocket.

The problem was, his wrists were tied behind his back. He couldn't get at the knife.

Sam shifted position, careful not to make any sudden movement that would warn the warriors. He could move his hands as far as his hip but no further. The pocket was inches away. It might as well be on the moon.

Sam stretched his arms and his fingers, but he was still short. He loosened his shoulder by wriggling it but only gained a quarter of an inch, if that.

Sam's life depended on that knife. He had an inspiration. To test if it would work, he commenced to buck and struggle, kicking his legs and thrashing. The Comanches were amused. They knew he was tied tight and couldn't get free. A thin warrior mimicked his movements, which the rest thought was hilarious.

Good, Sam thought. Rolling onto his back, he thrust his boots at the sky and flapped his bound legs up and down and back and forth. The Comanches loved that. They laughed and clapped each other on the back.

There was a purpose to Sam's antics. He thrust his legs as high as he could, his eyes never leaving his upended pocket. One end of the clasp knife poked out. He thrashed harder and more of it slipped free. Frantic, he pumped in a frenzy, and the clasp knife slid out and fell at his side.

The Comanches hadn't seen. They were having great fun at his expense.

Sam let his legs drop and slumped in fatigue with the knife behind him. He groped and found it. Opening the blade wasn't hard. Reversing his grip, he pressed the edge to the loop around his wrists.

They'd used pieces cut from his own rope to tie him. He bought the rope at the start of the roundup, and new rope was always harder to cut.

Sam moved the knife like a saw, back and forth, back and forth. His wrists began to hurt. The angle was awkward. But with his life at stake, he'd be damned if a little pain would stop him.

A warrior had taken the rabbit from the fire and the spit was being passed around. Each man tore off a piece and gave the spit to the next man.

Sam wished they were eating a buffalo. It would take longer. He gritted his teeth and cut and the pain grew worse. He risked glancing over his shoulder to see how he was doing but couldn't see his wrists. All he could do was keep at it. Eventually, the rope would part.

Sam thought of his folks, and his brother and sisters. And Lorette. He wanted to see them again. To hug them and eat and laugh with them, and be alive.

He was so intent on the rope, he didn't realize several warriors had risen and were coming toward him until their footsteps alerted him. He looked up.

The Comanche who had lost his son drew his knife.

Desperate, still cutting, Sam said, "Isn't there anything I can say that will change your mind?"

Apparently not.

The warrior bent toward him.

Chapter 63

Crouched as close to the Comanche camp as she could get, Lorette Kurst ran her thumb over the hammer of her Colt and waited for the other Burnetts to do their part.

Lorette had come up with an idea, but it was risky. Owen went along with it because he couldn't come up with a better one. Nor could Luke, who surprised her when they separated by shaking her hand and saying, "So long as you're serious and not out to hurt my brother's feelings, I'm fine with you being with him."

"I'd never hurt Sam in a million years," Lorette assured him.

Luke had stared hard at her, then nodded. "I believe you." He let go of her hand and patted his Remington. "Let's kill some Comanches."

That last comment bothered Lorette. Luke was too eager to start shooting. He didn't seem to care that they were outnumbered. She'd seen him practice, and yes, he was quick, but quick didn't count for much when you were outnumbered three to one.

Lorette gnawed on her bottom lip, a habit of hers when she was nervous. Another minute or so and Owen Burnett would set things in motion.

Her brother was with the horses. Wylie would bring them fast if shooting broke out. She only hoped it was fast enough.

Without warning, several warriors stood and moved toward Sam. One drew a knife.

Her breath catching in her throat, Lorette tensed to rush to Sam's rescue. She would drop as many Indians as she could and pray Owen and Luke got there to help before she and Sam were riddled with arrows.

Suddenly hooves pounded not far off. The three Comanches by Sam turned and those at the fire rose. Soon another Comanche galloped out of the woods, a quirt in his hand and an eagle feather in his hair.

Lorette prayed that Owen and Luke saw him, and waited. It wouldn't do to start things with the Comanches up and alert on their feet.

The rider didn't dismount. The warrior who had drawn his knife, and another, palavered with him. The warrior on the horse gestured a lot, toward the southwest.

In the direction, Lorette realized, of their herd. She wondered what it was about. Silsby and Iden were watching the cattle. Maybe the Comanches were going to attack them.

Presently half the warriors, including the one with the knife, climbed on their horses. Words were exchanged with those who were staying behind, and then those on horseback departed, led by the warrior with the eagle feather in his hair.

Part of Lorette wanted to go warn her brothers. But if she did, where would that leave Sam?

Awash in despair, she stayed where she was. It was the hardest decision she ever had to make: her own kin or the one she had given her heart to.

Maybe her brothers would be all right, she told herself. Maybe Jasper was back with them by now. Maybe her pa and Harland and Thaxter had gone back, too, for some reason. Maybe, maybe, maybe.

Think only of Sam, Lorette told herself. She looked toward where Owen and Luke were to commence the festivities but didn't see them. She figured they were waiting for the warriors who had gone to be out of earshot and for the remaining warriors to settle back down.

The seven warriors who had stayed returned to the fire. The rabbit had been eaten, some of its bones scattered about. Now and then one or another glanced at

Sam, but they showed no inclination to go over and do him in.

Hope flared in Lorette's breast. It could be they were waiting for the others to return.

Then a tall warrior drew his knife and set to sharpening it on a whetstone. He looked over at Sam, and smirked.

So much for Lorette's spark of hope. She half-turned, seeking some sign of Owen and Luke. They were taking too long to make their move.

The next moment, to Lorette's amazement, Sam was on his feet, a clasp knife in his hand. Racing to his dun, he gripped the saddle horn and swung up. He did it so swiftly that he was in the saddle and hauling on the dun's reins before Lorette could galvanize into motion to help him.

The Comanches were quicker. In the blink of an eye they were on their feet and rushing him, two nocking arrows to bowstrings.

Lorette hurtled into the open, cocking her Colt. She aimed and sent a slug into the warrior nearest to Sam.

The warrior clutched himself, and fell.

The others stopped in their tracks. Half whirled toward her.

One sent an arrow flying toward Sam, who ducked low over the pommel as the shaft was released. It missed him by a whisker.

Lorette focused on the three who were coming toward her. She banged off another shot but missed. She saw Sam rein toward her and shrieked, "No! Get away!"

Sam didn't listen. He jabbed his spurs and reached out his arm to scoop her into it when he reached her. He never saw the arrow that caught him from behind.

Lorette screamed.

Sam lost his grip and tumbled, rolling to a stop almost at her feet. The arrow had gone through his shoulder. He struggled to stand, and Lorette grabbed hold and got her other arm around him.

"I have you."

Together, they backpedaled toward the woods.

The Comanches were almost on them.

A fierce holler and the drum of hooves gave the warriors pause. Luke and Owen Burnett had exploded from the woods, Luke yelling at the top of his lungs to get their attention. The Comanches whirled, and Luke snapped a shot that caused a warrior to stumble.

Owen fired his Spencer.

Caught between Lorette and the charging Burnetts, the Comanches did the only thing they could; they ran toward their own horses, two helping the one Luke had shot. Luke shot another, and the warrior dropped.

Then the Comanches were on the fly. They made it to the cedars on the far side, and disappeared.

Lorette looked down into Sam's smiling face, and her heart seemed to fill her chest. "You've just been shot with an arrow, you lunkhead. What are you smiling about?"

"You came for me," Sam said.

"Did you reckon I wouldn't?" Lorette said, and kissed him.

Luke arrived, swinging off his horse before it stopped moving. "Sam! How bad is it?"

"I'm fine now," Sam said.

Luke helped Lorette lower Sam onto his side and Luke sniffed the tip of the arrow jutting from Sam's shoulder. "I don't think it's tainted."

Lorette remembered that Comanches were notorious for coating their arrowheads with rattler venom or dipping the tips in dead animals so a wound would become infected.

Owen trotted up and commenced to reload his Spencer. "We drove them off, but they might come back. Get that arrow out, Luke, quick."

His teeth clenched, Sam mustered a chuckle. "I can't believe I'm alive. I thought for sure I was a goner."

"We have to get that arrow out quick," Owen repeated. "These hills are crawling with Comanches. I have a suspicion the worst is yet to come."

The devil of it was, so did Lorette.

Chapter 64

The caw of a crow brought Luke Burnett to a stop. It didn't sound natural. His hand on his Remington, Luke rose in the stirrups. He spied a figure in shadow and started to draw, then realized it was the shadow of a tree and not a Comanche.

Luke frowned. He was seeing Comanches where there weren't any. This made three times now.

"Something?" his pa said behind him.

"It's safe," Luke said. Only for the moment; they could run into more Comanches at any time.

"This is taking too long," Lorette complained. "Your brother is in bad shape and should be resting."

Luke turned. They'd extracted the arrow and torn an old shirt of his he'd taken from his saddlebags for bandages. The wound was severe, and his brother sat slumped over, resting his weight on his saddle horn. Beside him, Lorette was holding him steady.

"It can't be helped, Miss Kurst," Owen said. "We have to go slow and keep our eyes skinned for hostiles."

"We haven't seen a redskin in hours," Lorette said. "Let's stop and rest for Sam's sake."

"I'm fine," Sam said weakly.

"Don't lie to me," Lorette said.

Sam slowly straightened. "We have to keep going. Your brothers and Jasper are at the camp. They can help protect you."

"I don't need no damn protecting," Lorette said. "It's you I'm thinking of."

"Language, my dear," Owen said. "I never let my girls talk that way."

"I'm not one of your girls," Lorette said, "and I'll talk as I please."

Luke was tempted to swear, himself. "Stop your bickering. Sam, can you go on or not? Tell me true."

"I can," Sam said.

"He's only saying that on my account," Lorette said.

"He says he can and I believe him," Luke said. "If he shows signs of passing out, let me know and we'll stop."

"You promise?" Lorette said.

"A Burnett keeps his word," Luke said, irritated that she'd think otherwise.

Except for that caw, the hills were strangely still, as if everything sensed that trespassers with violent intent were abroad, and the wildlife was holding its breath in anticipation of the bloodbath.

By Luke's reckoning, their cattle camp was less than two miles away. Not all that far, really, except that he never knew but when a feathered shaft might catch him in the back.

Eventually they reached the hill where they had found the dead warrior weeks ago. As they wound around it, a sense came over Luke that they were being watched. He peered into every thicket, into every pool of shadow, but saw nothing.

"Luke?" his pa whispered. He was looking around, too.

"I know," Luke said.

The cedar scrub ended and grass spread before them. For the first and only time that Luke could recollect, not one longhorn was lying down. Every last animal was up and bunched together, their hindquarters toward the creek, their heads—and their horns—pointed toward the hills that ringed them.

"What do you make of that?" Owen said.

Luke didn't know what it portended. He was more

interested in two figures standing midway to the campfire, holding the reins to their mounts.

Harland and Thaxter had returned. They were supposed to be with their pa, but there was no sign of Gareth. At the moment they appeared to be arguing about something. Harland poked Thaxter and Thaxter put his hand on his six-shooter.

"What in the world is that about?" Lorette said.

"Beats me," Wylie said.

Only the Kursts, Luke reflected, would squabble with Comanches all around. He rode past the longhorns and when he was close enough, hollered, "You two!"

Harland didn't seem pleased to see them. "So you pulled your little brother's fat out of the fire, did you?" he said, not sounding happy that they had.

"Where's Pa?" Lorette demanded. "How come he isn't with you?"

Harland looked at Thaxter and back at her. "Pa's dead, sis. The Comanches got him."

Lorette put a hand to her throat. "No," she said. "Where's Iden and . . ." She looked past them toward the smoldering fire and stopped, her eyes widening.

Luke had already seen the bits and pieces of bodies strewn amid stains and pools of dry blood.

"Iden?" Lorette gasped. "Silsby?"

Harland shook his head.

"Jasper Weaver, too," Thaxter said, pointing. "That's part of him yonder."

"All that's left is us and these Burnetts," Wylie said. "We should fan the breeze while we can."

"And leave the herd?" Harland said.

"Forget the cows," Wylie said. "Our lives are more important."

"Forget all the work we did?" Harland said. "Forget how long it took to round them up?" He motioned at the longhorns. "Those critters are money on the hoof. All we have to do is drive them to Kansas. With Pa and our brothers gone, the Burnetts can even lend a hand."

"You son of a bitch," Wylie said.

"Why wouldn't we help?" Owen said. "We're in this together."

"Sure," Harland said.

"All you care about are those damned cows," Lorette said. "Did you even shed a tear over Pa or Iden or Silsby?"

"I don't see you bawling," Harland said.

"I will. Don't you worry," Lorette snapped.

Luke was dumbfounded. Now they were spatting over who was going to cry? "Do you ever listen to yourselves?"

"Tend to your lover and leave the cattle to us," Harland said to Lorette. "Don't concern your little female head over them."

"How dare you?" Lorette said.

"You tell him, sis," Wylie said. "Harland must reckon he can lord it over us like Pa did."

"Don't you start up again," Harland said.

Luke wasn't aware they'd had a falling out of some kind. "You're forgetting the Comanches," he reminded them. "We're in danger out in the open like this."

He scanned the nearest hill and thought he saw a Comanche off in the trees. He blinked, thinking he'd imagined it, but no, the warrior was still there, staring at them with his arms folded. "What the hell?" he said to himself.

The Comanche did an odd thing: he smiled.

Luke went to tell the rest but before he could, the Comanche raised an arm over his head, gave voice to a savage war cry, and melted away.

"What was that?" Owen said.

From the far end of the herd rose more cries, a chorus of hate that grew steadily louder.

"The Injuns!" Thaxter exclaimed. "What are they up to?"

A stirring of the herd gave Luke the answer. "Oh, my God."

"What?" Sam said.

"They're trying to cause a stampede to trample us to bits."

Chapter 65

Sam was weak from his wound and felt feverish. He wanted nothing more than to lie down and drink water until it came out his ears.

Turning toward the longhorns, he saw that his brother was right. The bedlam raised by the Comanches was driving the entire herd away from the war party—and toward their camp. The motion was slow at first, the longhorns confused and uncertain.

"What are all of you waiting for?" Wylie Kurst said. "We have to fan the breeze."

Sam agreed. But hurt as he was, he was in no shape for a hard ride. He doubted he would last a mile.

Harland and Thaxter were staring at the longhorns as if they couldn't believe what they were seeing.

"Mount up," Owen urged. "Hurry, you two."

"Those are our cattle," Harland said. "We can't let them be spooked."

"We can't stop it," Luke said.

"All of us working together can," Harland said. "We'll spread out and fire our six-shooters. That should hold them back." He drew his own. "We don't, we lose all that money."

"Will you forget your damn riches?" Lorette said.

Harland gestured at Thaxter. "Come on." They climbed on their horses, hauled on their reins, and rode toward the herd, Harland waving his revolver over his head and whooping.

The longhorns were moving faster, all those hundreds and hundreds, coming straight toward them.

"Ride, boys," Owen said. "Ride like anything."

Sam was momentarily startled when his pa suddenly reined over and smacked Sam's mount on the flank. The dun burst into a gallop, and he barely firmed his hold on the reins and the saddle horn to keep from being unhorsed. He heard Lorette cry his name and saw her rake her spurs to follow. Luke and his pa were right behind her. Wylie Kurst came last.

Harland and Thaxter, incredibly, were still galloping toward the herd. Both were hollering and firing their six-guns into the air.

The longhorns weren't slowing. A veritable sea of horns stretched to the east, the Ghost deep in their midst, towering over the rest.

Thaxter slowed, but not Harland. Harland barreled right at them, determined to stop them no matter what.

The longhorns broke into a rumbling run. An irresistible phalanx of horn and muscle and bone, they bore down on the pair in a living tide that would sweep away everything in its path.

Thaxter must have realized that. He suddenly wheeled his mount and raced away.

Harland went on another ten to twenty yards. When he glanced back and saw Thaxter riding off, he tried to flee, but his horse was only halfway around when the leading ranks of the longhorns smashed into them. The horse whinnied. Harland screamed. Flailing and thrashing, the pair were swept under the flood of driving hooves. Scarlet splattered, and some of the longhorns stumbled.

Sam was almost to the woods. Out of the corner of his eye he was horrified to see that the longhorns comprising the south edge of the herd were a lot closer than he'd reckoned. He would be cut off before he could ride clear.

Hauling on his reins, Sam fled due west. His only hope now was to outrun them. He was aware of Lorette to one side but he had lost sight of his pa and Luke. He lashed his reins, the effort compounding his pain.

Sam had never ridden so recklessly. Limbs tore at

him. Logs and boulders threatened to bring the dun down. He had gone only a short way when he began to tire. The thought of pitching off and being crushed to bits under a host of pounding hooves lent him the strength to cling on.

In his wake, the rumbling swelled to thunderous proportions. Brush crackled and splintered. Small trees were shattered and went down.

Singly, a longhorn was formidable. In a herd of over two thousand, they were a force of nature that couldn't be contained.

And that force was nipping at Sam's heels.

He looked back aghast at a moving wall of heads and horns and driving legs. He was barely twenty yards in front of them and they were gaining.

"Ride, Sam!" Lorette bawled. "In God's name, ride!"

What did she think he was doing? Sam thought. His shoulder throbbed and he was breathing heavy and his arms were becoming leaden but he was riding the best he could. He avoided a cedar, went through some oaks.

The rumble grew louder. He was afraid to look, afraid that the longhorns were almost on top of him.

Lorette yelled something but Sam didn't catch what she said. A feeling of light-headedness came over him. He found it difficult to focus. He shook his head to clear it, but that only made the feeling worse.

Sam was on the verge of passing out. His wound, the loss of blood, was taking its toll. He thought of his ma and his sisters and choked down a sob. He would have liked very much to see them again. The light-headedness grew worse. The woods spun. His gorge rose and he tasted bile. His hand slipped off the saddle horn. He tried to clamp his legs tighter to keep from falling. He failed.

Sam heard Lorette scream. The last thing he felt was her hand on his arm. He tried to say her name but a black pit opened and he fell headlong into it. He didn't fall far. A jerk pulled him back into the sunlight.

He was still on his horse. His reins were in Lorette's hand.

Ahead reared an enormous boulder. Sam figured she

would go around it, and she did, but she reined up on the other side. Springing from her saddle, she gripped his arm and his shirt and yanked him down beside her. He almost fell. The world spun worse, and the next thing he knew, he was on the ground, on his back. Lorette's arm was under him and she was cradling his head to her bosom. In her other hand were the reins to the dun and the mare.

The horses were side by side, quaking with terror, their eyes wide and their nostrils flaring.

Sam became aware of the loudest thunder yet, an assault on his ears that threatened to burst his eardrums. He heard bawling and snorts and tasted dust in his mouth. The reek of cattle was overpowering. He was sure he was about to be trampled into the dirt.

His eyelids fluttered, and for a few moments he couldn't make sense of what he was seeing.

The giant boulder, almost as high as a barn door and just as wide, was all that stood between them and the horde of longhorns sweeping past on either side.

The cattle barely noticed them. The panicked animals would run miles before they tired.

Sam put his hand down and felt the earth under him shake. The dust got into his throat, and he coughed. He didn't mind when Lorette pulled him closer, didn't mind when she kissed him on the forehead.

The thunder went on and on.

Sam tried to sit up but he was too weak.

Finally the rumbling faded. The number of longhorns dwindled, becoming a trickle and then only one or two at a time. Not until over a minute had gone by without a longhorn running past was it apparent they were safe.

The woods were blistered and broken. Flattened brush formed a carpet of crushed plants. Busted branches were scattered about. Here and there, dust rose.

"Let me help you," Lorette said. Letting go of the reins, she propped him against the boulder, paying special mind to ease his shoulder gently. "There," she said, and touched his cheek. "How's that, handsome?"

"You saved me," Sam said.

Lorette smacked the boulder. "This here saved the both of us. We were almost goners."

"You could have gotten away without me but you didn't," Sam said. Clutching her hand, he caressed her fingers.

"Oh, my," Lorette said. "What's this?"

"I think I love you," Sam said.

"You think?"

"You know what I mean," Sam said hoarsely.

"Yes, I do," Lorette said. "About time you admitted it."

Sam was too mesmerized by her beauty to say anything.

"All it took was an arrow through your body and a stampede to bring you to your senses."

"I won't fight it anymore," Sam said. "I'm yours if you want me."

Lorette bent, looked him in the eyes, and grinned. "Forever and ever," she said.

Chapter 66

Within moments of jabbing his spurs, Luke Burnett realized they weren't going to reach the hills to the south before the longhorns reached them. "Head west!" he hollered, and reined around.

Luke hoped the others heard him above the cattle. He didn't look to see if they had until he was almost to the woods. He saw that his pa and Wylie Kurst were following him, and further back, Thaxter—but to his dismay, Sam and Lorette were still trying to reach the scrub to the south.

"Sam, no!" Luke shouted.

Whether Sam and Lorette heard or turned on their own, they changed direction. He lost sight of them once they entered the trees.

Luke was well ahead of the herd and intended to keep it that way. The first hill he came to, he went up it as if it wasn't there. His sorrel possessed superb stamina, and he had confidence it would leave the cattle eating its dust.

Wylie Kurst had a good horse, too, and wasn't far behind. "We should let Thax catch up!" he hollered.

Luke shook his head. Thaxter and Harland had been fools to think they could stop the stampede.

"Didn't you hear me, Burnett?" Wylie yelled.

"I heard you," Luke shouted.

"Slow down."

"You wait for him if you want."

Luke wasn't slowing for anything. He must keep his lead on the legion of horns and hooves that would gore and pound him to a pulp.

"Damn you, Burnett!" Wylie hollered.

Luke realized he hadn't heard anything from his pa and looked back. His father wasn't there. Fear gripped him, and he slowed, calling out to Wylie Kurst, "Where's my pa?"

"Go to hell," Wylie said.

One of the few mistakes his pa ever made, Luke reflected, was becoming partners with the Kursts.

Wylie was beckoning to Thaxter, who was scarcely a dozen feet ahead of the herd.

Luke faced front just as a dry wash appeared out of nowhere. Luke jabbed his spurs and the sorrel leaped with its front legs flung forward. They reached the other rim, but it was close. The sorrel came down hard, its weight causing the earth to buckle. For a few wild instants Luke thought the sorrel would tumble and take him with it, but somehow the sorrel regained its footing and sped on, its mane flying.

Luke patted its neck. "Good boy," he said in its ear.

Thaxter had caught up to Wylie and the pair were riding like madmen. After them roiled an ocean of hides and horns.

Luke had never heard of cattle stampeding through woods. Always it was on a plain. But there was a first time for everything.

He wished his pa had never heard about the new cattle drives. Wished that his ma had been able to talk his pa out of it. She had been right all along. The cattle business wasn't for them. It was too dangerous. They should stick to what they know and forget any fancy dreams of being wealthy.

All the hard work he and the others went to, and for what?

Behind him a horse screamed. Not a whinny. Not a nicker. It uttered a very humanlike scream.

Thaxter's mount had jumped the dry wash and landed badly. Losing its balance, it fell onto its side and slid.

Thaxter pushed clear and leaped to his feet.

The horse slammed into a tree. A leg splintered, and jagged white bone ruptured out.

Wylie wheeled to his brother's aid. He leaned down, his arm wide. Thaxter anticipated him and had his own arm up. As slick as could be, Wylie scooped Thaxter into the air and swung his brother on behind him.

Luke didn't stop. They were on their own.

The ride that ensued was a whirlwind of reining and ducking and dodging and not letting the sorrel slacken once.

He must have gone over a mile when he noticed a change in the din raised by the cattle. The rumbling wasn't as loud. The longhorns, at long last, had expended their fright. They were slowing. Far fewer were behind him. Soon there weren't any at all.

To be safe, Luke held to a gallop a while more.

The sorrel was lathered with sweat and gamely would have ridden itself into exhaustion if Luke didn't finally slow to a walk. Shortly thereafter, he drew rein.

Wylie's horse was worse off. Bearing double, it rasped like a blacksmith's bellows, its head hung low. It came to a weary halt.

"We did it," Luke said. "We survived."

"No thanks to the Comanches," Wylie said.

Thaxter was glaring at Luke. "I heard my brother yell to you. Why didn't you wait for us, you son of a bitch?"

"What would that have done us?" Luke said.

"I could have switched from his horse to yours when his tired."

"You're alive, aren't you?" Luke said.

"Don't prod me, Burnett."

Wylie held a hand out toward each of them. "Enough. We barely lived through the stampede and you're at each other's throats."

"I never have liked him," Thaxter said.

"The feeling is mutual," Luke said.

"I have half a mind to settle your hash here and now," Thaxter growled.

"No," Wylie said.

"Who are you to tell me?" Thaxter said. Sliding off Wylie's horse, he took several steps to his right, his hand brushing his holster. "How about it, Burnett? Want to settle this once and for all?"

"The Comanches might hear the shots," Luke said. And swarm down on their heads.

"There will only be one shot, and it will be mine," Thaxter said. "Climb down, you bastard."

"Don't do it, Burnett," Wylie said.

"Whose side are you on?" Thaxter demanded.

"All our sides," Wylie said. "We've lost Pa. We've lost Iden and Silsby. We've lost Harland. Jasper, and his son. We don't need to lose any more."

"Just him," Thaxter said, with a nod at Luke.

"What's gotten into you?" Wylie said. "You pick *now* of all times?"

"I've hated his guts since I can remember," Thaxter said. "With Pa and Harland gone, I'm the oldest, and I can do as I please. And it pleases me to put a window in his skull for not helping Harland and me try to turn the herd and for not helping you and me when my horse went down."

"Don't bite off more than you can chew," Luke warned.

"I'll show you," Thaxter snarled. "Climb the hell down."

Luke slipped his boots free of the stirrups, and without taking his eyes off Thaxter, he swung his right leg up and over and slid to the ground.

"Thaxter, I'm begging you," Wylie said.

"Stay out of this," Thaxter replied. "I never realized what a weak sister you are."

"Damn you," Wylie said.

Thaxter half-crouched, his hand poised over his Colt. "This is it, Burnett," he sneered. "You and me."

Luke was ready.

"Wylie, count to three," Thaxter said.

"Go to hell."

"All right, then. We'll just do it," Thaxter said, and his hand flashed to his six-shooter.

So did Luke's. He drew without thinking, his arm seeming to move on its own. Smoothly, lightning-quick, he cocked the hammer as he swept the Remington up, and fired from the hip.

Thaxter was clearing leather when the slug slammed into his chest. Jolted onto his boot heels, he tried to raise his gun hand, and Luke shot him again, the lead coring Thaxter an inch to the right of the first. Thaxter staggered and once more attempted to raise his arm, and Luke shot him a third time, fanning the hammer.

Thaxter Kurst melted where he stood. His body twitched a few times, and was still.

Luke pointed his Remington at Wylie, but Wylie was staring sadly at his crumpled brother. "What about you?"

"I've never hated you Burnetts like he did. He brought this on himself."

"It's over?"

"It's over."

Luke believed him. He set to reloading and didn't comment when a tear trickled down Wylie's cheek.

"Damn him, anyway. Damn Harland, too. And Pa while I'm at it." Wylie pressed a hand to his forehead. "I was never for this cattle business. It was Pa who wanted to do it. Now's he dead, and all the others. There's just me and my ma and my sister."

"I'll help you bury the bodies later on," Luke offered.

"I'm obliged," Wylie said, and gave a start. "My sis! The last I saw of her, she and your brother were riding for their lives."

"What about my pa?"

"He turned south a ways back," Wylie said. "Probably going after Lorette and Sam. I didn't see what became of them."

Luke turned to his sorrel and climbed on. "Let's find out."

Chapter 67

Owen Burnett wasn't the best rider in the world. He was a farmer. He spent more time behind a horse pulling a plow than on a horse in the saddle.

So now, after turning south and then west when he caught sight of his youngest and Lorette Kurst, it was all he could do to rein clear of obstacles and not be swept from the chestnut by a low limb.

It didn't occur to him that by changing direction he had put his own life in greater peril. Only when the clamorous pounding of hundreds of hooves boomed in his ears did it hit him that the longhorns had halved the distance.

Owen had met a rancher once who'd told him that nothing on God's green earth rivaled a stampede for what the rancher called "thunderation." He'd never understood that until now.

Owen swallowed, and whipped his reins. It didn't help that the chestnut was an ordinary saddle horse. It wasn't exceptionally fast. It couldn't gallop forever.

The herd was gaining.

Owen bent low. The wind in his face, the blur of the vegetation—when he was younger he would have loved to ride this fast. Now he only wanted it over.

The cattle, though, showed no signs of flagging.

He emptied his head of all thoughts except to ride, ride, ride. A branch swept at his head and he ducked. Another tore at his left shoulder, ripping his shirt and almost knocking him off his horse. An oak reared and he streaked around it.

He no longer saw Sam and Lorette. They had been to his left but no longer were. Fear froze the blood in his veins. Fear they had been caught and ridden down.

Surely he would have heard screams and cries? They must still be alive, somewhere ahead of him.

I'm coming, son, Owen thought. He recalled the first time he held Sam in his arms, how small and helpless Sam had been. Babies. How anything so fragile could grow to be so big and strong was a wonderment.

Another low limb arced at his face. Owen pressed onto his pommel but it wasn't low enough. There was a sharp sting; his hat went flying. His head stayed on, and that was something.

Owen straightened, and heard a snort. He risked a glance behind him, and his heart leaped into his throat.

The Ghost was after him. The biggest of them all, the lord of the herd, an engine of destruction, all muscle and horn, and intent on his destruction.

Owen flailed his reins, raked his spurs. But the chestnut was already galloping full-out. It had no extra stamina to call on.

The Ghost snorted and bellowed.

Owen considered yanking his Spencer from the scabbard and trying to shoot the monster before it reached him. He didn't, though. He wasn't much of a shot, and even if by some miracle his shot scored, the chance of it bringing the Ghost down was slim. Most likely he would wound it, and wounded animals were notoriously vicious.

"Help me," Owen breathed.

A thicket flew by, and several boulders, and the chestnut started up another hill. The slope was treacherous but the chestnut game and they reached the top and raced down the far side.

A louder snort caused Owen to dare another look.

Barely three feet separated the chestnut's tail and the Ghost's flared nostrils. The bull's eyes were hellish pits of brute fire.

Owen sensed his doom. With nothing to lose, he reached for the Spencer but he only had it half out when a tremendous blow to the chestnut's hindquarters elicited a squeal of terror from the horse. He lost his hold on the Spencer, felt the chestnut buckling, and kicked free of the stirrups. Unable to control his fall, he cartwheeled, not once but several times, and crashed to earth with such force, his vision went briefly dark.

A whinny brought Owen back. Not much time had passed. He was on his side with oaks all around, his ribs in agony, his left arm bent under him. Dazed, he raised his head and wanted to cry.

The chestnut was down, too, and struggling to stand as the Ghost drove his long horns in again and again and again.

The rest of the herd had divided and was pounding past, raising a cloud of choking dust.

Pressing flat and curling into a ball, Owen closed his eyes and prayed his end would be swift. The ground under him quaked. The dust became as thick as fog. The thunder went on and maddeningly on, to the point where it seemed it would never end.

Every bone rattled, every sinew was taut.

Owen's ears rang so loudly, he didn't realize silence had fallen. Cautiously, he raised his head. The chestnut was pulverized meat and bone.

The Ghost, and the herd, were gone.

Owen slowly sat up. His left arm was broken, but by holding it against his stomach he lessened the pain. He bet several of his ribs were fractured, too.

Using an oak for support, Owen stood. He shuffled a few steps in one direction and then a few steps in another, unsure of which way to go. Swatting at the dust, he coughed and moved in a circle.

"Thank God," he said.

Sam and Lorette and their mounts were coming out of the cedar. Sam was handling his own reins, but he was pale and his shirt was stained with blood. "Pa," he said, and smiled.

"Mr. Burnett," Lorette said. "I kept him alive for you."

"I can see that," Owen said, and wanted to hug her.

Sam looked at the ruin that had been the chestnut, and grimaced. "We were lucky."

"Luckier than blazes," Lorette amended.

"Amen to that," Owen said.

Chapter 68

Owen insisted on making camp as night fell so Sam's arm could be tended to. He also insisted Sam rest.

"Put a splint on me and we can keep going," Sam argued. "The sooner we get home, the better."

"Do what your pa says," Lorette said, "or you'll have me to answer to."

To Owen's surprise, Sam meekly gave in. He kindled a fire while Lorette rigged a splint. She used two tree limbs, trimmed down, and a length of rope. She also fitted a sling over Sam's arm.

"So it won't flop around when you're riding and hurt more," she said when Sam told her the splint was enough.

Owen smiled when his son gave in a second time. "You two have become pretty closely acquainted, I take it?"

"She'll be Mrs. Sam Burnett before the year is out," Sam said.

"Darned right I will," Lorette said.

All Owen could think of to say was, "Your mother will be plumb surprised."

Later, the fire crackling softly, stars twinkling in the firmament, Owen hunkered on his heels and sipped coffee from Sam's tin cup. Sam was lying propped on his saddle, a blanket pulled to his chin.

Rustling in the brush brought Owen to his feet. He'd lost his Spencer, but Sam had given him the Walker. "Who's there? Speak up or we'll shoot."

Lorette leveled her gun.

"It's only us, Pa."

Into the firelight rode Luke and Wylie Kurst. Both were caked with dust, and Wylie was downcast.

Luke beamed as he alighted and gave Owen a hug. "We spotted your fire. I never thought I'd see you again."

Owen had to swallow a lump in his throat to say, "I was worried sick, too."

"How bad?" Luke asked, indicating the sling on Owen's arm.

"Busted up a little. Lorette made it for him. She's a right handy gal to have around and we'll be having her around a lot."

Luke went to Sam. "And you, little brother?"

"Never better," Sam said.

Lorette moved past Owen to her brother's horse. Wylie hadn't climbed down yet.

"Where's Harland?"

"Didn't you see? The stampede got him."

"Thaxter?"

Wylie looked at Luke. "The longhorns got him, too."

Owen saw his oldest glance at Wylie as if surprised. "At least the two of you made it safe."

"If you say so," Wylie said.

None of them were hungry. Their ordeal had sapped their appetites.

Weariness drove them to their blankets early. Owen slept fitfully. His arm bothered him. So did his ribs if he moved a certain way. Toward morning he got an hour or so of solid sleep, but it wasn't near enough.

Breakfast consisted of coffee and venison jerky. Sam was eager for them to be on their way, but Owen said no. "You're as pale as paper yet. You need more rest. Until noon, at least."

"Tell him I'm fit enough to ride," Sam appealed to Lorette, who had pressed a palm to his forehead.

"I'll do no such thing. You're warm. You might have a fever coming on." Lorette pried at the bandage. "I hope to God your wound isn't becoming infected."

"I have three mas now," Sam said sullenly.

"Would you rather we don't check and you become so sick, you die?" Lorette asked.

Sam didn't answer.

Owen chuckled. "I'm growing right fond of you, Miss Kurst. You have a knack for handling him."

"He's male," Lorette said. "I only say what's best for him and he knows it, so he gives in."

Luke spoke up from over by the fire. "My sisters tried the same thing when we were younger, and he never listened."

"Sisters aren't the same as wives."

"You're getting head of yourself," Luke said.

"Not by much."

"That wouldn't have worked with Pa," Wylie said. "He never let Ma tell him anything."

"That's because Pa spent his whole life thinking he knew better than everyone else. He wouldn't listen to anybody. Least of all her." Lorette suddenly stood and pointed to the southeast. "Look yonder. Riders are coming."

Owen whirled. He'd been worried the Comanches would return and finish what the stampede started. But the men coming down the slope wore hats and clothes and six-guns. Twenty, in all, and at their head a lean figure in buckskins with hair as white as snow and more wrinkles than Methuselah. "Ebidiah Troutman, by God."

The old trapper brought his horse to a trot. If his smile was any indication, he was genuinely glad to see them. When he dismounted, he clapped Owen on the arms and happily declared, "You're alive! These townfolk and me reckoned the savages would have done you in by now."

"They tried," Owen said. He recognized the marshal and the blacksmith and a clerk at the general store and the man who ran the feed and grain, among others. "All of you came all the way out here looking for us? How did you know we needed help?"

"The Comanches have struck a dozen or more homesteads. Yours and the Kursts' and the Weavers' among them."

Icy terror rippled down Owen's spine. "Philomena?"

"Safe in town," Edidiah said.

Luke brushed past Owen and gripped the trapper by the front of his buckskin shirt. "Mandy and Estelle? What about them?"

"Safe as well," Ebidiah said.

"This old goat is too humble," the marshal said. "He's the one who pulled their fat out of the fire. If not for him, they'd have had their throats slit, or worse."

"Mrs. Weaver wasn't as fortunate," Ebidiah said.

"Wait a minute," Wylie said, coming over. "What about our ma? She was home alone, too."

The expressions on many of the men gave him his answer.

"I'm sorry," Ebidiah said. "I tried to warn her, but the Comanches got there before me."

Wylie looked as if he'd been walloped with a hammer. "Ma, too?" he said dazedly. "This gets worse and worse."

Lorette uttered a low whine and put a hand to her throat. "No," she said softly, her eyes glistening. "Not her. She had no backbone, but she was my ma." Turning, she sank to both knees and Sam put his good arm around her.

"We took a chance coming after you, and we have to head right back," the marshal said. "Only half the men in town are left to defend it."

"Not even Comanches would attack an entire town," Owen said.

"Don't ever put anything past them," Ebidiah advised. "When they put their mind to something, they don't stop this side of Creation."

"You heard them, Pa," Sam said. "Are you going to make me sit here, or can we head back?"

Owen thought of Philomena and the girls. "As soon as Miss Kurst cleans your wound, we'll fan the breeze."

"What about your cattle?" Ebidiah asked. "We saw where they'd stampeded."

"Forget them," Owen said.

"After all the trouble you went to?"

"If I ever see a longhorn again, it will be too soon."

"You're talking nonsense, Pa," Luke said.

Maybe he was, Owen mused. After what they'd been

through, who could blame him? All those who died, and what did they have to show for it? Nothing. "We nearly died, son."

"The ones who did," Luke rejoined, "did they die for nothing? Mr. and Mrs. Weaver and Reuben? Mr. Kurst and his boys? Because if we give up, that's what it'll amount to."

"It's just cattle," Owen said. "They're not worth more lives."

"No, before they were cattle," Luke said. "They ran wild and free. Now they have our brand on them. Twenty-five hundred of the critters, just waiting to be taken to market."

"There's not enough of us to make the drive."

"We can hire men," Luke said, "and pay them out of the money we make. I'll put a notice in the newspaper, and we'll have more hands than we know what to do with."

"I'll be healed by then and raring to go," Sam said.

"And where he goes, I go," Lorette said.

Wylie glanced at her and shook his head. "And where she goes, damn it, I go too."

Ebidiah Troutman chuckled. "Sounds to me, Mr. Burnett, as if you'll be making that drive whether you want to or not."

"Heaven help us," Owen said.

Postscript

Lorette Kurst married Samuel Burnett two months to the day after the stampede. Her brother Wylie gave her away.

Owen Burnett hired on eight men and spent six weeks scouring the hills. They gathered up nearly two thousand of the branded longhorns along with another forty-three that needed branding.

Their cattle drive was the first by settlers, not a rancher. They followed the Chisum Trail, as it was being called. The only incidents of note were when one of their cowboys was bit by a rattlesnake but for some reason no venom was injected into the man's blood, and later when a small band of Indians asked for three cows to let the herd pass through their territory. Luke wanted to drive the Indians off at the point of his six-shooter, but Owen gave them the cows.

"I've had enough of killing to last me a lifetime," was how he summed up his sentiments.

They reached Kansas without losing a man. Or their lone woman.

The buyers offered forty dollars a head. After Owen paid his hands and split the proceeds with the only two Kursts still breathing—even though, by rights, Lorette was now a Burnett—that left him with almost forty thousand dollars. He gave ten thousand to each of his sons.

Sam went off to California with Lorette and prospered in the dry goods trade. They came back to Texas once a year, and Owen got to bounce five grandchildren on his knee.

Luke became a deputy in Kansas and later a lawman in Wyoming. He never shot another living soul.

Owen and Philomena stayed on their farm. They built that addition she'd dreamed about, and Owen splurged on a carriage to take them to and from town. In their senior years they rocked on their porch every evening and reminisced about the old days.

Now and then the cattle drive came up. On one occasion Philomena reached over and placed her hand on Owen's. "Was it worth it, you reckon? All those lives that were lost?"

"We got a fine daughter-in-law out of it, and enough money that we never have to worry."

"Money isn't important. Family is," Philomena said. "Don't you agree?"

"I always agree with you, dear."

Philomena smiled. "If you learned nothing else in life, you learned that, at least."

"Every husband does," Owen said.

Philomena laughed, and smacked him.

Read on for an excerpt from

OUTLAW TOWN

a Ralph Compton novel by David Robbins
available in January 2016 from Signet in
paperback and e-book.

"Where the blazes are we?"

Chancy Gantry gazed out over the sprawling expanse of brown country they were passing through. "That's a good question." He tilted his head skyward and squinted at the blazing sun from under his hat brim, but only for a moment. The glare hurt his eyes. "All I can tell you is we're heading north."

"That's not where, pard," Oliver Teal said with a grin. "That's a direction."

Chancy grinned. Ollie and he had been partners for going on six years. They were both from San Antonio but that was about the only thing they had in common. Chancy was tall and lanky; Ollie was short and broad. Chancy had straight black hair and brown eyes; Ollie had reddish hair with a lot of little curls, and wide, frank green eyes. Chancy's chin sort of came to a point; Ollie didn't have much of a chin at all.

Their taste in clothes was different, too. Chancy went in for plain work clothes and a hat with a single crease. Ollie liked to wear a brown rawhide vest even in the hottest weather, while his hat had a crease in the center and two more to either side.

They didn't tote the same revolvers, either. Chancy was fond of a Remington. Ollie favored a long-barreled Colt.

"We're somewhere in Indian Territory," Chancy clarified.

"The Injuns can have it," Ollie said in disgust. "It's a heap of nothingness no one else would want."

"From what I hear, they don't want it, either," Chancy said. "The government made them come here."

"That's the government," Ollie said. "Always telling folks what they should do even when the folks don't want to do it."

Chancy changed the subject before his friend started on his usual rant. Ollie's pa had been conscripted during the War Between the States, and Ollie, a youngster at the time, had never forgiven the government for taking his pa away even though Ollie had been one of the lucky few in that his pa had made it home in one piece. "Ten days or so and we should be in Kansas."

"Addy told me this morning that he heard the trail boss say it was more like fourteen or fifteen days."

Chancy couldn't wait to reach the railhead. Back in Texas the notion of taking a herd north had been exciting. A trek of more than seven hundred miles, with all sorts of dangers along the way. He'd imagined tangling with Comanches, or having to stop a stampede, or running into owlhoots. All sorts of things could have gone wrong. But nothing had. The drive had been as uneventful as a Sunday stroll in a San Antonio park.

It was Chancy's first trail drive, and if he had to pick one word to describe it, that word would be "dull."

Lucas Stout was the reason. Stout had a reputation as one of the best trail bosses around. He had a knack for finding water and grass, and got the cattle to market with few losses. Not only that, but he had a knack for overseeing men, too. No one ever gave Lucas Stout trouble. Not twice, they didn't. Small wonder that hardly anything ever went wrong on any of his drives.

"What's that?" Ollie suddenly said.

Chancy looked up.

In the distance, riders had appeared, their silhouettes distorted by the heat haze. They were hard to make out until they came closer. There were seven, all told, and they spread out as they came.

"Why, speak of the devil," Ollie said.

"What?" Chancy said. It galled him a trifle that his friend had the eyes of a hawk and could make out things a lot farther off than he could.

"Injuns, by gosh."

Chancy sat straighter and placed his hand on his Remington. "Are you sure, pard?"

"Well, they've got long hair and some of them have bows and their faces are kind of dark." Ollie paused. "I never did savvy why we call them redskins, though. They're not really red. But then we're not really white, are we? We're sort of pink."

"One of us should ride back and let Stout know," Chancy suggested. They were riding point, well ahead of the fifteen hundred longhorns.

"It might not be smart, only one of us staying," Ollie said. "What if they're hostile?"

Chancy scowled. He'd never fought Indians. For that matter, he'd never fought anyone. Of the fourteen cowboys on the drive, not counting the cook, only two were any shucks with a six-shooter. Jelly Varnes shot two men once in a saloon fracas. And then there was Ben Riginaw. Gossip had it he'd killed at least three and wounded a few more. Maybe he had and maybe he hadn't, but the matched pair of Remingtons he wore wasn't for show.

"I reckon you're right," Chancy said, drawing rein. "We hold our ground and see what they want."

Ollie followed suit. "Three of those redskins have bows. One has a lance. He'll be the one to watch out for."

"Since when are you an expert on Indians?"

"I know a lance is a lot bigger than an arrow," Ollie said. "If that redskin raises his arm to throw, I'm plugging him."

"Listen to you," Chancy said. "Wild Bill Hickok."

"So what if I've never shot anybody?" Ollie said. "I'm not about to let them stick me."

Chancy studied the Indians as they drew near. Truth was, he couldn't tell one tribe from another. But he could tell old from young, and with one exception, the seven were long in the tooth. Over half had gray hair and were scrawny, to boot. Four wore leggings, the others a mix of white clothes that had seen better days. "They don't look very fierce."

"Neither does a dog until it bites you."

Sometimes, Chancy reflected, his pard said the silliest things. "Keep your six-gun holstered. We don't want to provoke them."

"Could be they're already riled," Ollie said. "Three of them have arrows nocked."

It could be caution on the part of the redskins, Chancy reflected, or it could portend trouble.

"They lift those bows, we'd better shoot."

Chancy prayed it wouldn't come to that. He plastered a smile on his face to show he was friendly, but none of the Indians returned the smile.

The warriors drew rein about ten feet out. The youngest, in the middle, wore a black hat with a round crown and cradled a Sharps rifle in the crook of an elbow.

Chancy held his left hand up, palm out, and said, "How do you do, gents? We're friendly if you are."

"What makes you think they speak our lingo?" Ollie said. "They probably only know their own."

"Doesn't hurt to try," Chancy said.

The warrior in the middle gestured sharply. "We want cows."

"How's that again?" Ollie said.

"We want cows," the warrior repeated.

"I don't blame you," Ollie said. "They beat pigs. Pigs don't give milk and taste too salty. I've always liked cow meat more than pig meat. Chicken meat, too, for that matter. Snake meat I can do without. I won't eat any critter that crawls."

The warrior cocked his head as if confused, then said, "One cow for each." And he pointed at every single warrior in turn.

"I don't happen to have any cows on me at the moment," Ollie said, and chuckled at his little joke.

"No cows," the warrior said, "you not go by."

"Well, that's rude," Ollie said. "You and your geezer friends should move out of the way before our outfit gets here. Some of them won't be as nice to you as I am."

"Cows," the warrior said, and thumbed back the hammer on his Sharps. "Or you be sorry."

National bestselling author
RALPH COMPTON

"A writer in the tradition of Louis L'Amour and Zane Grey!" —*Huntsville Times*

Available wherever books are sold or at
penguin.com